Montana SANCTUARY

JOSIE JADE

MONTANA SANCTUARY: RESTING WARRIOR RANCH

To Denise Hendrickson...
Happy huge milestone birthday!
Thank you for your help and encouragement with this project. It (and so many other books) wouldn't have made it to print without you.

Chapter 1

Evelyn

The sun shone down on my face as I walked to the coffee shop. It was my favorite part of the day, this morning walk. My little taste of freedom. But for the first time in a while, there were other things that competed for my favorite part of the day.

The scent of dry air and the distant sound of traffic. The glint of sun off sweating stucco and rushing water in a nearby arroyo.

Albuquerque hadn't been high on my list of choices, but I was pleasantly surprised by the flat city that was bordered by mountains. The people were down to earth and didn't ask questions. I'd found friends quickly, and the past six months seemed like they'd lasted forever. Hopefully, they continued to feel that way.

I'd always heard that phrase "it's a dry heat" about the Southwest, but I hadn't understood what it meant until living here. The temperature climbed into triple digits during the summer days, but it didn't feel that way given the absence of water in the air. Back home in Florida, eighty-five degrees could be unbearable if the humidity was high. This, I could live with.

I turned the corner, and the Sandia Bean coffee shop came into view. When I'd first gotten to town, I'd stopped there on a whim to get a cup of coffee and noticed the help wanted sign. Once I'd stepped inside, it was all over. It was an adorable little space with a wall of windows that showcased a gorgeous view of the mountains. The place had turned into home more quickly than I expected.

I was a manager now. That was new, but welcome. I'd never thought I would love working in a coffee shop this much, but I did. Something about being able to make even the grumpiest customer smile with the blessing of caffeine. And now, I was finally putting down some roots.

The little bell over the door chimed when I entered followed by a chorus of hellos. No customers currently, but one of the baristas, Jess, was at the espresso machine. She was determined to perfect a new concoction that she swore would be a bestseller. She hadn't found her version of perfection yet, but her results were delicious enough that no one—the owners included—minded her experiments.

"Hi, Ava." Jess waved to me from behind the counter. "Unbearable out there yet?"

I laughed. "No, not yet. It's actually gorgeous out. I parked far away on purpose."

"Of course you did." She shook her head. It was an open secret that I liked to walk to work, but I also lived on the other side of the city across the river. So I made a compromise and parked my car a few blocks away when I drove over.

Plus, it kept my car from being associated with the shop. Just in case. But Jess didn't know that part.

A crash broke through the air like thunder, and I jumped, diving under the nearest cafe table.

"Sorry!" Jess called. "Just me being clumsy. I swear this machine keeps moving or something considering the number of times I've knocked things over in the past week."

My heart pounded in my chest, and my breath was short. A pair of giant hands squeezed my lungs until there was nothing left. Adrenaline pulled me down into a vortex that was far too familiar. I couldn't breathe. I needed to run.

With far too much effort, I forced breath into my lungs.

Calm down, Evelyn. He is not here. You are safe.

It took another three full breaths for me to force myself out from under the table and stand up. Steamed milk flowed across the floor behind the counter where Jess had knocked it over.

I cleared my throat. "Sorry. Must be a bit jumpy this morning."

"It's my fault," Jess said. "Don't know how these things manage to make as much noise as they do when they fall, but *c'est la vie.*"

"It always seems that way." I smiled, but my breath still felt tight in my chest, and the smile itself was forced. Fake it until it's real. It's the way I'd had to live for far too long. The panic would pass soon enough, and I could go back into the happy bubble that this place provided for me.

I started toward the back office, stepping over the spilled milk as I went. "How's the latest experiment?"

She made a face. "How is it ever? Not perfect."

I laughed.

"Oh, Ava, I forgot. Someone delivered something for you about an hour ago. I put it on the desk."

"They say what it was?"

She shook her head. "No."

Not completely out of the ordinary. Probably a sample of some kind. Local suppliers sent the managers samples by name, hoping that we'd take a chance on them and start using a new product. Sometimes we did, but more often we didn't.

I flipped on the lights in the office. A small, rectangular box sat on the desk I shared with two other managers. Maybe an instant coffee sample?

My name was on the box in neat black script, but nothing else. No shipping label. No return address. It was a hand delivery.

My heartbeat kicked up into a new rhythm, even though it had just settled down from the scare. I scolded myself internally. There was no reason to freak out. Maybe a local had decided to do a hand delivery for a more personal touch and gotten unlucky with their timing.

But the other part of me whispered to my growing panic. It couldn't be . . . right? Everything had been fine, no signs of anyone following me, nothing. He couldn't have found me here after I'd been so careful.

I picked up a letter opener from my cup of pens and Sharpies and split open the box. And that was when the walls started to crumble around me. I couldn't breathe, those iron hands squeezing my lungs again, my heart pounding like I was in the final mile of a marathon where I'd been chased by a lion.

Fuck.

This couldn't be happening.

Deep down, I'd known what would be inside this box, and every time it happened, it felt a little more like dying. Which was exactly what he wanted.

A scarlet jewelry box sat within the cardboard, like the present every woman wanted to get for Valentine's Day or

Christmas. I would prefer to never see another jewelry box ever again.

The gold bracelet inside the box was brutally familiar. I had a whole collection of them. A curving cuff of gold etched with subtle images. This time the picture was of the Sandia Mountains—the view I could see if I walked outside.

I turned the bracelet over, the sight not getting any easier.

A va Meadows
1992-2022

Another grave marker for a name I'd hoped I would be able to keep. Fuck. The engraved letters spurred me into action. I had been *so careful* this time, and this was the longest I'd ever been able to stay in a place without a sign of Nathan.

"Hey, Jess?" I called. She appeared in the doorway to the office. "The person who dropped off the package. What did he look like?"

She thought for a moment. "Really tall, blond. Good-looking too. I was tempted to ask him to stay, but there was already a line."

I forced myself to smile at her disappointed pout. But I had to grind my teeth to keep that smile in place.

It really was him, and he hadn't sent anyone to drop this off, he'd done it himself. I had to go. Now. It was probably already too late. If he was here, between me and the car . . .

I couldn't let myself think that way. Head down, move quickly.

Words tumbled out of my mouth as I said something to Jess about an emergency at home and pushed out of the shop and into the summer heat. I couldn't run. Running would make people notice and ask questions. But I walked as fast as I dared, heart pounding in sync with my steps. If I could make it to the car, I had a chance.

I forced breath into my lungs and back out. I'd practiced this, and it only worked if I kept breathing. But the panic was crawling up my throat and threatening to suffocate me. The feeling of eyes on my skin made it crawl, and the phantom pains started.

Not now. Please. Just let me get out.

One more breath hauled into my lungs. And another. One more block to the park. There were some kids playing on the playground and their parents with them. He wouldn't try anything in front of kids, would he?

Stupid question. I'd learned to never question Nathan's boundaries. He didn't have any. I'd learned that the hard way, which is why I had an escape plan in place, one I'd had ready since the first day I'd gotten to Albuquerque six months ago.

My hands shook as I shoved the key into the lock and sat in the heat. I was still holding that damn bracelet, and I tossed it onto the passenger seat. I'd never gotten enough courage to leave one behind. All the same, I felt its presence like a brand as I peeled out of the parking spot and drove far too quickly from the place that had seemed so safe an hour ago.

The mountains loomed closer as I pushed my car as fast as I could through the streets without getting pulled over—that was the last thing I needed—toward the edge of the city where it broke into flat desert.

There was no need to go back to my apartment. The bag I needed was already in the trunk. I hadn't lived anywhere in the past few years without that bag in whatever car I was using at the time.

The lot on the edge of the city looked abandoned, and for all intents and purposes, it was. Surrounded by a chain-link fence that I barely stopped to unlock, the space was a graveyard of things better left forgotten. The owner didn't care about the land and rented pieces of it for storage. It was littered with broken cement pipes and piles of leftover springs from an infrastructure project gone wrong. Old and defunct phone booths stood in the corner, lined up like toy soldiers. And then there was my little piece of junkyard paradise.

A car-shaped lump under a cover coated with desert dust. From a distance—even up close—it looked like a thing long abandoned to the elements. But it wasn't.

I parked my car and tore back the cover, revealing the secondhand car I'd purchased when I'd gotten here. It wasn't anything fancy, but it would do the job. And right now, the job was getting out.

The panic that had gripped me was still present, threatening to claw back into my brain and drown me. But it had receded in the face of my determination and the cold blankness I'd associated with this routine. It was what I had to do. I would push it down until I could breathe again. Until I'd left yet another false life behind.

I popped the trunk on the car to make sure that everything that I'd stored was still there. Emergency cash, false IDs, some clothes that couldn't fit in my first bag, and a box filled with gold bracelets.

Something made me keep them, even though every time I saw the box it filled me with dread. Maybe it was confirmation that I wasn't crazy, and that it was all really happening. Maybe it was some strange sentimentality—the only things I had left from all of those lives that I'd created.

I asked myself *why* every time I had to leave, and I never found a better answer. Now, I didn't have time to dwell on why. Tossing the newest bracelet into the box and the bag into the trunk, I slammed it shut.

It took me only seconds after that to complete the familiar routine. Down onto the ground to check underneath the car. Grab the spare key from its magnetic hiding place. Get in and start the engine.

I didn't bother to close the gate behind me.

There had been times when I'd planned more ahead than this. I'd picked a new location and had everything laid out from the beginning. But I had let hope get the best of me this time. I'd thought that maybe I'd done it. Escaped. That I could have a life.

Stupid.

I would consult a map when I got clear of the area. Contact Melanie and let her know that I'd had to move on. I let the car pick up speed, and the iron fists squeezing my lungs loosened. I was out. He hadn't gotten me this time. I was still safe. For the moment.

Dust billowed behind the car in my wake, and I didn't look back.

Chapter 2

Lucas

The stallion reared, lashing out, and I dove to the side to avoid a hoof to the head. That wasn't the way I wanted to spend my afternoon.

The sound of him galloping across the paddock made me sigh. Damn it.

I'd thought we were making progress.

Pulling myself up off the ground, I brushed the dirt off my jeans. In the two years we'd been doing this, I'd never had so much trouble with a horse. He wasn't acclimating well to people at all, and he'd been here for weeks.

Not that I blamed him. He'd been rescued from a place that wasn't good to its animals. A place I tended to avoid thinking about because of the anger that came with it. The result was a horse that was too skittish for his own damn good and who was thoroughly convinced that all humans were out to get him.

Which made this process . . . less than easy.

But I'd seen worse than him come back. I could see the potential in him. When he was alone in the stables, unaware that anyone was watching, the sweetness underneath was obvious. He would make a good companion animal. If I could get through his fear.

And besides, I knew what it was like to be always looking over your shoulder and expecting the next hit. I would make this work.

If there was one thing I'd learned about myself over the years, it was that I was damn stubborn. I didn't give up on things. Even, arguably, things that I *should* give up on. But in situations like this one, it served me well.

This horse *needed* to settle. We needed him. I hadn't met the client yet, but Rayne had told me that the requirement was a steady animal that would be around long-term. He was the only horse we had on site that wasn't already scheduled to be shipped elsewhere.

I had to get it right.

Leaning against the fence, I watched him across the paddock. He tossed his head like he didn't have a care in the world, but he was watching me. I pretended not to notice him at all.

"Come on," I muttered under my breath. "You know I'm not going to hurt you."

He pranced against the far fence, teasing in his defiance. If I could harness that attitude and bring out his gentle side, he'd be the perfect therapy animal.

"Still trying to get him to calm down?" Liam's voice came from behind me.

I sighed. "Always."

"When are you finally going to get control of him?" He was teasing me too, poking at the sore spot. Everyone on the ranch knew about my trouble with this horse. And the longer it took to break him in, the longer it would take for me to live it down.

"I'll get it," I said. "Just gonna take some time. Something will click."

"Have you given him a name yet?"

I shook my head. "No. You think that's part of the problem?"

"I mean, if I was walking around and you were calling me 'horse' all day, I know I'd have a problem with it."

"Smart-ass."

"Of course." Liam leaned against the fence, bracing his arms. "You know, some animals aren't cut out for this."

"He is. I know he is. Rayne tell you about the client?"

He nodded. "Yeah, I saw her up at the house. Kid. Teenager. Had some fucked-up shit happen to him, I guess. From what I could gather. Not like she could tell me all that much."

"Yeah." The horse had settled down on the other side of the paddock, calm now that I wasn't close to him. "He needs a therapy animal sooner rather than later, so I have to crack it."

"You'll get it," he said. "And if you don't, then we'll have Daniel come and replace you."

I rolled my eyes. "Like hell. He barely trusts *me*. You think introducing another person to this equation makes it better?"

He shrugged. "Don't know. But it might help if everything is on the table."

I couldn't argue with him. We were getting to that point.

"I'm not out here to bust your balls."

"Could've fooled me," I said, smirking.

He laughed. "Well, partially that. But there's a woman here to see you."

I turned to him then to see if this was another joke. He looked serious. "Really?"

"Yeah."

It had been a long time since a woman had come looking for me. Been a long time since I'd interacted with any woman seriously. And there was no woman I could think of who had reason to come here to talk to me. "She say why?"

"Nope," Liam said, popping the word. "But you should definitely come find out."

I sighed. "Can you take care of it? Or one of the other guys? I'd like to keep trying here."

"They're all out or busy. Besides," Liam said, climbing over the fence and dropping down next to me, "she specifically asked for you."

Something deep resonated with those words, an unnamed instinct perking up and sensed something. And that was strange because once I'd come out here to Montana, I'd left all those instincts long behind. "Fine."

Slowly, Liam helped me approach the horse from opposite directions. He'd helped me get him under control and into the stables a few times over the past several weeks. And the horse was predictable. He reared again upon realizing that he was being cornered, but I managed to get ahold of his bridle. "We're not going to hurt you," I said softly.

A harsh breath came out of his mouth. He didn't believe me. That was all right—he didn't have to. We would show him that we could be trusted. Liam stayed back as I led the horse into his stall in the stables, ready to jump in if the animal decided he wanted to make a run for it. But, thankfully, he didn't do much more than shake his head and try to prance out of my grip a couple of times.

I sighed as I closed the door to his stall. "Horse is going to be the death of me."

"Hopefully not," Liam chuckled.

We headed back to the main ranch house. None of us lived there, but there were rooms for client meetings, the communal kitchen and dining room, and both the security station and business office. "You left her inside?"

"Yeah," Liam said. "In the kitchen."

"Any first impressions?"

He shrugged, hands in his pockets. "Not many. Seemed nervous, maybe. But she didn't seem crazy if that's what you're asking."

I honestly didn't know what I was asking. Instead of going straight inside, I walked around the house to another set of stairs that led up to the wraparound porch—and the window that would let me see her without her noticing.

There she was, exactly where Liam said he'd left her. The second my eyes fell on her, those long-dormant instincts roared to life. The way she was sitting, she was aware of everything around her. Attentive in a way that most civilians were not. That awareness called out to me. And it reminded me of things that I would much rather forget.

Long, dark hair fell around her shoulders in waves, but her skin coloring was so pale, I wondered if that was its real shade. She was stunning, but also doing her best to disguise that fact. Her clothes didn't fit well and drew away from the shapes underneath them. Misdirection. I had seen it enough to recognize the signs.

And Liam was correct—she was nervous. Her fingers never stopped moving. Making small circles on the arm of the chair and then on her knees. Picking at an invisible cuticle. Little subconscious movements that only someone with training would be able to hide.

"She didn't say why she was here?" I asked again.

"No," Liam said.

"And she asked for me by name?"

He nodded. "Your guess is as good as mine."

Okay, then. It was time to see why she was here.

Deep inside, my instincts were screaming, but I couldn't pinpoint the reason. The urge to protect and to soothe was there, along with a prickling sensation at the back of my neck like someone was watching.

I hoped she had answers. Because now that I'd seen her, I needed them.

Chapter 3

Evelyn

This was taking way too long.

I forced my body to stay seated despite my nerves telling me I should get up and leave. My fingers wouldn't stay still. I couldn't stop them.

I should drive away and find some other place in town that promised a steady job. But this was too perfect not to give it a chance, even if it was a long shot.

It was hard not to let myself hope, but I wanted this to work. Garnet Bend seemed like the perfect place to hide. The few times I'd let myself be online during the trip— libraries and internet cafes only—I'd settled on the small town.

Being in a big city hadn't prevented him from finding me, so it was time to try the other option. Maybe that would do the trick. I doubted it, but that spark of hope was there all the same.

Whenever I picked a new place, I tried to be as random

as possible without also being predictable in my randomness. Last time I'd run, I'd gone diagonally across the map from Rhode Island to Albuquerque. This time, I took a straight line north. Montana seemed like an okay place to try living in a small town. After all, there was nothing out here, right?

It had certainly seemed that way from most of my driving.

I'd sorted towns by population and picked one that was on the smaller end while still being big enough to blend in. The other advantage to a smaller population was that it was easier to see someone like Nathan coming. He'd managed to sneak up on me in Albuquerque. Too many places to hide.

I'd picked this place mostly for the name. And the fact that it was only a couple hours from one of the larger Montana cities, so it wouldn't be impossible to get to an airport if I needed to. But it was off the beaten path enough that I hoped I wouldn't be an easy target.

For all those reasons, I needed the job listing that I'd found in town. It was definitely too good to be true, but I had to try. If not, I'd stay at a hotel and see if there was anything else before moving on.

The man and woman I'd spoken to on the way in had been kind, even though I was here to speak to someone else. Another man. That alone made me nervous. But jobs that provided housing didn't come along very often, and when I'd seen that this place was on the outskirts of town . . .

I needed it to work.

A silhouette darkened the screen door, and I froze, learned impulses making me go still. A man pushed inside, and he was huge. Tall and broad like a linebacker and definitely, one hundred percent, one of the biggest men I'd ever seen in real life other than Nathan.

Should I have expected that? This was Montana, filled with people who worked the land and spent a good amount of time outdoors. It probably wasn't a place that bred small, unintimidating men. That didn't change the creeping dread that slithered up my spine and spun in my gut.

He didn't move, and neither did I, both of us simply observing each other. And then he sat across from me, well out of reach, and my body relaxed. I was suddenly aware of air in my lungs again—I'd been holding my breath.

If he noticed my nerves, he didn't say anything. He just looked at me, and once I had enough breath in my chest, I looked back. Not only was he huge, he was *gorgeous*. Like he could star in a Montana ad campaign featuring a cowboy. Brown hair, warm eyes, and a jaw sculpted with a hint of lazy stubble. He was beautiful.

I stopped any further thoughts on that. I'd been fooled by beautiful men before, and I knew better than anyone that beauty didn't have anything to do with whether or not someone could be trusted.

Nathan was beautiful. Look where that had gotten me.

The man in front of me cleared his throat. "My name is Lucas Everett." His voice was low and smooth like dark whiskey. The kind of voice meant for intimate nights spent next to a fire. "I'm who you asked for. What can I help you with?"

I was still so taken with his voice that it took me a second to process the question. Right. The reason I was here. I pulled the faded piece of paper from the pocket of my sweatshirt. It had been tacked up on a community bulletin board in one of the local coffee shops.

"I found this," I said, clearing my throat in an attempt

to make the words firmer. "I was wondering if the job is still available."

The paper outlined a job at the Resting Warrior Ranch. A person to cook meals and clean the guest houses and communal areas, housing included.

Leaning forward, Lucas took the paper from my hand. I made sure that our hands didn't touch. He glanced at the paper with a frown. His eyes flicked up to mine and back down. "Where did you find this?"

"A community board."

His lips pressed together in a line. "This listing is more than a year old. It shouldn't have been up on any bulletin board."

Shit. My stomach twisted. I knew it was too good to be true. Standing, I brushed invisible dirt off my clothes. "I'm sorry for the inconvenience. I'll go."

He held up a hand. "You don't have to leave. Just because this position is filled doesn't mean I can't help you. Would you like some tea?"

I eased back down as he rose. He went the long way to the small kitchen to avoid walking past me. So he had noticed my nerves. "Sure," I managed.

"What work experience do you have?" he asked, pouring water into an electric kettle and flipping the switch. But my thoughts were swirling. He wanted to help? How? Why?

In my experience, people didn't want to help without an ulterior motive, and that had my senses reaching for what was wrong.

Stop it. Hear the man out. Listening is not a commitment.

"What's your name?"

"Evelyn." The word flew out of my mouth before I could stop it, and I closed my eyes. Crap. He was throwing me off so much I'd given him my real name. That alone was a bad thing. I had planned to be Elizabeth for this run. Guess that was out the window now.

"And your work history?"

I took a breath. "Most recently, I was a barista. And one of the managers for the coffee shop. I've done some office work—admin stuff." There'd been so many places and jobs over the past few years, it was honestly hard to narrow it down. "I've been working consistently, but it's kind of . . . an eclectic collection. If you want, I can put together a full list."

The tiny clatter of porcelain to my right made me jump. Lucas was standing right there. Inches away. Holding out a teacup. There hadn't been any sound to tell me that he was approaching. Everything in my body was telling me to jump and run. Create distance *now*.

I was vaguely aware that my body had turned to stone, so stiff that if I fell over I would crack and break. But I managed to stay in my seat, and even though there was almost no chance, I prayed that Lucas hadn't noticed the reaction.

"Thank you." I forced the words out and took the cup from him.

"You're welcome."

Why did his voice have to be so distracting?

I shook off the stillness in my body, feigning nonchalance. The look on his face told me that he didn't buy it, but as long as he didn't call me on it, I could live with that.

Lucas returned to the seat across from me and leaned forward, elbows on his knees. The pose was engaged and his eyes roamed over me with a sharp interest that I didn't understand. "So," he said. "What brings you to Garnet Bend?"

I took a sip of tea. "I'm sorry?"

A small smile and his eyes danced with amusement. "You're new to the area, right?"

"Yes."

"And that's why you're looking for work?"

I nodded.

Lucas's head tilted to the side as he looked at me. What did he see? I hadn't tried to project any particular image, except making myself seem not particularly feminine. I never did that until I knew I was around people I could trust.

As it was, I was still getting used to dark hair. I'd redyed it in the motel bathroom on the drive up here, and though I'd been dyeing it for years, I'd never had a color this dark. On the one hand, it was striking. On the other hand, it didn't really feel like *me*.

"Well," he said, "I'm sorry we don't need anyone for that position anymore. But I know the owner of the local coffee shop, and if that's something you're interested in, I'll happily put in a good word for you."

I looked up at him. "Really?"

"Of course," he said with a smile. "And since you're new to the area and we have the room, you're welcome to stay in one of the guest houses here until you're on your feet."

"Oh, I—"

He stood and moved to the wall where a rack hung like something out of an old-fashioned hotel: a wooden frame of rectangle cubbies that each held a key.

"You're free to think about it," he said, picking up one of the keys and walking it back to me. "There's no pressure, and no one will be offended if you say no. But you won't be bothering anyone either."

He held out the key, and I took it, in a daze. This whole

meeting had thrown me sideways, like I'd gotten caught in a tornado.

"This is for the Bitterroot House. Follow the road down, and you'll see a sign on the left. I hope I'll see you around, Evelyn."

He strode away from me to the stairs across the room and disappeared up them without so much as a look back. I blinked. Maybe I'd imagined the whole thing. But no, I was still standing in this house with a key in my hand, which meant that Lucas was real.

Beautiful and real.

I didn't know how to feel about that. Or about the key in my hand.

But what I did know was that even with my nerves, Lucas didn't make me feel afraid in the way I was used to. And that was saying a lot.

Chapter 4

Lucas

I forced myself not to look back at her as I walked up the stairs. She needed the freedom to make this decision without the weight of any expectation from me. But I was hoping that she said yes.

Evelyn was a mystery. My instincts hadn't stopped screaming, and she was clearly hiding something. But I didn't think she was dangerous, or that she was here to do Resting Warrior any kind of harm. I think it was simply good luck that she'd stumbled into a place where we could help her.

Pushing open the door to the office, I ignored the fact that Daniel and Harlan were clearly on a call. Daniel raised an eyebrow as I passed. Whatever Evelyn decided, I needed to see it.

"Okay, thanks," Daniel said. "Do you need anything else or can we follow up with you next week?"

"That's fine," the voice on the call said.

"Have a good day," Daniel said, and the call ended with a click. "What's going on?"

I watched the front of the lodge like it was a target. Evelyn was running from something. The fact settled on me, satisfying the itch of my questions. I would bet a lot of money on the fact that she was on the run from something bad.

She was used to hiding her reactions, but I'd seen them. When I'd startled her, she'd jumped so hard I'd thought she might bolt like that horse down in the stables. All in all, she'd played it off well. Clearly, she'd had a lot of practice. But that didn't change the fact that she was so stiff a harsh breeze could have knocked her over.

The movements were brutally familiar. My mother had spent so much of her life covering the fact that she was on edge that I'd never forgotten the way it looked.

Someone had hurt Evelyn.

Rage flooded my system, and I held myself still so I didn't go vaulting back down the stairs to demand she tell me who it was.

What the fuck was that?

The surge of protective energy drilled through my veins. I crossed my arms and froze. I'd never felt anything like this before, and certainly not for someone I didn't know.

My mind went over her reactions. And her face. She was beautiful, even though she was trying to hide it. I didn't want to scare her. I wanted her to feel safe with me. And that's why I couldn't look away from the window now. I needed to know what choice she would make.

"You alive in there?" Daniel asked, stepping next to me at the window.

Behind us, Harlan chuckled. "He's got his eye on something."

"A woman showed up and asked for me. I was working with the horse, and she asked for me by name. Turns out she found a paper from last year—the listing that we hired Mara for."

"That's strange," Daniel said.

Harlan made a sound of agreement. "Thought we took all those down. She must have been digging deep to find that."

I nodded. "My thoughts too, and more, I think she's running from something, though I don't know what."

"So why are you standing up here staring at the driveway like you're about to snipe something?"

"I offered her the Bitterroot House until she gets on her feet. And I offered to talk to Lena for her to see if I can get her a job."

I didn't need to turn and look at them to feel their surprise.

"You sure?" Harlan asked.

The guest houses weren't usually used for things like this. Normally, they were reserved for people visiting Resting Warrior for physical therapy or PTSD treatment. Right now, we had a couple of people in residence, but we still had plenty of room. And everything in me was screaming not to let Evelyn walk away. That she needed to be here.

"I'm sure. She needs it. Even if she doesn't realize it yet."

"Why do you—"

I cut Daniel off. "I can see it. Trust me. It's something I'm . . . more than familiar with."

Neither of them pushed me. Each of us had our own pain, and it was an unwritten rule among the men of Resting Warrior that you didn't encroach on another man's past. If he shared with you, that was fine. But each person's journey was theirs to share or not. And both Daniel and Harlan knew enough about my past to put at least something together.

"It's not just for me," I said. "With what we do, we can't let her walk away. She doesn't know what we do yet."

Below us, a dark head of hair appeared, and my breath stilled in my chest. Evelyn walked down the steps off the porch and toward the car that must be hers. It was an old, beige sedan that had seen better days. How far had she come? And *where* had she come from?

My mind wouldn't slow down, whirling with questions for her and about her.

The floor creaked behind me, and Harlan let out a low whistle. "You sure you want her here for therapy, Lucas?"

I grit my teeth and kept my eyes on Evelyn.

"Maybe you're right," Daniel said. "He can't take his eyes off her."

I cut a glare at Daniel then turned back to the window. What would she choose? Would she stay or go? She stood next to the driver's side of the car, and just . . . stopped. Thinking.

I would kill to be a fly on the wall of her thoughts.

Evelyn straightened her spine and opened the door and slid into the car.

Stay.

I thought the word at her, holding my breath.

Stay.

Every inch of my body was taut, resisting the urge to go *make* her stay. She needed to choose this on her own. But I was still holding my breath.

The car rumbled to life and pulled forward. She didn't turn around. The breath fell from my lungs, and Daniel laughed, clapping me on the shoulder. "If she needs help, we'll help her. You know that."

I looked over at him. "But?"

"But be careful about getting in too deep. Especially with something that might hit close to home."

"Come on, Dan," Harlan said with a grin. "Let the man live. Lucas finally being interested in a woman after all of that? That's something to celebrate."

I forced a smile at Harlan, holding any reaction in check. Even when he grinned at me so wide I wanted to smack it off his face. "I got it," I said, looking back at Daniel.

And I did. I understood what he meant, and I didn't disagree. But I also knew that it didn't matter. The second I'd seen her startle over a teacup, I'd known I was going as deep as I needed to help her.

No matter what.

~

T he drive from Resting Warrior Ranch into town had always been one of my favorites. It wasn't far, but the stretch of fields spread against the background of the Mission Mountains never failed to impress me.

Before the ranch, I'd never imagined living in a small town like Garnet Bend, and I'd certainly never thought that I would live in Montana of all places. I was a city boy through and through. Or so I'd thought.

But the pace of life out here suited me more than I'd expected, and being surrounded by peace and quiet had eventually brought *me* peace. Or at least it did most of the time.

I'd spent last night staring at my bedroom ceiling and trying to untangle Evelyn's threads. There was no way I could—I didn't know enough. But that didn't stop my brain from trying. What would bring her out here so far?

This wasn't a place that you ended up by accident. How bad was it, and what had she suffered?

The idea of someone hurting her brought on that same roaring pressure in my chest. The need to make sure that she was protected at all costs. And fuck, that was confusing. In the work we did, I'd seen plenty of women with trauma and horrible pasts. I'd felt sympathy for them and did what I could to help. Why was she so different?

I'd never experienced this kind of ache to make something right.

Pulling into town, I parked in front of Deja Brew—easily the most popular coffee shop in town. It was a place filled with soaring windows, comfortable chairs, and used books. A place you could spend a couple of hours and be at ease. Plus, Lena made sure that everyone felt welcome.

The scent of both coffee and freshly baked bread hit me as I walked through the door. It was warm in the way that reminded you of family holidays and good memories. No surprise to me that everyone loved this place.

The owner herself stood behind the counter and waved, a smile on her face. "Well, if it isn't Lucas Everett. I thought you must have disappeared into the mountains to become a hermit for all I've seen you around here."

I smiled. "Hey, Lena. Sorry about that. Been working with a horse that's giving me trouble. Haven't strayed far from home in a bit."

"As long as you remember there's life outside the ranch," she said, laughing. "Coffee?"

"Please."

Lena stepped away from the counter and grabbed a cardboard cup to fill with coffee. She'd been a huge supporter of the ranch when we first opened and remained a good friend to all of us. I'd been surprised that someone like her had stuck around in Garnet Bend.

Lena was quirky.

While most of this town was straitlaced and painfully normal, Lena dyed her hair with red streaks and wore outfits in colors that barely avoided clashing. But she was a force of nature, determined to a fault, and kind. She would make it wherever she chose to live.

"Here you go." She placed the coffee down in front of me, and I handed her a few bills.

"So I have a confession."

Lena gasped. "You're in love with me? I knew it, Lucas. You've come to sweep me off my feet." There was a sparkle in her eye, and I laughed.

"I'm sure you'd break my heart if I were here for that, Lena. But I did have something other than coffee I wanted to talk to you about." It was an open secret that Lena liked Jude, one of the other members of Resting Warrior, and I didn't miss the blush on her face when I'd said that she'd break my heart.

"What's on your mind?"

I took a sip of my coffee. "I was wondering if you were looking for any extra help here in the shop?"

A flare of interest lit up her eyes. "Why?"

"A woman showed up at the ranch yesterday looking for work. She found an old paper with the job Mara has now. But she says she has barista experience." Lena looked at me, and I sighed. "I offered to let her stay at the ranch until she gets on her feet."

It looked like Lena had questions, but she didn't ask them. As it was, she likely saw too much. "Hmm, I haven't been actively looking, no. But we have been a lot busier lately. And I've been wanting to spend more time on the bakery side of things."

In addition to a coffee shop, Deja Brew sold baked goods. They weren't a full bakery, but they were easily the best baked goods in town. We got at least one loaf of bread from her every week when Jude came to pick it up. I chuckled. "No one at Resting Warrior will say no to more baked goods."

She smirked. "I didn't think so. Tell her to come over for an interview, and I'll see what I can do."

"Really?"

"Sure." Lena smiled. "Things have a way of working out. Maybe this is a sign that I should be baking more."

I laughed and dumped a packet of sugar into my coffee. "Well, I appreciate it."

"Before you go," she held up a finger, "take this with you. Just in case Jude doesn't get to town later this week."

Lena handed me a fresh loaf of bread in a paper bag. We kept whatever Lena sent us in the lodge kitchen, and I don't think any of the guys would ever admit how quickly we went through it. "I'm sure he'll be here. As far as I know, he hasn't missed a week since he started coming." I pretended to ignore her second blush. "I'll send Evelyn over tomorrow."

"Sounds good," she said. "Make sure to stop by again soon."

"Will do."

The drive back to the ranch always seemed shorter than the drive away. But today, I was glad for that. I wanted to tell Evelyn the news. And more than that, I wanted to see her again to know if the reaction I'd had yesterday would be the same today.

As far as I knew, she hadn't left the Bitterroot House. She could. I hadn't mentioned that to her, but I would. I didn't want her to think that because she was staying here she had to be locked in the house like some kind of prisoner.

I parked near her car and knocked on the door. It took

a couple minutes, but there was a soft shuffling inside before Evelyn pulled open the door. She'd been sleeping—that much was clear—dark hair messy and eyes still bleary. That was also something I recognized. If she was running from something, she would be exhausted and probably needed to catch up on what she'd missed in her flight.

I felt bad for waking her. "Hello."

"Hi," she said, stepping back from the door. It was deliberate, to put as much distance between us as possible. Not exactly a surprise. I wasn't a small man, and there wasn't any way for me to hide that. If Evelyn was a victim of abuse, then my silhouette in her door probably wasn't a comforting sight.

"May I come in for a moment?"

"Sure."

I didn't close the door behind me all the way, intentionally making sure she saw it. I wanted her to feel comfortable. More than that, the very idea of her being afraid made me sick. I didn't want that.

"Thank you," she blurted out. "For letting me stay."

"It's no trouble," I said.

"Maybe not, but it . . . means a lot to me." She seemed better than yesterday. She was still nervous, but I could see something more now. A spark under all the nerves.

"I just got back from town, and I spoke to Lena Mitchell—the owner of Deja Brew. You're welcome to go there anytime and have an interview. I mentioned that you might come tomorrow."

Surprise was clear on her face. "Oh. Wow. Thank you."

Interesting. I had promised I would put in a good word. So she wasn't used to people keeping their promises. "As far as food, I'm sure that you saw there's a kitchen in here. So feel free to do whatever you like. However, we do host communal meals a couple times a week for the ranch residents. Tonight is one of those, actually. Everyone contributes to the cooking and cleaning. No pressure at all if you're not up to it, but you're welcome to join the meal tonight, and get on the cooking and cleaning schedule if you enjoy it."

She looked at me, blue eyes hitting me square in the chest. There was so much in her eyes it was practically pouring out of her. "Will you be there?"

"Yes." It wasn't my turn to be at dinner, but the word was out before I'd registered saying it. Even if my mind had given me a chance to think, I still would have said yes. I wasn't about to turn down a chance to see Evelyn in a natural environment.

She didn't respond, and the silence stretched thin between us. I couldn't help but notice again that she was beautiful. Delicately made and soft. But whatever she'd gone through had hardened her edges. She was thin and there was fear in her eyes that I wanted gone. No one should look that haunted.

I kept my voice low. "While you're here, if you want to talk to someone about what you're running from, you're welcome to. Resting Warrior works with therapists for exactly that reason."

Evelyn's spine snapped straight and there was fire in her gaze. "I'm not running from anything. And if I were, it would be none of your business."

Our eyes locked, and she didn't look away. There were no nerves now. Only anger. I liked that fire, and the sudden strength. I nodded.

The air between us went tight, and suddenly, it felt like there was no distance between us. I didn't want there to be. I'd never been so viscerally attracted to anyone, like a magnet buried deep in my gut was pulling me toward Evelyn.

I wanted to crack her shell and know what was wrong. To see the problem and fix it. To pull her close and tell her that she was *safe* and that everything was going to be okay. To whisper those words into her ear as many times as she needed to hear them.

I shoved the instinct down. She had enough going on. She didn't need to deal with my attraction. "I'll see you at dinner," I said and closed the door behind me.

I might not be able to tell her that everything would be okay, but I was going to make sure it was true. Even if she didn't know that yet.

Chapter 5

Evelyn

My car bounced as I took one of the dirt road's potholes too fast. I'd left the ranch a few minutes behind, and I didn't want to show up late on my third day of work.

The past couple of days had been a whirlwind, and it was crazy how quickly things could change.

Despite my nerves, I'd gone to the communal dinner on the ranch and met the other people staying there. An older gentleman who had trouble walking, a quiet, local teenage boy, and a middle-aged woman. No one mentioned *why* they were there, and it didn't feel polite to ask.

Lucas was there, too, with his giant body and easy smile, along with Daniel, one of the other owners of the Resting Warrior Ranch. Lucas pretended like any awkwardness between us had never existed, which I appreciated. But my heart still raced when I thought about his suggestion.

It wasn't a bad one. Talking to someone might help. But I couldn't risk talking to anyone and bringing hell down on them, because Nathan would hurt anyone I was close to.

And more than that, the fact that Lucas *saw* me like that made me panic. If a man I barely knew could see it, then I wasn't doing a good enough job hiding it. Then again, I supposed that showing up out of nowhere and looking for work could give someone pause. Especially with the way I'd reacted to the teacup.

Lucas had been kind and friendly at dinner, managing to put me at ease even when I'd thought that would be impossible. I'd thought that it might be nice to see him around more.

Now, it seemed like I saw him everywhere.

I'd seen him when I'd driven off the ranch to go to the interview and when I'd stopped by the lodge to sign myself up for the communal dinner rotation. He was working with the horses when I went out for walks in the evening, and I'd spotted him doing repairs around the ranch.

Whenever I saw him, he was ready with a smile and a wave, but he'd never forced me to talk to him. In fact, he seemed determined to give me as much space as I needed, and I appreciated it. Though I was starting to admit to myself that I was curious about him.

I shouldn't be.

Pulling up to the coffee shop, I sighed. It reminded me of the Sandia Bean in a lot of ways. There was a mountain view and a comfortable atmosphere. But Deja Brew felt like walking into a friend's house. Sparkling crystals hung in the windows and overstuffed armchairs sprawled around an ornate fireplace that frankly had no place in a coffee shop. Somehow, it all worked, pulled together by Lena.

She'd hired me on the spot, and I already liked her. She was vibrant and open. She neither took shit from anyone nor gave it. She wore her heart on her sleeve in a world where the rest of us were hiding. Admirable.

Tinkling crystal chimed as I pushed in—on time.

Lena sat in one of the chairs with a red-haired woman, but there was no one else in the store. She looked up and smiled at me. "I'm glad you're here. This is someone that I want you to meet. If you're going to be in Garnet Bend and working for me, you guys need to be friends." She stood and waved in a "get on with it" gesture.

I laughed. "Hi, I'm Evelyn."

The redhead looked up at me. She was beautiful, but her shoulders were heavy with something. People who held pain could recognize it in others. "Grace Townsend," she said, holding out a hand.

"Nice to meet you."

She smiled. "Lena has been singing your praises. I think once she got used to the idea of having more free time, you became her favorite person."

"I'm happy to help. And to have a job."

"Well," she took a sip of her coffee, "if you ever get tired of this place, you can always come work for me. I'm always looking for more female employees."

"What do you do?"

Lena appeared with a cup of coffee and set it down next to me like I was a customer and not supposed to be tying on an apron right now. "Don't you dare poach her already. I will have to lay down the law, Grace. And yes, by lay down the law I mean that I will have to kick your ass."

"You're welcome to try," Grace said, smirking. She

looked back at me. "I own a ranch. It's a pretty typical answer around here."

"Oh, where? I'm staying on a ranch right now. Until I get settled."

"North of town. The Ruby Round Ranch." She smiled, but this time it didn't reach her eyes. "It was my husband's way of poking fun at the name *Garnet Bend*."

"Clever." I glanced at her left hand. Her ring finger was empty.

"I should go," she said abruptly.

Lena placed her hand on her friend's shoulder. "You don't have to, Grace. I have a hard enough time getting you here as it is."

"I know. I promise that I'll be better about it. If not, you can come drag me into town on a leash."

Lena rolled her eyes. "Fine."

Grace stood and turned to me. "You should come out to the ranch sometime. We can have dinner. Maybe you can get this one to come with you." She nodded at Lena.

"I'd like that, thank you."

"Us girls have to stick together, right?"

I laughed. "Right. And feel free to stop by for dinner too. I think we might be close to each other if you're north of town."

"Oh?"

"Yeah," I said. "I'm staying at Resting Warrior. And there are dinners a couple times a week. Though I do have a kitchen in my house if that's not your thing."

I'd spent enough time controlling my reactions to know when someone else was doing it. Grace's entire energy changed. It turned cold, her body stiffening. "I'll think about that. But let me know if you want to come out my way."

"Sure."

She gathered her purse and Lena walked her to the door. They shared a few quiet words and hugged before Grace slipped out the door to the sound of the tinkling melody.

I closed my eyes, savoring the rich scent of coffee and a hint of baked sugar. If I could bottle this scent in a way that made it smell like it *didn't* come from a bottle, I would do it. But this kind of smell only came from the real thing.

"I'm glad you got to meet her," Lena said. "I was worried she was going to bolt before you came in."

Grace hurried down the street away from us. "I'm sorry. Did I say something wrong?"

"No, why?"

"She seemed bothered when I mentioned Resting Warrior."

Lena waved a hand, and I followed her behind the counter. "No, you were fine. Grace has a history with one of the men there, and they haven't exactly worked it out yet. But don't worry, I've folded it into my *Reintroduce Grace to the World* plan."

My apron hung on a hook next to Lena's, and I loved it. When she'd hired me, she'd taken me to one of the back rooms and pointed me at a box that overflowing with brightly colored aprons. The one I'd chosen was a vibrant teal, and Lena's was deep violet. The aprons alone embodied the spirit of Deja Brew.

It had only been two days, and I already loved it here.

Because of that, it was hard not to run. Did I really want to get attached and have to leave again? Did I want to break people's hearts and leave them wondering?

I'd sent an email to the managers of Sandia Bean resigning and saying I had to leave town indefinitely for a family emergency. It was always the same lie, one that kept the people I left behind from filing missing person's reports that would make my life that much more complicated.

The shop was already spotless. There wasn't much to do until the noon rush, so I leaned against the counter and turned to my new friend and boss. "Why do you need that kind of plan?"

Lena winced. "Grace's husband died six months ago. Car accident."

"Oh, shit."

"Yeah. She's been kind of isolated since then. Understandably. But she and her husband—Charles—had an interesting relationship. It wasn't really a romantic thing, though she doesn't like to talk about why. And I know that he wouldn't want her to spend her time all alone on the ranch. Especially when everything there reminds her of him. So I try to get her into town as much as possible."

I nodded. "Makes sense."

"And now, you can help me," she said. "You guys don't know each other well yet, but you're going to like each other."

"Good to know." I smiled and took a sip of the coffee that she'd given me.

"It is, and you know that I'm never wrong."

"Is that so?"

Lena grinned. "Well, I am your boss, so you have to say yes."

"Absolutely. You *are* always right. How could I forget?"

The door's chime sounded, signaling a customer, and we went back to work. This part was all familiar, and I was grateful for it. I could slip into the ease of small talk and cheering people up when I united them with their beloved caffeine.

The noon rush came and went, and the afternoon sun turned golden. Light flooded through the windows, casting rainbows across the space. It was hard not to think that this place was magic when it looked like this.

"So how is it at Resting Warrior?" Lena asked. "I know it's only been a couple of days. But are you liking it?"

I nodded. "Yeah, it's been nice. I'm still not sure why they're letting me stay there. But I signed up to help with the communal meals, so I feel like less of a burden."

"You're not a burden. That's what they do."

"What do you mean?"

Lena tilted her head. "They didn't tell you what the mission of the ranch is? There aren't exactly a lot of cattle on their property."

No, there weren't, from the parts that I'd seen. I shook my head. "Lucas mentioned something about them working with some therapists, but I—" I cut myself off, not wanting to say too much. "But we moved on quickly."

She smiled warmly. "Well, I'll let them tell you when they're ready. Or you're ready. But trust me, you're not a burden."

I hung my apron on its hook, comforted by the small reminder that I would be back. It was a nice thing for Lena to say, but I couldn't believe it. Not until I had more proof.

"I'll see you tomorrow?" I asked.

"You bet. Have a good night, Evie."

I smiled at the nickname. She'd just started using it, and I didn't mind. There was a warm pressure in my chest as I walked to my car. Roots were forming quickly, and that was dangerous. But I *liked* it. I was tired of being lonely, and so far, everyone here had been kind and friendly.

A healthy amount of cynicism still lived in me, but for once, I tried to push it aside. I wanted to believe that people could be kind without another motive. I wanted to believe that I could be safe and happy. For now, I was going to ignore the warnings in my gut to run before I got hurt. I needed rest, and if anywhere, the Resting Warrior Ranch seemed like the place to do it.

The sun was sinking into evening when I pulled up to the Bitterroot House. Though it was the middle of summer, there was a bite of chill in the air that woke up my lungs and made me want to explore. I couldn't bear the idea of going inside yet.

I'd gone for a couple of short walks around the property but had been driven back by nerves and the ever-present feeling of eyes on my back. Today, I felt neither of those things.

I walked west toward the setting sun where the lake was. This property really was stunning, with open fields and patches of woods set against the backdrop of the mountains. But the thing I didn't think I would get used to was the *silence*. I didn't realize how much ambient noise there was in towns and cities until I'd felt the absence of it, and this was the first place I'd been where there was almost nothing.

Only the crunch of my footsteps on rocks and grass and the rush of wind. Maybe the occasional sounds from the animals here—horses, dogs, sheep, and even some alpacas. But those were natural sounds. And it was still so much quieter than the city.

I couldn't remember a time when I'd been comfortable in silence. Silence meant punishment, that things were building to an explosion that would hurt. And after so long, that was a hard habit to let go of. But here, under an open sky blazing bright with orange and pink, the silence felt peaceful instead of foreboding.

For long minutes, I breathed as much of that peace into my lungs as I could. I was greedy. I wanted all of it in case this was all I could get.

A distant voice startled my eyes open. Lucas was across

the field with a horse. One that I'd seen him with before. It wasn't a well-behaved horse, and it was clear that it was fighting Lucas's hold on his bridle, but Lucas didn't react.

I stepped into a copse of trees, making sure not to announce myself. Every time I'd seen Lucas, he'd seen me too. There hadn't been an opportunity to watch him alone. People were different alone. If I'd gotten a chance to observe Nathan in complete isolation, would I be here now?

Lucas stopped and turned to the horse. He was smiling and reached out to stroke a hand down the horse's neck even though the animal was clearly skittish.

God, how long had it been since I'd ridden a horse? Over a decade, for sure. Though I'd been obsessed as a kid and teenager. I'd spent every weekend at the stables and as many nights as I could con my parents into. I missed it. There'd been a time when I'd thought animals would be my life.

I stopped the thoughts before they dragged me away from the present. The evening was too beautiful for that.

The horse yanked away, trying to rear up and back, but Lucas held firm. Across the distance I heard the murmur of his voice, calming and gentle. Not even a flash of temper.

You could tell a lot about a person by the way they dealt with animals, and Lucas didn't send up any red flags.

Had I expected something different? Nothing I'd seen so far had given me any reason to think that Lucas could turn violent.

The part of my mind that I hated whispered, *You thought the same thing about Nathan.*

It was true, and it was a lie. If I was honest with myself, I'd ignored signs in favor of being in love. I hadn't seen any signs with Lucas. Yet. I wanted to know that the man who'd offered me shelter wasn't going to turn on me.

He worked with the horse for a while, walking him around the field and letting him have some space out of the barn while still forcing him into human proximity. It was a good idea. But inevitably the horse became too jumpy, and Lucas turned back to the barn with him.

Before he reached the path that would take him out of view, Lucas turned, looked directly at me, and waved once.

Shock rolled through my system, and I was suddenly aware of everything at once. The breeze on my skin and the rustle of leaves and the smell of hay and manure in clean air. He didn't linger and was gone before I could take my second breath.

He'd known I'd been there the whole time. So why hadn't he let me know earlier? Why hadn't he called out and asked me to join him or try to talk to me? Force me out of hiding?

The answer rooted me to the ground. It was the same reason that he hadn't pushed me to talk the other times I'd seen him. Somehow, Lucas knew that I needed space—that I needed to hide. And he didn't judge me for it or try to change it.

Terror clung to my insides and washed down my spine. Being seen for what I was, that was more frightening than being chased by a madman.

But at the same time, so deep I couldn't locate the source, there was relief.

Chapter 6

Lucas

The ceiling of my bedroom was one of the most familiar sights in my life, and I hated that. I'd been staring at it for at least an hour, waiting for my heart to calm and the surrounding air not to feel so dangerous.

But it wasn't any use. My mind was now on alert, and things kept jumping out of the shadows.

Fuck.

I sat up, scrubbing my hands across my face. The sheets clung to the sweat from the dreams, dragging across my skin. I'd really thought I was past this.

I hadn't had one of the fucking nightmares in a long time, but the past few days . . . they'd been happening again. A big regression—that's what Rayne called it. She'd probably tell me that something had made me more sensitive to my past, and it was bringing all this shit up.

Didn't matter that I'd thought I'd dealt with all of it. And it wouldn't matter. Working here and through all of my issues many times, it would still keep coming up. And unfortunately, I knew what was bringing it back.

Evelyn.

I started my nighttime routine for when this happened, walking through my house and turning on every available light. Shadows were not good right now.

This time, I'd lasted longer than normal. When I'd woken up with the sound of machine guns firing in my ears and the phantom weight of Emmett in my arms, I couldn't stand the darkness. In the early days of living in this house, my power bill had been through the roof, with all the lights on nearly every night.

The other guys never said anything. They all had their own demons.

All the lights were on now, but it wasn't nearly enough. Tonight, I craved air, and even though outside meant more darkness, I knew my mind well enough to know that forcing myself to stay here would only make it worse. So I dragged on sweats and a T-shirt before heading outside.

The clock told me it was after midnight. But it wouldn't be the first time one of us had wandered the ranch in the middle of the night. Jogging down the stairs from my porch, I headed away from my house and into the darkness of the nearby field.

The weight began to lift off my chest, cleansed with the cool night air. And I could finally bring my mind back to the problem at hand.

Evelyn.

I reframed the thought. She wasn't a problem, but she was clearly affecting me. And in a way, it all fit together. The deep, roaring instinct to protect her hadn't lessened even though I currently had to do it from a distance.

I'd let her watch me earlier this evening because I'd known she felt safer from that distance. But that didn't mean it was easy to stay away. And given the dream I'd just had . . .

Yeah, it made sense. I hadn't been able to save Emmett, and now this drive to protect Evelyn was bringing up the guilt I always felt when I thought about him. I didn't want to have the same guilt with Evelyn. It didn't matter that I barely knew her—she was mine to protect.

I knew that. In a deep, caveman, I-shouldn't-say-those-words-out-loud way.

But I still had to discover more about what was drawing me to her. She was fucking gorgeous, and she'd invaded very different kinds of dreams, no matter how hard I'd tried to keep her out of them. But it was more than that. Something below the surface was yanking me toward her with all the speed and subtlety of a freight train.

Across the ranch, a light was on in one of the guest houses. When I was out here at night with nothing but the stars, every artificial light was a beacon. My stomach did a swoop both of dread and excitement. It was the Bitterroot House. So I wasn't the only one having trouble sleeping.

Earlier today while I had been walking the horse, it had occurred to me that the process for approaching Evelyn was the same. Obviously, Evelyn wasn't an animal, but slow, consistent exposure was the only way either of them would let go of the nerves they carried.

Cutting a wide berth around one of the other guest houses, I made it to the road. Evelyn was sitting on the porch of the house in a pool of light, and my anxiety eased. But that same instinct that had told me she was more comfortable at a distance told me that I shouldn't sneak up on her in the dark. She was safe. That was enough for me.

"Who's there?"

She was looking in my direction, body now fully alert. I'd underestimated how much she'd be listening. And staying silent wouldn't ease anything for her. "It's Lucas."

She relaxed. "Oh."

I walked closer—close enough that she could see me in the porch light, but far enough to respect her distance. "I'm sorry, I saw a light while walking, and I wanted to make sure you were all right. I wasn't planning to bother you."

She blew out a breath. "I'm glad it was you and not like . . . a bear."

"A mountain lion would probably be more accurate." Her face fell, and I chuckled. "I'm mostly kidding. There are mountain lions, but they're actually pretty shy and stay away from humans. And we have electric fences."

"So . . . sitting on the porch in the middle of the night is a safe idea?"

I laughed again. "Yeah, you'll be fine."

"Good to know." She leaned back against the chair.

She was wearing comfortable clothes made for sleeping, and it was the first time I'd ever seen her in something that showed skin. The tank top revealed her arms. And then I had to force myself to keep still.

Evelyn had scars. I wasn't close enough to see their true shape, but there were a lot of them, drifting down her arms in seemingly random patterns. They didn't look like they were self-inflicted, which confirmed my suspicion. She was running from something—or someone—and I'd bet money it was what had given her those scars.

"You were out walking?"

I nodded, loosening my jaw enough to speak. "Needed some air."

"Most people are sleeping by now."

"You're not."

A small smile that felt like a victory appeared on her face. "Fair enough." A small silence intervened. "Couldn't sleep?"

I shook my head.

"Me neither. And I've never seen stars like this. So why would I stay inside when I could watch them out here?"

Looking up, I saw what she meant. The vast Montana sky made the stars so clear it felt like you could touch them. You could see them twinkling. The moon hung low on the horizon, just a sliver that didn't overpower the stars. It was stunning.

On impulse, I took a step closer. "Do you want to see the best view of the stars?"

Her eyes met mine, cautious. "Where's that?"

"Top of the lodge," I said. "It's built for stargazing. Well, not exactly for stargazing, but we built it with the intent for it to be used. Sometimes, we take the grill up there and barbecue."

Another small smile. "Men and their barbecues."

"Damn right."

"Does barbecuing on a roof really make it that much better?"

I shifted my hands into my pockets. "No, but it makes it easier to see in all directions in spite of the smoke."

None of us had really said that out loud when we'd thrown around the idea of a flat deck on top of the lodge. We weren't hipsters—we hadn't dragged a grill all the way up three stories on a whim. No, all of us needed the security of being able to see our surroundings while the air was filled with the scent of burning.

"What are you watching for?" Evelyn's gaze rested on me, its weight tangible.

I knew that she was running from something, so it was only fair she knew that I had scars too. Not all of them were visible. "What am I not watching for would probably be the better question."

"Doesn't that get exhausting?" she asked. "Always watching everything?"

"You tell me."

Poking that sore spot was a risk. But she didn't turn to anger this time. "Yes. It's exhausting."

A layer slipped off her. Her fragility was suddenly visible, as well as that same exhaustion that drove us both from sleep. Her dark hair curled around her shoulders, and her fingers wove together only to break apart again.

The thin tank top made the curves she'd tried to hide obvious. She was stunning. My hands balled into fists in my pockets, fighting the urge to reach for her. I wanted to feel her skin, and those curves, under my hands. I wanted to just . . . hold her so that we could both rest.

But that's not what she needed right now. "How about the stars?"

Evelyn stared at me, no part of her body moving. I didn't move either, feeling her process whatever she saw and weigh the risks. If she said no, I wouldn't blame her. And I hoped I'd given her enough space for her to understand that I wouldn't be upset or hurt her if she said no.

Then she rose. "Okay. Not like I'm going to sleep anyway."

I smiled. "That makes two of us."

Chapter 7

Evelyn

I followed Lucas through the lodge and up to the roof, and holy *shit* he was right.

The roof itself was exactly as he'd described it. A large, flat, open area bordered with a low wall before the roof sloped away. But it barely held my attention.

Even though we were only three stories up, the sky felt so much clearer here, away from my little porch light and anything else that could get in between me and the stars.

Lucas crossed to a bench seat and opened it. "We keep pillows and blankets in here in case anyone feels like doing this. And to protect them from the rain."

He handed me a pillow and blanket and immediately moved, spreading his a few feet away from mine to give me some space. But it didn't feel like he was avoiding me or was disgusted by me. He was being careful.

That was nice.

I tried to tell myself that even if he were disgusted by

me, I wouldn't care. But that wasn't true. Lucas had been nothing but kind to me, and I liked him. I *shouldn't* care what he thought of me, but I did.

I'd hesitated coming here with him. It was a risk. But he didn't know that there was pepper spray in my pocket or that I very much knew how to use it. I also knew that I wouldn't have to.

Spreading out my blanket and pillow, I looked up at the stars. The sight made me think I should have tried hiding in the wilderness a long time ago. A blue so rich it was nearly black was painted with swaths of stars that you could never see with city lights.

"Some nights, it's so clear you can see the Milky Way down here," Lucas said. "But if you really want to see it, the mountains are the place to be."

"Elevation?"

"Yup."

The quiet between us didn't feel oppressive or like it was charged with something waiting to happen. Another easy silence, the kind that lifted the weight off my shoulders and let me breathe.

"I haven't talked to you much the past few days," Lucas said. "I'm glad it went well with Lena."

"Me too. She's . . . great. And I love everything so far. It reminds me a lot of my last job, which I loved. She seems happy too."

He chuckled. "Lena is a force of nature. When we opened the ranch a couple of years ago, there was some resistance in the community since we're not exactly a traditional operation. She was immediately on our side and fought with everything she had to get the town to accept us. We owe her a lot."

"Why wouldn't they accept you?"

He shrugged. "People around here can be pretty traditional. And sometimes that means they're resistant to change. But they're good people, and they came around once they saw that what we were doing actually helped the community."

"What do you do? You never really told me." I had an inkling, given that he'd told me that they worked with therapists, but I hadn't looked into it further.

Lucas looked over at me and smiled. "We help people who need it. Mostly through training service animals or opening our property up for people who need to get away for a while—a chance to rest like the ranch name says. All of us who live or work here, we've been through things, and we know what it's like to not have anywhere to go. Especially if you're . . . running from something."

I swallowed and said nothing. But I didn't look away either.

"But in some ways, it's easier to show you. Next time you're around in the afternoon, I'll give you a tour. All official and everything."

"I'd like that. Can we see the alpacas too?"

He grinned at me. "No tour of the Resting Warrior Ranch would be complete without showing the alpacas."

I found myself smiling. It was easy to smile around him. Probably too easy, but it felt too good to stop. Lucas was the first man I'd said more than a couple of sentences to in years. The first one I'd voluntarily been this close to.

"How's the house working for you?" he asked.

It was great. A godsend. I'd stayed in far worse places during my first weeks in a new town. "It's wonderful. Really. Thank you for letting me use it. I'll be out of there as soon as I can find a place in town."

Lucas smiled. "Take as much time as you need."

"I don't want to be a burden."

"You're not. Like I told you. We help people."

Still, the feeling of imbalance swam uneasily in my gut. They helped people . . .

For a fraction of a second, I entertained the thought that they *could* help me. And I shut it down like I was slamming a door in place. They couldn't help me. Even if they wanted to, I didn't want to put them in Nathan's path.

A cool breeze floated across the roof, carrying the scent of fresh air and mountains. There was a certain sweetness that permeated the air here sometimes, and I couldn't put my finger on what it was. It came out of nowhere, no consistent plants or flowers when it was near. So I'd come to the conclusion that it was simply . . . Montana.

Lucas's voice was quiet when he spoke. "Are you comfortable talking about them?"

"About what?"

"Your scars."

My whole body went stiff. I'd gotten so comfortable with him that I'd completely forgotten my arms were exposed. He could see the constellations of scars that ran down my arms, small dots and larger circles. Lines. The drawings of a madman on my body.

There were more scars under my clothes, but he didn't need to know that.

I forced a smile. "Oh. Those. It was a long time ago. An accident. It doesn't matter."

He said nothing, and when I dared to look over at him, he was staring back. In the pale light of the stars, his eyes were pure darkness, and he was looking right through me. I don't think he bought my excuse any more than I did. It didn't sound real out loud. But I wasn't ready for that.

What would Lucas think of me if he knew?

Terror gripped me along with a memory. In my third hiding place, a couple of coworkers had seen my scars by accident. I'd spilled something in the break room and pushed up my sleeves to clean it up. I'd done it without thinking, and then I'd heard the gasp from behind me.

I'd decided to take a risk and tell them the truth. I would never forget the looks on their faces. Their first reaction hadn't been sympathy or pity—it had been disgust. Why had I stayed with someone who had done that to me? Why hadn't I left? Why hadn't I seen that he was a fucking psychopath earlier?

They were all questions that I had asked myself thousands of times. But that wasn't what broke me. It was the pity and disbelief in their eyes. The certainty that what had happened to me would never happen to them, because surely, they would see it coming.

"I saw you signed up to help with meals."

"Yeah," I said, blowing out a breath at the subject change. "I had a good time. Everyone was really nice."

"I'm glad. It's actually my turn to cook this week. You might have to rescue me."

I smiled. "Really?"

"I'm hopeless."

"I don't know, you seem like the kind of guy who knows his way around a kitchen."

He chuckled. "I can feed myself, but it won't be fine dining."

"Simplicity is good. Underrated, in most cases."

"That bodes well for me," he said. "It means I might be able to impress you with my mediocre cooking skills."

"I'll keep an open mind."

I'd rolled on my side to face him, and he'd done the same, like a mirror. We were so close now that we could touch if we wanted. Lucas could lean closer and kiss me without a second thought.

The world spun, and there was suddenly no air. Close.

Too close. Why had I let him get this close? "I think I'm tired enough to sleep now. Thank you."

I sprang to my feet so quickly that I stumbled and nearly fell again. Lucas reached out to catch me, but I stopped him. "I'm fine. I'm fine, I promise."

"Evelyn—"

"Thank you for showing me this," I said. "It was lovely."

He stared at me in that way that made me want to sprint toward the mountains and not come back. The way that told me that he saw too much and I couldn't hide anything from him.

Finally, "Goodnight, Evelyn."

I kept my steps slow until I reached the stairs and gave into my instinct to sprint. I'd let him get so close, and I hadn't noticed. My guard was slipping. I couldn't afford to let that happen. Not with what was at stake.

The fact that I wasn't afraid of Lucas was what made me afraid. I couldn't remember a time when I hadn't been afraid of a man or of coworkers I knew were safe. There was always an undercurrent of worry.

Not with Lucas. He made me feel . . . better. Like I could breathe and everything was easy.

But just because I wasn't afraid of him didn't mean that he could be trusted. I was the last person who should be called on as a judge of character. In spite of all that, as I hurried back to my house and crawled into my bed, regret clung to my skin like mist. It wouldn't leave.

I shoved it down with the rest of everything that was buried. Regrets were something I could survive. And that was all that mattered.

Chapter 8

Evelyn

The crystal chime rang above the door, and I looked up as Grace entered the store. She was smiling, and her whole demeanor was lighter than the last time I'd seen her.

"Hey," I called.

"Hi." Her eyes flicked to Lena coming out of the back. "See? You didn't have to come out to the ranch to drag me into civilization."

Lena laughed. "I'm so proud."

"What will you have?" I asked.

"Coffee, and one of the chocolate chip cookies if there are any."

"Hell yes, there are," Lena said, ringing up the coffee. "I just made a batch so you can have a hot one."

Grace groaned. "You know my weakness."

"Yes, I do."

"I'll grab it," I said with a smile. They were all cooling

on a rack in the kitchen. They made the place smell amazing. Lucas had been right when he'd told me that these were the best baked goods around. I could tell that, and I hadn't been anywhere else in town yet.

I picked one up, grateful that they were cool. Lena had tried to tempt me into the kitchen to help with the baking, but she hadn't pushed me when I'd told her that ovens made me nervous. Ovens. Hot water. Stoves. Fire. Anything that could burn. I dealt with it when I had to but avoided it when I could.

The yawn hit me as I came out of the kitchen—they'd been catching me all day. Staying up half the night looking at stars and then lying awake for hours after that hadn't been great for my energy level today. But maybe I would get a good night's sleep tonight.

"Damn, girl," Lena said. "You okay? You've been yawning all over the place."

"I'm fine," I said as I handed Grace the cookie in a paper sleeve. "Just didn't get that much sleep last night."

"I hope it was the fun kind of getting no sleep," Grace said. "That makes it all worth it."

The blush was instantaneous, and any chance they wouldn't notice was gone.

"Oh my gosh, what happened?" Grace placed her elbows on the counter and propped her chin in her hands like she was ready for story time.

"It's nothing."

Grace snorted mid sip. "Sure. It's nothing, all right."

"I . . . okay." I recapped my excursion to the roof with Lucas while they stared at me with their mouths open. I skipped over the part where I freaked out and left and just said we parted ways. "See? It's nothing."

"Is it though?" Lena asked.

"Yes." I sighed. "I think he feels responsible for me. He

wanted to make sure everything was okay when he came to see why my lights were on. It's not like he came over with the intention of taking me stargazing."

"Who knows?" Grace's face was a sneaky grin. "Maybe that's exactly what his intention was."

"It wasn't." I looked down at my hands, pushing aside the regrets I had about leaving and ignoring the way my body *felt* when remembering it. I couldn't ignore the calmness that filled me when I was in his presence. And they wouldn't understand how tempting that was. But my stomach fluttered when I thought about Lucas now, and I hadn't decided if that was terrifying or amazing. It was all too confusing. And confusion could get me killed.

Lena put her hand on my shoulder. "We're only teasing, Evie. But if it ever turns into *not nothing* I better be the first person to know. Got it?"

"Got it," I said, laughing. She would in fact kick my ass if I kept it from her. Lena was like that. Barely a week of friendship, and she was all in. And it made me want to be that way too.

A glinting reflection caught my eye across the street through the windows. A man walking, hands in his pockets, like nothing in the world mattered.

The ground disappeared underneath me, and I was on the floor. All the air was gone, my lungs on fire. Why couldn't I breathe? Why was I burning? Pain flared up my arms and stretched across my back like a familiar, brutal caress.

No.

He couldn't be here. He couldn't have found me already. It wasn't possible. There was nothing on the grid since Albuquerque except the emails to Melanie. And I had done everything I could to keep those anonymous. Was that enough?

But that was him. Was it him? Was I seeing things now?

My heart pounded in my ears, every beat sending more panic through my veins. Terror was cold. It froze you in place and weighed you down and rendered you helpless. I'd spent forever trying not to let terror get the best of me, but I couldn't move.

Voices came from somewhere. Grace and Lena asking if I was all right. But there was no way I could respond to them. Not with vines of adrenaline climbing up from the floor and tangling with my limbs. Holding me down.

I was bound in the dark. I couldn't breathe. I needed to *breathe. He's coming back. He's going to do it again.* What other parts of myself would I have to hide under clothes once he got his hands on me?

Pain flared along with my skin, springing to life through memories so real that I would never forget them. Ever. And he wouldn't stop, he wouldn't stop, he wouldn't stop—

Hands touched me, and I fought back. I wouldn't let it happen. This time I would fight. I was telling him to stop. Telling him no. But he wasn't fighting back. Good. A hand caught my wrist, not doing anything but holding it. Gently. Firmly.

"Evelyn."

That wasn't his voice. This voice was dark whiskey and chocolate and safety. My vision cleared of haze and found warm brown eyes close to mine. Lucas was crouching in front of me. Crouching because I was on the ground. I'd fallen behind the counter, back pressed up against it like I was ready to lash out. And I was.

Lena stood behind him, looking down at me with worry. I'd had an attack. I hadn't had one in years. Why

58

now? My cheeks flushed hot, but I still couldn't move or run. I wasn't out of the spiral yet. Not completely.

I closed my eyes for a moment, pressing down the horror that they'd seen this part of me. I didn't want these people to react with disgust or pity. That would . . . I didn't think I could take it. They didn't need to see this.

Slowly, I took long breaths until I didn't think I was going to cry. Lucas said nothing. He'd only said my name. That was what had brought me out of the spiral. My wrists were still in his hands. Because I'd tried to hit him.

"I'm sorry," I whispered.

Slowly, he released my hands, placing them on my knees. "Did you hit your head when you fell?"

"No." At least I didn't think so.

"Anything injured at all?"

I searched my body for any pain, but there was none. At least none that was real. There were still phantoms and flickers that my mind was tricking me with. But there wasn't anything that I could do about that. "No, I don't think so."

"That's good." His voice was quiet. Low and smooth so that only I could hear him talking. "How's work been today? Busy?"

I shook my head. "Pretty average."

"Average is good. Anything stand out as unusual?"

"Um." Trying to think was like wading through mud as thick as caramel. "I was kind of clumsy. I almost spilled an entire pot of coffee. The mess would have been bad."

A small smile. "Then I'm glad you saved it."

I took another breath, and the panic receded a little more. He was bringing me back to myself. Grounding me. Which meant he'd done this before. He knew how to break someone out of a panic attack. I wasn't sure if that made him witnessing this better or worse.

"You know," Lucas said, "I've never asked you what your favorite color is."

I met his eyes again. "Why do you want to know?"

"Humor me."

"Teal," I said. "Like the ocean."

He smiled wide this time. "Like your apron. I'll remember that."

I took a full breath, and the adrenaline keeping me tight faded, and I sagged against the back of the counter.

"Evelyn," Lucas said softly. "You're in Deja Brew. No one else is here but me, Lena, and Grace. Can you tell me what triggered you?"

Just the thought brought the walls crashing down. The oxygen shred itself in my lungs and I was suffocating.

"Evelyn," Lucas said again. "You're still here."

I was. And he was still here with me. Lucas hadn't moved, but I had. I'd reached for him in the second wave of panic, the fingers of my right hand grasping his belt and one of the loops of his jeans, like he was an anchor.

He must not have noticed it, because he looked down in surprise, and then back at me. The air between us charged. Something that wasn't pain crackled in the air, but neither of us moved to break it open.

It wasn't a conscious thing, reaching for him. But it wasn't something that I could take back either. A part of me saw him as safe, and he was the closest thing I had. My cheeks flamed in a blush. I couldn't read the look in Lucas's eyes, but it wasn't disgust. Or pity.

"Can you stand?"

I swallowed. "Maybe."

"Will you let me help you move to the back patio where you can sit?"

I nodded.

Lucas took my hand and helped me up, but my knees

didn't make it, buckling before I was upright. I never hit the ground. Lucas's arm swept under my legs, and I was suddenly in his arms.

Panic tried to swallow me, and the instinct to fight him locked all my limbs in place. I hadn't been touched by a man in years. But deep down, I knew that he wouldn't hurt me. I knew it on a level so deep that I couldn't question it.

My own judgment wasn't something I trusted anymore, but that instinct kept me still in his arms as he carried me to the patio. The way he held me was effortless, and it was hard to ignore the true surge of safety I felt resting there.

Warmth and the scents of both pine and mountain air wrapped around me. I could fall asleep here, rest my head on his shoulder and let go because he would catch me. Yearning hit me so strongly that tears came to my eyes, and I had to blink them away.

He set me in one of the chairs on the patio in the sun. I hadn't realized how cold I was until I was pressed against his body. The warmth of the sun was nice, but it was nothing compared to the furnace that was Lucas.

A teacup was set in front of me. Lena.

Oh my God. I'd had an episode at work. At a brand-new job. I had really liked this one too.

"Lena, I'm so sorry. That hasn't happened in a long time. I didn't know it would."

"Don't worry about it, Evie."

"I'm serious," I said. "It's not a normal thing, and I'm so sorry. I get it if you don't want that kind of thing around the shop—"

Lena held up a hand, stern kindness on her face. "Don't be ridiculous. I'm not angry at you, and I'm sure as hell not going to fire you. Go home and rest, and I'll see you tomorrow. And only if you actually feel up to it."

"But—"

"No buts. You come back when you're one hundred percent, or I'll lovingly kick your ass and send you home again."

"Okay."

Grace stepped forward and slipped me a piece of paper with a phone number. "If you need to talk, I'm around. I've been through some stuff too."

That same sadness was back from the day I'd met her. I wasn't sure I was ready for that, but of anyone, Grace might understand. "Thank you."

The two of them disappeared back into the shop, leaving me with Lucas, who was staring at me. I suppressed a wince. This was the part where he brought up the fact that I'd lied about running from something. Not once, but twice. Where he threw it in my face and asked me to move out sooner rather than later.

"Do you mind if I call you Ev?" He asked. "Lena called you Evie, so I wondered if you were okay with nicknames."

Ev. I rolled it around in my brain. I'd never had anyone call me that before. Granted, I hadn't gone by my real name in years. I was less comfortable with the full version of it, so nicknames felt more natural. "That's fine."

A breeze hit my back, and I shivered. I hadn't spent much time out here on the patio, but it was a pretty space. Lights were strung above, forming a roof that would glow prettily in the evening. Flower boxes surrounded the brick pavers, and there were wrought-iron tables and chairs. It was cute and eclectic in the same way the rest of Deja Brew was.

Lena steeped herself into everything that she did. I wished I could do that.

"You're cold," Lucas said. "The tea will help."

I took a sip and tried to remember what had set me off.

It was Nathan. Or at least someone I'd thought was Nathan. But if he was here, then I couldn't be here. I needed to find out if what I had seen was real.

"So how are you liking Montana, in general?"

I blinked, the question throwing me off. "It's nice. Very beautiful. I don't know what makes it smell so good half the time."

He chuckled. "I'm not sure either. It's just the way it is."

"I do like it here though. More than I thought I would."

"Is that a bad thing?" Lucas looked at me like the answer meant more than a simple yes or no. I didn't know if it was a good or a bad thing right now. It was bad because if I had to leave, then it would hurt. And it was good because I'd enjoyed my time here so far.

My hands shook as I played back the memory of that stranger walking across the street, and my stomach flipped. Even if it wasn't him, could I afford to take that chance and put everyone in danger? Lucas, Lena, Grace, everyone at the ranch?

"So teal," Lucas said, referencing my favorite color. "I haven't spent much time by the ocean. Do you like it there?"

"Yes," I breathed. When I was by the ocean, I felt complete. It was hard to explain. The mountains were beautiful, and I could enjoy living in them. But the ocean felt like home. Part of growing up in Florida, I guess.

I tilted my head. "Why the random questions?"

He smiled a little. "Distracting you. Is it working?"

Surprisingly, it was. My hands weren't shaking anymore, and I did feel warmer. "A bit."

"Can I take you home, Ev?"

The casual way he said it made something deep in me

ache. *Home* sounded so nice right now, even if it was a guest house. "Yes, thank you."

I kept looking around as he walked me to his truck, determined to run at any sign of Nathan, but there was nothing. Everything in Garnet Bend seemed almost painfully normal. Like nothing had happened at all.

"What about my car?"

"I'll take care of it," he said as he held open the door and helped me up. His touch was gentle but it felt like a brand—heat through my clothes. I told myself that it was because I was still cold.

The rest of my mind knew better.

Lucas didn't ask me any more questions on the way back to the ranch, but the quiet between us was comfortable. Comforting. Lucas had a steady presence that helped me relax. I was glad that he was driving. If I'd gotten in my own car, I might have driven out of town and not looked back.

I still wasn't sure that I shouldn't.

He drove me all the way to my house and jumped out of the truck to help me down. He walked me to the door, alert the whole time. Even on his property, he was looking for any danger.

He stopped when I reached the door and unlocked it. "Evelyn—" The look on his face was a mixture of wanting and anger and something else. It was too much to decipher. It looked like he wanted to say everything and nothing. He took a small step forward into my space, so close that I could almost feel his heat again.

My heart kicked up a rhythm, either panic or something else, but I didn't move. For the first time in a long time, I didn't want to.

Lucas started again. "Evelyn, the ranch is secure. We have one of the best security systems there is, and all of us who run Resting Warrior are former SEALs. We take security seriously." He paused before looking at me again. "You are *safe* here."

Emotion hit me. An ache and an itch in my chest that made me look away. He couldn't know what those words meant to me. What hearing them felt like. But he also didn't know Nathan. And I doubted I would be safe anywhere. Not anymore.

He moved slowly, pulling out a piece of paper with writing on it. "This is my number. You can call me any time you need to. Day or night. Okay?"

I swallowed past the lump in my throat. "Okay."

Lucas waited until I was inside and the door was locked before he walked away.

Chapter 9

Lucas

The second that Evelyn closed the door behind her, I was moving. Movement was the only way I wouldn't go insane. The drive to protect and claim was warring with my control, and I was close to losing it. I needed to make sure that what I'd told her was true. That she was safe here.

My truck flew down the road that circled the property. It wasn't a small loop, but I wasn't taking any chances. It didn't matter to me that whatever or whoever had triggered her was in town, Evelyn needed a space where safety was sacred. And I could make that happen.

The fences that surrounded Resting Warrior weren't normal ranch fences. Those were simple, made of wood or wire, and only intended to keep cattle from wandering off. But that didn't work around a place run by seven navy SEALs all struggling with trauma.

No, our fences were high and electrified. They were

part of the reason the town hadn't been thrilled about us moving in right away, like I had told Evelyn. To them, the high fences and security meant we were doing things that we shouldn't. But once we'd explained that we were helping people and animals who needed to feel as safe as possible, they'd been nothing but supportive. That was good.

I needed to tell Evelyn the true purpose of Resting Warrior. I'd been avoiding it because of her first reaction to me suggesting therapy, but today's events made it clearer than ever that she was meant to be here.

I'd never heard Lena's voice like that. Panicked and desperate. "It's Evelyn. *Please*." I'd been moving before she finished the first sentence.

She'd been on the floor, and I'd thought she'd hurt herself, but whatever had triggered her had made her look like she'd seen death incarnate. And the thing that she didn't seem to remember—though I would never fucking forget—were the words she'd said over and over.

"It's him, it's him, it's him."

Clearly she'd seen someone who had triggered that response, and that was enough to make me furious. No one should have to live with that. Especially not her, with those scars on her arms. If this person was the one who'd hurt her and made her run—who had put the fear in her eyes—I wasn't sure what I'd do.

Ev reaching for me had hollowed me out inside. She'd held on to me because she'd had nothing else, and because she'd known I was safe. Something about that had broken me at the same time that I'd wanted more.

I forced my jaw to unclench and my hands to relax on the steering wheel of my truck. The fence was intact. No visual signs that anything was broken. But that wasn't good enough.

Back at the main lodge, I threw my truck into park and took the stairs into the house two at a time. The security room was empty, so I sat down in front of the wall of monitors and started flipping through our cameras. Digital security wasn't my strong suit, but we'd all trained in how to use this when we'd started the ranch, so I could find my way around.

Nothing had been broken or even touched. No signs of any digital attack to take down the fence's electricity, and the whole perimeter fence was responding perfectly. We were secure here. But the anxious itch to solve the problem didn't disappear.

I pulled out my phone and dialed.

"Daigle Security."

"Hey, Jerry," I said. "It's Lucas over at Resting Warrior."

His tone changed from professional to jovial. "Well, hello. Been a while since I've talked to anyone from the ranch." He chuckled. "Which doesn't surprise me; you guys run a tight ship over there. What do you need with small-town security?"

Jerry was a retired cop turned private security, and he ran all of the cameras in town. It was a good living in a town this size, and everybody loved him. He was a kind man who went out of his way to help people while also calling out bullshit. A rare combination.

"I was wondering if you could give me coverage from this afternoon, all over town, but specifically around Deja Brew. Literally everything you have."

There was silence for a second. "Got a time frame?"

"Give me one o'clock to four o'clock."

Jerry made a sound. "I can get that to you, but it'll take some time to get it all. Earliest I can get you that amount of footage is tomorrow morning. That work for you?"

I sighed silently. It wasn't exactly a surprise, but I'd been hoping it would be sooner. "Yeah, that'll work. I'll owe you one."

"Nah, you won't. But is there something that I should be looking for?"

Jerry had been a good cop, and he knew how to pry information out of someone even when they weren't looking to give it. He liked to be informed about what was happening in the town, and this would only pique his interest, but it was a risk worth taking. "Nothing specific," I said. "But if I find something that you need to worry about, I'll let you know."

"I appreciate that. Normal email good for the footage?"

"Perfect. Thanks, Jerry." I hung up.

"You're calling Jerry?" Harlan's voice came from behind me. Shit. I was so distracted that I didn't even hear people coming up behind me now. "Yeah."

"Why?"

"I don't know yet. I'll tell you if it turns out to be something."

Evelyn's story wasn't mine to share, and I didn't want to get the guys as riled up as I was if it turned out that it wasn't anything. My gut told me that it wasn't nothing, but I needed to be cautious. I was tiptoeing on the edges of a boundary already by getting the footage, and I wasn't going to step over that line before I had to.

Or before I talked to Evelyn about it.

Harlan shook his head. "You don't have to tell me, but you've got to do something, because you're so tense you're about to snap."

He wasn't wrong.

"Come on, Lucas. Let's go."

"Where?" My tone was dark. I didn't want to go anywhere right now.

"The gym. Because you look like you need to beat the hell out of something, and I need a workout anyway."

Evelyn was safe in her house, the property was secure, and there was nothing I could do until I got the footage. If I kept all this energy inside my body, I was going to explode. This was better than nothing. "Fine."

We had a gym on the property behind the lodge, a huge building with state-of-the-art equipment and a space where we could do exactly what we were about to do: whale on each other. I grabbed an extra pair of clothes from my locker and taped my hands. But each movement was in a daze.

I couldn't do anything to help Evelyn until she told me what she was running from. But why would she do that? I was nothing to her. She had no reason to trust me beyond not making her life miserable the past week. Why should she trust me? I was a stranger who'd shown her the sky and accidentally seen her scars.

But it didn't feel that way to me. I felt like I knew her, even though that was utterly impossible. I wanted to save her. I *needed* to save her. Since I hadn't been able to save my mother. And I hadn't been able to save—

Harlan came at me, and I had to duck under the force of his blow. I didn't need to warm up, I was already too warm with the intensity and the roaring in my ears.

This wasn't a graceful sparring match. It was raw and elemental. Pure instinct and exactly what Harlan had said I needed: beating the hell out of something.

Thoughts about how I needed to save Evelyn to make up for my past kept rising up, and I kept punching them down. This wasn't the time to deal with my own pain. It lived in me all the time; it could wait a goddamn minute for me to figure this out. Evelyn was more important than my failures. I couldn't fail *her*.

I landed a punch to Harlan's side. He grunted but took it in stride before he came at me again. We weren't the most equally matched partners. I had a good four inches in height and probably thirty pounds on him. But that didn't stop him from putting me on my ass regularly when we sparred. He was fast, and determined, and right now he was holding back.

"You don't want to hit me?"

Harlan shook his head while bouncing on his toes. "The whole point is to let you hit something. I hit you plenty."

"If all I wanted to do was hit something, Harlan, we have five fucking punching bags twenty feet that way. Fight me."

"This is about her. Isn't it?"

I grit my teeth and swung. The blow went wide as he ducked and spun behind me, tapping me on the shoulder to show me that he could hit me, and wasn't.

"The woman staying in the Bitterroot House."

We circled each other, and I glared at him. "Her name is Evelyn."

"Good to know. This is about her?"

I pressed my lips together. "Nothing's changed in the past half hour, Harlan. It's not mine to tell right now."

He nodded and stepped closer, looking for an opening. "Well, at least I know it's about her."

"Mind your own business and fucking hit me."

He swung, and I jumped back out of the way. "I'm not trying to overstep. All I'm trying to do is figure out if you're in over your head. You know we're here for you."

I landed two more glancing blows before he dodged, and I nearly stumbled from my momentum. "I'm fine."

"Really? You don't look fine."

"I'm fucking *fine*," I growled.

Or I would be. I had to be. I'd let Evelyn stay here. I'd helped her get the job at Deja Brew, and that was on me. If I hadn't done those things, maybe I wouldn't have seen that terror in her eyes or the way she'd crumpled to the floor.

And then she wouldn't be here, and I'd never have shown her the stars.

But it was my fault that she was here, and triggered, and I needed to fix it. Because if I didn't, if it happened again—

Light flashed behind my eyes, pain slamming through my jaw. I hit the mat like dead weight, nearly knocked out with the force of Harlan's punch. At least the ceiling I was staring at right now wasn't the one in my bedroom.

Harlan chuckled. "You said to hit you. But I thought you'd block it."

"Distracted," I said, still lying on the floor. Normally after a blow like that, I'd be nursing my ego, but my mind was still racing too much for me to care.

"Yeah, no fucking kidding." Harlan held out his hand and helped me off the mat. "Now I'm not asking you to spill your secrets, Lucas. And I'm not telling you to give me information that you can't. I'm asking as your friend if you need help."

I looked at him. He was breathing hard like I was, but his gaze was clear. I wasn't sure why I was surprised. The seven of us had been through enough, both separately and together, that we could take each other at our word. But when faced with things like this . . . it was hard to remember that we had each other's backs.

I sighed. "I'll know more tomorrow, I think. But I'll let you know."

"Okay." He held up his hands in surrender. "All I needed to know."

My cell phone rang from my clothes. "Thanks, Harlan."

He nodded and headed off.

I grabbed my phone from the pocket of my jeans. It wasn't a number I recognized. "Hello?"

"Lucas?" It was her voice, and it took the breath out of me just hearing it.

"Evelyn. Are you all right?"

"Yeah," she said. "I'm fine. I was wondering if you could take me to get my car?"

I frowned. When she'd asked, I'd told her that I'd take care of it. What had changed? "I'll be right over."

It only took a few minutes to get my truck over to her house, and as soon as I saw her on the porch I knew that something was wrong. Evelyn looked cold. Not in temperature, but in temperament. She looked steeled. "You don't have to worry about it," I said. "I'll get someone to drive it back."

Her spine was straight as she looked at me. "No, I'd like to go get it now, please."

The shape on the porch behind her distracted me. A suitcase. Her suitcase. She was going to run again. "Evelyn—"

"I need to do this, Lucas."

"Do you?" I pushed down my fear for her and took a breath. "I will take you right now to get the car. If you're sure." She opened her mouth to say something so I kept going. "I don't know what you've gone through, Ev. But I do know what it's like to be constantly looking over your shoulder, never able to breathe. And I want to help you."

She stared down at me from the porch, and the look on her face was far from convinced.

"I want to make sure that you feel safe. That you *are* safe. And you'll never feel that if you keep running from every reminder of what happened."

"Why?" The word was small.

"Why what?"

Evelyn huffed out a breath. "Why do you want to help me? I'm nothing to you. No one."

"Because you're *someone*." The words came out more forcefully than I'd intended. Taking a step forward, I made sure that she was looking right at me before I spoke again. "Because no one should have to live like that."

She said nothing, but she couldn't keep looking at me. Her fingers drifted to the railing, picking at the wood. One little sign that her resolve was breaking.

"Please," I said. "Give me some time. Let me see if there's anything I can do. Give me a name. Let me help. Let me—" I cut myself off before I said too much.

There was something buried in my gut that was drawing me to her. I didn't understand it, but I couldn't ignore it. Evelyn needed me, and despite Daniel warning me, I was already in way too fucking deep.

But I couldn't force her. If she wanted to leave, then I had to let her go. No matter if it broke me open and brought back every nightmare I'd ever had. No matter if I'd always wonder if she was safe for the rest of my life.

Long minutes passed until, finally, Evelyn looked up at me.

"All right. I'll stay."

Chapter 10

Evelyn

I woke up in the bed at the Bitterroot House. It wasn't something I'd ever thought I'd be doing again. But that look on Lucas's face, and the desperate way he'd asked me to stay . . .

It seemed like he wanted to help me. And I was so tired of running.

My immediate instinct was to go to work, but I still felt jittery, and odds were that Lena was going to send me home anyway, so I stayed on the ranch, giving her a quick call to let her know.

But while I was here, I didn't want to be cooped up in the house. Lucas had said that the ranch was secure, and I believed him. It would be safe enough to walk around here. At the very least there wouldn't be strangers that surprised me.

I craved the quiet and the open air that I knew I could find outside, and it almost made me laugh, how quickly I'd adapted to needing and wanting this atmosphere. It was warm and sunny, which felt good. The air no longer felt suffused with the sum of all my panic.

After Lucas had dropped me off here last night, I couldn't stop thinking about whether or not Nathan was here. And if he was here, him hurting everyone would be my fault. I didn't want to leave, but leaving was the only way to fix it. Nothing would protect them from him except removing myself from the equation.

But I was still here.

I walked toward the stables, and I saw Lucas almost immediately. He was working with the same horse that he'd taken out to the field. Good. I'd been hoping to see him. The mere thought of him made me blush now. I could count on one hand the number of people who'd seen me go through an episode. And I wished that he hadn't. I didn't want him to look at me like that—like I was broken.

As if a magnet spun between us, Lucas looked over at me. He waved and started guiding the horse back toward the stables. Now that I was here, I wanted to run back to the safety of the house, but I held my ground, waiting for him to come back. I was glad he took his time with the horse so I could get myself under control. But as he walked toward me, I couldn't seem to get over this new shyness.

"Hey," he said, leaning on the fence from the other side.

"Hi." I prayed he wouldn't notice how hard I was blushing.

"How are you?"

I looked at the ground. How was I doing? I honestly didn't know. Fine, but still spinning? Worried that I'd made the wrong choice? Weirded out that I suddenly enjoyed silence?

Lucas climbed over the fence and dropped down in

front of me. He was close now, which did nothing for the state of my blush, but I managed to look up at him. There was nothing but concern in his eyes. "What's wrong?"

"I—" I stopped the lie that nothing was wrong from coming out. If I was going to let him help me, I had to be honest with him. At least about this. "I wanted to apologize about yesterday. I'm . . . embarrassed. That you had to see me like that."

"Embarrassed? Ev, you don't have to be embarrassed about that."

"I don't want you to think of me like that. I'm not broken."

Lucas shook his head. "I promise you, Evelyn, I would never think you are broken. No one is broken."

I bit my lip. I was, but I couldn't bring myself to say it.

"Remember when I told you that Resting Warrior helps people?"

"Yes." I nodded.

"Well," his mouth curled up into a half smile, "we actually help people like you. People with post-traumatic stress disorder. We also train animals for use in therapy for that specifically."

I shook my head. "I don't have PTSD."

Lucas's eyebrows rose. "I'm not a medical professional, and I would never pretend to be. But I have a lot of experience with PTSD, and what happened to you yesterday is right out of the book."

"But it's not possible," I said. "I'm not a soldier. I can't have that."

"You don't have to be a soldier to have PTSD. There are lots of things that cause it. And they cause flashbacks. Panic attacks. A whole shit ton of other fun symptoms too."

I'd never considered the possibility that that's what all

of this was. It was just the way things were in my brain now. I barely remembered a time when my mind didn't have a constant thread of worry and panic running in the background.

"That's what the others are here for?"

He nodded. "We work with people in Garnet Bend. A couple of therapists, physical therapists, and psychiatrists. The ranch provides a place to stay and for animal-led therapy. And of course, the training."

My chest tightened. How was it that I'd ended up here randomly? Serendipity, maybe? A light clicked on in in my brain. "That's why you offered me the house. You saw something was wrong."

"I did."

I swallowed. "Well, thank you."

Lucas was so close that either of us could reach out and touch the other. But I didn't. Still, that same crackle of electricity was in the air between us as when I'd reached out and grabbed his belt. Something huge and desperate and unspoken.

And for the first time, I allowed myself to really notice Lucas as he was. Tall and broad and beautiful. Right now he had a shadow of stubble on his sharp jaw—a jaw I wanted to touch. His warm brown eyes were watching me, and the way he looked at me didn't feel terrifying. It felt . . .

Like something I hadn't felt in a really long time.

The sun shone down on his hair, making it seem more red than brown. And his body—the size that had made me instantly fear him—now made me feel safe. What would it be like to be touched by him? More than touched.

I blushed again, and the charge between us grew painful. Lucas's gaze dropped to my lips, and for the briefest moment I thought he might lean down and kiss me. And I thought I might let him.

The only person I'd ever been with was Nathan. And he'd kind of ruined the whole idea of being with anyone. But looking at Lucas now was like waking up to whole new possibilities.

"Where would you have gone?" he asked, voice lower, like he was struggling not to reach out the way he wanted to.

"If I had left?"

He nodded.

"I don't know," I admitted. "Normally, I have a plan, but this time, I didn't. I had the overwhelming urge to get out, so I would have just started to drive. Probably east."

His head tilted a little. "What's east? Family?"

"Yeah." I crossed my arms over my chest. "I have a sister I haven't seen in a while. It hasn't been in the cards, but I really miss her."

I wasn't telling him the whole truth, and he knew that. I could see it. But this would have to happen in stages if I wanted it to happen at all. But true to form, he didn't call me out for it.

"Okay," I said. "That was all I wanted. To apologize, but also to say thank you. For being there. For distracting me and bringing me back."

"It was my pleasure."

I pressed my lips together for a moment, struggling to contain strong emotions—hope and relief and something else entirely. "Guess I'll head back now."

Lucas reached out a hand and froze. I froze too. He looked like he was trying to figure out the right words to say. "Yesterday, when you grabbed my belt."

Embarrassment rose, hot and visceral. Like I'd stepped into a room that was ten degrees warmer than where we were standing. "I'm sorry."

Lucas shook his head. "I'm not angry. I just—" He

sighed and looked at me. "I want you to know that I don't take that for granted."

His hand was still outstretched, and I stared at it for long moments. It almost felt like I was watching from outside my body as I stepped closer to Lucas. Inside the range of that arm that was reaching for me the same way that I reached for him. And I watched from a distance as Lucas wrapped his arms around me.

And then I was very much present in my own body. Lucas was just as warm as he'd been yesterday, just as hard and strong. I closed my eyes and let him hold me.

The scent of pine surrounded me, along with the tangible scent of mountain wind, and then he was holding me closer. With a rush of breath, Lucas *held* me. One arm came hard around my waist and the other slid up my spine and into my hair. It was the kind of desperate motion that was barely conscious.

The rush of emotion took me by surprise. It wasn't until this moment that I realized how starved for touch I'd been. Tears flooded my eyes, though thankfully he couldn't see them. God, how long had it been since I'd been touched by anyone at all? I never wanted to move from this spot. It was a release. Like Lucas touching me freed me from the anxiety that I'd been carrying for years.

Lucas's arms curled further around me, cradling me to his chest like I meant something. More than that, like I meant *everything*.

Grabbing a belt loop with each hand, I held on to him. The breaths I took felt like the first full breaths I'd taken in forever. Nothing but Lucas could touch me here. This place was a refuge, and I knew that even after he let me go, I would return to this moment.

I didn't know how long we stood there together. It felt like eternity but yet only seconds at the same time. But

Lucas took a step back, and now there was something between us we couldn't go back from. And I didn't mind.

"See you for dinner later?" he asked.

It was the day for his communal dinner. I'd nearly forgotten about it. "Yeah, definitely."

There were unsaid words on both of our lips, but I didn't know how to say them. I didn't know if I *could* say them. But there was no way I would be missing dinner.

When I got back to the Bitterroot House, I looked at the suitcase that was still sitting by the door, opened so that I could fish out my pajamas and toothbrush.

I picked up the suitcase and carried it back to the bedroom. With the lid flipped open on my bed, I unpacked it. Completely. Every single thing that I had in the suitcase I put into a drawer. And then I put the suitcase into the small closet.

There wasn't a time since I'd started to run that I'd had an empty suitcase. Too often, it wasn't worth it.

I wasn't going to pretend that the idea of staying here —committing to staying here—didn't make me anxious. It did. I was terrified of what would happen if Nathan found me again. And what that would mean for the people around me. But I would do it.

And in spite of the terror singing in my gut, that empty suitcase made me feel lighter. Better. And any step in that direction was a good one.

Chapter 11

Lucas

Another sleepless night left me tired, but I would take every sleepless night I had to in order to keep the progress that I'd made with Evelyn.

The fact that she'd let me touch her yesterday gripped my thoughts. The way she'd stepped forward and into my arms—it had been her choice. The way she'd melted against my chest, and the way I'd almost let myself go too far when I'd pulled her close.

God, I didn't know what this was yet, but it was powerful. Who would have thought that a finger in a belt loop could be so significant? She'd stayed, and she'd taken the first step. Little by little she was coming out of her shell, and maybe soon she might trust me enough to tell me everything.

She'd retreated at dinner, which I'd expected. After something as intense as that embrace, I'd known that she would need space again. But she'd still been there, and she'd smiled as she helped me cook.

This morning, I'd refreshed my email before I'd gotten out of bed, hoping that Jerry had emailed the footage. He had. It had taken me a good couple hours to go through it. But there was nothing out of the ordinary. Just people walking down the street, no one intentionally making circuits around Deja Brew or acting like they had an unnatural interest.

And unfortunately, even though I knew when Evelyn had been triggered, there was nothing I could isolate. There had been multiple people outside the shop at the time, and with things like this, it could have been anything. I doubted that she was ready to talk about it.

I'd taken down descriptions of the people outside the shop just in case before I'd come into town. But now that I was here, all I wanted to do was go back and check on Evelyn.

Crowding her wasn't a good idea, but I wanted to see her. As soon as I had the thought, it was like the universe delivered. I glanced behind me in the rearview mirror and did a double take. Was that Evelyn? In town?

Errands had built up until I couldn't ignore them anymore, so I'd come to town to take care of them. But Ev didn't work today. So why was she coming out of the library? Coming into town alone had to make her nervous after what had happened. Was that why she looked like she was shaking?

I pulled into a parking spot on the side of the street and stepped out. It was her, and she didn't look good. Pale, and hurrying in my direction, though she hadn't seen me yet. "Ev," I called, and she startled before seeing that it was me.

Her smile was nervous as I approached.

"I didn't know you'd come into town today," I told her.

She shrugged, pretending to be casual in spite of the tension in her body. "I had a couple of things I needed to do."

"Are you okay?"

She hesitated. "Yes."

It was a lie. Clearly. There was a sheen of sweat on her forehead and though she was already pale, her skin was nearly translucent. I tried to push down the rising frustration. "Are you sure?"

"Yes."

Fuck. I'd thought that we were making progress, but it was obvious that she still didn't trust me. There wasn't anything I could imagine that would make me judge her. I had a hell of a past too. I breathed through the urge to push her harder. This would take time. "Have you seen much of the town yet?"

"Not much. Took me a while to even find the library."

"Can I show you around? Some of the humble sights?"

She took a half breath, and I thought she might refuse, but she nodded. "Okay."

"Perfect." She was on edge, and as long as Ev was nervous, there was no chance in hell that she would talk about anything. But maybe I could get her to relax enough to remember that I wasn't her enemy. That she could trust me. As much as I wanted to know everything, I could and would be patient.

All I wanted to do was help her.

We walked south along the main road toward Mission Park. It was probably the prettiest spot in town, with gorgeous flowers and landscaping. One of the few public spaces in Garnet Bend that the town actually spent time and money maintaining. The view wasn't half bad either.

This part of Montana, which butted up against the Mission Mountains, was relatively flat with isolated hills and mountains. But as Garnet Bend was in the foothills of the towering range behind us, we could see for miles over all that flatness. And now in the height of summer it was all a beautiful green. The sky was clear today, dotted with white clouds that seemed too perfect to be real.

"This is beautiful," Evelyn whispered.

"It is," I agreed. "I thought you might like it."

She whipped her head around at me. "Why?"

"Because you seem like a person who loves beautiful things." I wasn't sure where the words had come from, but as I said them I knew they were true. Or maybe it was because she was beautiful and deserved to be surrounded by the same.

"Everybody loves beautiful things," she whispered. The way she said it made me think there was more to it than she would admit, but her body was more relaxed since we'd walked into the park, and her color was coming back a little.

We walked all the way to the edge, where the land dropped off in a gentle slope that rolled out into the distance. Beside me, Evelyn inhaled. "You smell it?"

"What?"

"It's that thing I told you about," she said with a smile —a real one. "That weird sweetness in the air I can't figure out. Maybe it's the flowers here, but I feel like it's everywhere."

I focused on the air around us. Evelyn was right. There was a sweetness to it, nearly sharp. Now that I'd been here a few years I didn't notice it as much, but when I'd arrived, it had struck me the way it did her. This place seemed different from the rest of the world.

But what struck me now was *her*. Evelyn's eyes were

closed, head tilted back, enjoying the breeze that swept up to us. This was the freest I'd ever seen her. The smile on her face was pure and open, and in this moment . . . I could see who she was. The real Evelyn without the things that she was running from and that were weighing her down.

She turned and looked at me, that smile still on her face. The smile landed in my gut. I wanted to see it on her face all the time, and I knew without forming the thought that I would do whatever it took to keep it there.

"I've never seen anything like this," she said. "And I've lived in a lot of places."

"A lot of people say that Montana is the last best place."

"With this view, I can't disagree." She walked to a nearby bench and sat.

Her posture was the opposite of what it had been coming out of the library. And damn if that didn't make me desperate to know what was going on with her. I sat next to her, keeping a careful distance, but closer than I would have yesterday.

For a while we sat and watched, enjoying the sunshine and wind. She had her eyes closed again, a faint smile on her face.

"Evelyn?" When she returned my gaze, her eyes were soft. "I hope you know that you can trust me."

Her face shuttered, and I hated myself for taking away the little peace that she'd found in this place. She took a long, slow breath before she met my eyes again. "I know. I do. But that . . . doesn't come easily for me."

"I know." I angled my body toward hers. "And I would never push for anything you're not comfortable with. I'm here to help."

Her voice was quiet. "You have helped. Really."

I held myself still as she looked back at the view. This felt fragile, and I wouldn't do anything to break it.

"I've been—" She stopped. "I'm sorry that I lied."

A blush turned her cheeks pink, and I forced myself not to focus on the color and how it might look elsewhere on her or how I could make her turn that color again. Because fuck, that blush was everything. But the reason why she was blushing was not. "Never apologize for something that's keeping you safe."

Evelyn nodded. "Still. It's not like you couldn't tell that I was lying."

I couldn't stop my smile. "I have a lot of practice with that."

"I swear I'm actually a better liar than that. She turned on the bench and sat cross-legged in front of me. The breeze caught her hair; she caught it and tied it back before it went wild. I'd felt that hair yesterday, and I wanted to again. "It's just with you."

"What's with me?"

Another blush. "The lying. You . . ." She made a gesture with her hands. "You throw me off and I can't manage to make myself convincing. I wasn't planning on telling you my real name, but it slipped out."

That was something interesting. "What were you going to say it was?"

"Elizabeth Cunningham."

I smiled. "You're not an Elizabeth."

"Liz?"

"No." I shook my head. "And definitely not Beth. Lizzie, maybe."

"Noted." Her hands fidgeted in her lap. The only sign that she was nervous.

"How many names have you had?"

"Fake ones?"

I nodded.

She blew out a breath. "Thirteen."

I couldn't hide my surprise.

That was a lot of aliases for someone who wasn't in the business professionally. As a SEAL, I knew my fair share of people who had them, and I knew how to create them. Make them airtight if I needed to. And it wasn't cheap to have quality false IDs made. Granted, I didn't know if she'd done that. But it was still impressive. And worrisome.

"That's a lot."

"Yeah," she said. "It is." Evelyn wove her fingers together and pulled them apart again. "You've probably already guessed part of it. Seen it."

"Your scars."

She nodded. "Yes. It was a long time ago, but some-one . . . hurt me. Someone I trusted. And I haven't been able to escape it. I've been running ever since, but it always catches up to me."

"Like the coffee shop."

"Like the coffee shop," she confirmed. "I keep hoping that a new place will be safe, but I haven't found one yet."

"Maybe this can be your place."

She looked up at me, face full of hope. "Maybe."

Without realizing it, we'd shifted closer to each other like that night on the roof. Then, that closeness seemed to scare her. But now, as my eyes dropped to her lips, she didn't pull away.

"Evelyn," I murmured.

"Yes?"

"If I kiss you, are you going to run away?"

She stopped breathing for a moment, and when she spoke it was in a whisper. "No."

I waited one more beat, to make sure that she believed it herself before I leaned in. The first brush of lips was gentle, and I'd meant to keep it that way. But when our lips touched it wasn't possible to keep it soft and simple.

Evelyn's mouth was sweet, and it unlocked that bone-deep instinct to protect her at all costs, along with a yearning that I'd never felt before and couldn't explain. Everything had me pulling her closer, gathering her into my arms as best I could.

She melted against me exactly as she had yesterday. She settled against me like she was comfortable there. Her body trusted me, even if her mind couldn't, and that was something.

One simple kiss, and I felt more alive than I'd ever felt in my life. More than when I'd been in BUD/S or in battle. My focus was sharper than when my team had been on missions that required stealth. I was aware of every breath she took and the hand resting on my leg. Of her velvet lips against mine. Of her pounding heart.

I wanted more. My body was hard, and I was grateful that we were here in the park where I couldn't be tempted to take this further. Down in that place where my instincts spoke, I knew that this was far enough. But the idea of having more nearly made me groan.

Evelyn was flushed and breathless when I pulled away. It did nothing to stop my imagination from running wild. I'd pulled her nearly into my lap, her chest pressed against mine, and her softness was enough to break me.

"I didn't run away," she said softly.

"No. You didn't. Should we see what happens if we try again?"

Evelyn was smiling when I kissed her a second time. Thank fuck, because it would have been torture not to. For the first time since she'd arrived, everything in me felt settled. This was *right*. I never wanted to let her out of my arms, and that was as terrifying as it was exhilarating.

"You're still here," I said with my mouth still against her lips.

"I'm still here."

Slowly, I let her go, already missing the way she felt.

"I—" She stopped and bit her lip before continuing. "I'm sorry that I'm not ready for the rest. To tell you."

I nodded. Of course there was more. Because running wasn't easy. Whatever horrors were living in her mind were bad enough to keep her on the move. "I'll be here when you are ready."

Evelyn shuddered. I wanted to find whoever had hurt her so deeply that even words of support shook her. That person and I were going to have a very serious conversation if I ever encountered them. If they were lucky, the conversation would not involve my fists.

"Can I walk you to your car?" I asked. She hadn't said anything, but it must have taken bravery and resolve to come into town. The least I could do was make sure she felt safe leaving.

Evelyn nodded. "Please."

We didn't speak on the way to her car. It didn't feel necessary. Simply being with her was enough. But when we reached where she was parked, I couldn't let her go without saying anything. "Are you all right?"

She smiled easily now. "Yes. No plans for running."

I laughed. She'd seen through the reason for my question. "Just promise me that if you want to, you'll call me first."

"So you can talk me out of it?" One eyebrow raised, she was nearly smirking.

"Maybe. Or kiss you out of it." I savored the blush that followed my words. "I'll see you at home."

Evelyn stared at me for a moment before getting in the car, and I watched her drive until her car was out of sight down the main road. This wasn't at all how I'd thought my trip to town would go. But if this was the way they went from now on, I'd have to take them more often.

Chapter 12

Evelyn

Each day that passed uneventfully lifted the weight off my lungs a little more. I'd gone to the library in town that day to email Melanie. We had an email account we shared, only sending emails to the same address. I hadn't updated her since my frantic flight from Albuquerque.

But the message that was waiting for me had left me cold and shaking, and that was after already having to force myself to drive into town. I'd been terrified.

The email she'd sent was short.

Don't use this. He knows.

No more details than that.

Questions spun in my mind. Was Melanie okay?

Had Nathan threatened her? Sent her a message? I desperately wanted to call her and hear her voice. But we'd learned the hard way that Nathan was monitoring her calls. Even when she changed phones.

Because he was rich, and a genius, and the staff of West Tech would do anything for him without a second thought. So I was in the dark, with no way to contact my sister, and I'd already logged into the account *here*.

If he'd found that account and was watching its activity, he could know where I was. But I hadn't seen the phantom Nathan anywhere again. After a few days, I'd finally relaxed enough to believe that I was just on edge. There'd been no other signs that he was here or that he knew that I was.

A huge part of my relief was Lucas. Running into him after the email had been equally terrifying, because he'd seen through me like no one else had. But I couldn't deny the safety I felt with him, and the kiss . . .

I'd thought about that kiss more than anything else the past few days. The gentle press of his lips that woke things in me I had forgotten. The way it had grown deeper, like it was meant to. When he'd leaned in, I hadn't been afraid. I'd been worried that maybe I *was* broken in that way—that Nathan had taken the ability to want.

But kissing Lucas was a revelation, and I wanted more than one kiss.

The door chimed, and I smiled as the resident of my thoughts walked in the door. Lucas had started coming in halfway through my shift, every time I worked, like clockwork. We didn't talk too much; I got him coffee, and he asked if I was okay. I usually was.

Today, Jude was with him, one of the other owners of Resting Warrior, I'd met him a couple other times when he'd come into the coffee shop. He was a quiet man, though he was bigger than Lucas, if that was possible.

But the best part of Jude coming in was watching Lena. She blushed every time he appeared and her boisterous, sassy personality became shy.

"Hey," I called as Lucas and Jude came in. "Coffee today?"

"Yeah," Lucas said, and Jude nodded as well.

I stepped away from the counter. "I think Lena might have some stuff for you. I'll be right back."

She was in the kitchen, putting a tray of cookies in the oven, flushed from baking up a storm. There were a lot of custom orders this week, and Lena had been working like crazy to get them all done. I helped when I could.

"Jude is here with Lucas," I said, "if you want to see him."

Lena blushed a deeper shade of pink. "Why would I want to do that?"

I sent her a look. "Really?"

"He's not here for me," she said. "I'm glad he likes the coffee."

"Lena, that man has not come to your store every week for two years because he likes the coffee."

"It's his job to pick up their order," she said, but she didn't meet my eyes.

"At least come say hello to Lucas."

She made a face at me, not fooled at all, but she came with me all the same. Lucas smiled when we returned and I went about getting their coffee. "You surviving back there?" he asked Lena.

"Barely. I swear the whole town decided they needed baked goods this week. But Evie has been a huge help."

I finished pouring the coffee and put both lids on

before I turned around. "She's being modest. This week she's been a baking machine."

Lucas took both coffees from me, our fingers brushing far more than they needed to. "Are you okay?"

"I'm okay," I said, smiling. There was no way I'd admit how much having him check in helped. Knowing that he would be there kept me calm, and I looked forward to his visits, even as I felt guilty about them. There were probably things he had to do on the ranch that his visits were interrupting. But at the same time, I couldn't bring myself to ask him to stop.

"Don't burn yourself out, Lena," Jude said. "What will Resting Warrior do if you work yourself to death?" The way he was looking at her left no room for doubt in my mind. He was not here for the coffee.

Lena turned crimson, and she wiped her hands on her apron. It was her tell when she was nervous. Which meant it really only happened when Jude was here.

"I'll be okay," she said. "I'm making good progress."

"We won't keep you," Lucas said, finally handing the coffee to Jude. Then he looked back at me. "See you later?"

I didn't know if later meant tonight or tomorrow, but I would take either. "Yeah."

His answering smile made butterflies take flight in my stomach, and I watched him leave until he was out of sight.

The fact that he'd kissed me—that he wanted me in any way at all—was shocking. I was a mess, and no matter what he said, I would never live down the embarrassment of him seeing me triggered. But at the same time, I was so, *so* tired of running. Tired of knowing that fear could hijack my mind over nothing, all because of the things that Nathan had done.

But the idea of talking about those things out loud . . .

It was unthinkable.

The first time I'd tried, Nathan had made me pay, and I'd learned there wasn't anything to do but run. And so I had. For the first time since I'd left, I hoped that I could have a life. If I could push past that fear.

I didn't see Lucas that evening, and I was opening Deja Brew alone for the first time in the morning, so I went to bed early.

Garnet Bend was a different place in the early morning. The vast quiet of Montana that was already everywhere seemed greater when the sun was peeking over the horizon and painting the mountains gold. There was a hush in the air, like the world was still holding its breath, and I liked it enough that it made me want to wake up early more often.

There was a bouquet of flowers by the door of the bakery, and a small box. They must be for Lena, since I didn't usually work mornings. I hoped they were from Jude. The bouquet was all black roses, but Lena was a sweet little oddball, and frankly, black roses wouldn't be out of left field for her.

I left them on her desk in the office and started the process of opening the shop without thinking more about them. The morning rush passed quickly and easily, and like it had when I'd worked at the Sandia Bean. People were starting to recognize me, and I was starting to remember people's orders.

Shortly before Lena was supposed to arrive, the phone rang in the office, and I picked it up. "Hello?"

"Hi, it's me." Lena sounded out of breath. "I broke down on the way and Grace is picking me up. I'll be a little behind."

I laughed. This was the first time it had happened to

me, but apparently this was a regular occurrence with Lena. She drove a classic car that had been on its last legs ten years ago, but she loved it and kept driving it even though it seemed like it was dead set on stranding her. "Okay, that's fine. I'll see you soon."

She burst into the store a half hour later like a whirlwind, Grace close on her heels. "I'm here, I'm here. Sorry."

"It's been pretty quiet. But are you okay?"

"I'm fine. No big deal."

Grace rolled her eyes. "You need a new car, Lena."

"Bessie does her best."

I hid my grin as best I could. "You named your car Bessie?"

"A name that's as old as time itself? Seems appropriate," Grace muttered.

"Hush, or you're not getting any coffee."

I poured Grace a cup and slipped it to her across the counter before Lena could make good on her threat. There was no one in the shop, so Grace and I followed her into the kitchen.

"I have about two hundred cookies to make today. Tonight. Whatever. The senior center ordered chocolate chip for their party tomorrow. Though I don't know why on earth they need two hundred cookies. There aren't close to that many people. But that's fine, I'll take the money."

"Lena," I said, interrupting her rant. "Do you know you're still talking out loud?"

Looking up, she froze. "I was, wasn't I? Guess I'm more frazzled than I realized."

"Just tell me what to do, and I'll help," Grace said.

I nodded. "And obviously you can boss me around, boss."

"I need a second. I'm going to look at the order again

to make sure I'm remembering it right before I jump into doing something and realize that I've totally spaced." She disappeared into the office. "Evie, what's with the flowers?"

"Oh." I'd forgotten about them. "They were in front of the door this morning. Someone left them for you." I looked at Grace. "Black roses."

"Really?" She made a face. "Lena hates roses."

I didn't know that. There was a hitch in my chest but I pushed it down. It was fine. There was nothing wrong. Someone was playing a joke. A prank. Or we'd sold a bad pastry. It wasn't him. It *wasn't*.

Lena peeked her head out of the door. "But the card in them is addressed to you."

My stomach plummeted through the floor, and all the blood drained from my face. I grabbed the edge of the worktable to make sure I didn't hit the floor.

No.

It wasn't possible.

Everything in me fought against the truth, because the truth meant I would lose everything. Again.

"What's in the box?" My voice was flat and dead, and they were both looking at me like I might pass out again.

Lena took a step forward. "Are you o—"

"Lena," I said, "what's in the box?"

She pressed her lips together and stepped out of sight. Cardboard crinkled a moment later.

What could I do? Was it really him on the street the other day? If he was already here and watching the shop, the chances of me making it back to Resting Warrior were slim.

If he wasn't, I could make it. But where would I go? I'd already made the decision to stay. I didn't have a plan. Grief ripped through my chest and I fought off sudden tears. I didn't want to do this.

Lena came out of the office holding a jewelry box like I'd known she would. But it was smaller than the others. She lowered it down on the worktable next to me. "Evie, what does this mean?"

I swallowed before I opened the box. What would it be this time? The box was too small to be a bracelet.

A strange sense of calm surrounded me as I opened it. It was like I wasn't present in my own body. I was somewhere else, and another person was pretending to be Evelyn. Controlling her movements.

Nestled in the velvet of the box was a ring. Not just a ring, but a beautiful one. The gold band had decorative filigree surrounding a deep red stone. I knew with one glance that it was a garnet. My birthstone. Because of course it was.

Lena gasped, and Grace—now standing behind me—let out a low whistle.

The ring was a message, and a different one than he'd been sending. What was it this time?

That familiar feeling of desperate hollowness filled me as I reached for the ring. I was breathing, but it wasn't enough. The air felt thin. Flimsy. Those invisible hands I always imagined gripped me hard, squeezing the life and joy I'd found out of me. The only thing left was darkness and fear.

Lena and Grace watched me carefully as I picked up the ring and turned it over. There it was. The tiny engraving that I'd known would be there. But this time it wasn't a false identity with a date of death, it was me.

E velyn Taylor
   1992-2022

. . .

He'd never sent flowers before either. That was what had thrown me off. If it had just been the box sitting in front of the door, I might have known.

But shouldn't I have known?

Black roses. Love that's died.

I flipped open the tiny envelope. The words were printed in delicate script. He would never handwrite it. He would never leave anything that could be directly traced.

Last chance, *Evelyn. Till* death *do us part.*

So this was it, then. He was going to come for me and finish what he'd started. On some level, I'd always known that this would happen. That I couldn't run forever. Nathan was too smart and too powerful.

I still felt calm, at complete odds with the terror inside. Maybe I was too scared to feel it. Or worse, maybe I'd resigned myself to this a long time ago. Maybe all I'd done was delay the inevitable.

Lena picked up the card from where I'd placed it on the table. Her head snapped up when she read the words. "Is this a death threat?"

"Yes," I said. "I'm sorry, Lena. I never should have brought this into your life."

There was anger on her face, but it wasn't directed at me. "Like hell, Evie. This is from him? The man you thought you saw?"

I stared at her. "How do you know that?"

"When you fell behind the counter," Grace said. "The only thing you said was 'it's him.' Over and over."

My whole body went cold. "Oh."

"So is it?" Grace asked, more gently than Lena.

I nodded.

"I'm calling the police," Lena said.

"*No*." The word exploded out of me like lightning. "No, you can't."

She leveled her gaze at me, and if she weren't on my side, that look would kill. "Well, I'm sure as hell not going to stand here and do nothing."

My voice disappeared entirely. How did I explain that calling the police would make it worse? How did I tell her about years of trauma?

She sighed. "Okay, I won't call the police. Yet. Do you want me to call Lucas?"

His name was like the sun breaking through the clouds. Light. Safety. Warmth. I nodded.

Putting her hand on my shoulder, Grace guided me toward the office. "Let's get you sitting down. You look like you're about to pass out."

Half of me wished that I would. If I was unconscious, I couldn't feel. If I was asleep, I couldn't fear. Lena was already on the phone. And it was only seconds later that I heard the only words that could bring me relief. "He's on his way."

Chapter 13

Lucas

L iam stood across from me, staring down the horse. We were starting to push him a little harder. Gently, but pushing all the same. If we never confronted the barriers that kept him skittish, he'd never get better.

"He's stubborn, that's for sure," Liam called.

"Tell me about it," I muttered under my breath. I'd never met an animal so averse to change. But that only made me more determined.

My phone rang in my pocket and I pulled it out to silence it. Didn't need it spooking the horse. But the number on the screen stopped me midmotion. It was Deja Brew.

"Hello?"

"Lucas," Lena said.

I was already moving to the edge of the paddock. "Is she all right?"

"I'm not sure. It's not an episode like last time, but she needs you. You're the only one that she would let me call."

I waved to Liam, and he nodded, having heard my part of the conversation. "Who else did you try to call?"

"The police."

Swearing under my breath, I started to jog. My truck was parked at the lodge. "Why?"

"I think it's better that you see for yourself."

"*Why*, Lena?"

She sighed. "Because I don't want you getting in an accident on the way here."

"I'm coming," I said and ended the call.

Fuck. Visiting her at work the past couple days, I'd only become more invested. That kiss, the things that she was still hiding, Evelyn was a puzzle I wanted to solve.

But along with those things, the same urge to protect her overwhelmed me. It was *screaming* at me to get to her now. She had let Lena call me. Me. That made me run a little faster. I couldn't leave her alone—had to get there in time.

I skidded to a stop in front of my truck as Harlan came out of the lodge. "Where are you going?"

"Town."

"Lucas—"

I jumped in the front seat. "This has to happen later, Harlan."

He stood still for one second, then rounded the truck and got in the passenger seat. "Let's go."

"Get out."

"No."

I huffed out a breath. "What the fuck are you doing?"

"You don't think any of us know you well enough to see what's happening? That's fine, you don't have to tell me. But I can see it on your face. I'm going with you in case you need help. Now drive."

There wasn't time to argue with him. He wanted to come? Fine. But I was leaving his ass in town if Ev wanted to come home. I wasn't going to force her to sit between two men after something had happened. What had happened?

I tried to calm my spinning mind, put together what was going on. But I had no idea. The fact that Lena wouldn't tell me made me that much more desperate.

She was probably right to not tell me. I was skirting traffic laws as it was. The only thing keeping me within the speed limit was the thought that getting pulled over would slow me down.

There wasn't any parking by the coffee shop. I was about to double park when Harlan's hand landed on my shoulder. "I'll park, you go."

I did.

Lena was behind the counter when I walked in. "Where is she?"

"She's in the office," she said. "There's something you need to see first."

She led me into the kitchen and didn't need to guide me any farther. A massive bouquet of black roses sat on the table, beautiful, though morbid. And a ring.

"There's an inscription in the ring," Lena said softly. "And the card . . ."

I read them both, keeping myself deadly still.

Shock came first, then anger. Evelyn had PTSD, and it was obvious that she was suffering. I hadn't known she was *in danger*. No wonder she was fucking running.

The idea of Evelyn in danger cracked something open in me, a portion of myself that I'd locked away after

Emmett. A part I'd dealt with as much as I was able. But Evelyn had to be safe. I *needed* her to be safe.

I gripped the side of the table in an effort not to stride into the office and take her back to the ranch. Lock everything down. But I couldn't do that. She was probably scared out of her mind, and I needed to keep myself in control.

Grace slipped out of the office and saw me. She smiled, and then she didn't. "What the fuck are you doing here?"

The words weren't aimed at me, but at Harlan. He was standing in the door to the kitchen with my keys. "I came with Lucas, in case he needed help."

She scoffed, fire in her eyes. "I don't think anyone here is going to be helped by your presence, Harlan. Go home."

His face darkened, and then it sharpened into a smile. "You don't control where I go, Gracie. And I'll leave when Lucas, Lena, or Evelyn asks me to, given that they're the ones actually involved in the situation."

"You're such an asshole," Grace hissed, body taut like a spring. I wouldn't be surprised if she pounced on him.

"Enough," Lena said. "You guys have issues, we get it. If you need to work it out, get a room. But this isn't helping."

The two glared at each other but stayed silent.

"I'm going to talk to her," I said, slipping by Grace.

I wasn't sure what to expect, walking into the office. Would Evelyn be in a state of panic or fear? What I didn't anticipate was the utter calm. She was sitting quietly, still, staring into space. I shut the door behind me.

"Evelyn?"

She sat there frozen, not fidgeting, not moving at all. Given that she had just gotten a death threat, I didn't blame her. Finally, she looked up at me, but she wasn't there. Not fully in her body. Her spirit had gone.

"Hi," she finally said.

I crouched in front of her, holding myself back from begging her to tell me who it was so I could kill him. Later, I would get to the gym and beat the hell out of a bag with a phantom face on it until I was too exhausted for the dreams to come.

"I didn't know he was coming after you."

"Yeah."

"He's why you're running," I said again, because I needed the confirmation. "He gave you the scars?"

She nodded.

I stood and turned away, pushing down the fury that wasn't directed at her. Yes, I was angry that she hadn't told me, didn't trust me, but that was a different conversation. "Do you know how he found you?"

"I have an idea. Not for sure."

What next? If she was in danger, we needed to establish security and boundaries. Quickly. I wasn't about to lock her up, but I wanted to put her inside the ranch where we had cameras.

"I need to know something, Ev," I said. "Please."

She looked at me again, waiting. I hated the deadness in her eyes.

"Why didn't you tell me he was still coming after you?"

"Because you'd want to help me," she said. "You would go after him, and I can't put you—or anyone else here—on his radar. You don't know what he'll do."

Frustration scraped my insides like sandpaper. He'd made her feel powerless. So powerless that she'd had to leave her life and thirteen others besides, and through all that, she was still trying to protect people.

"I can take care of myself, Ev," I said softly. "I need you to hear that and believe it."

"I do. But you don't know him."

"Then tell me."

There was a soft knock on the door, and Lena opened it. "Lucas, let me grab you for a second."

"Okay."

Evelyn was coming back. I could see it in her face and body, but she didn't look like she was about to tell me shit.

"I just thought of something," Lena said after I pulled the door closed. "The package with the ring. It didn't have a return address on it. And the flowers weren't delivered during business hours. They were waiting when she got here this morning. Does that mean he's here?"

I clenched my jaw and focused on keeping my body still. "I don't know." As soon as Ev was home and safe, I needed to call Jerry again. This time, there had to be something.

"Keep her safe, Lucas," Lena said. "I don't give a shit if that means I'm working alone. Don't let this asshole— whoever he is—get to her."

"Not planning on it. Thank you, Lena."

In the shop proper, Grace and Harlan were facing off like they were about to have an old-fashioned shootout.

"I'm going to take Evelyn home," I told him. "Can you call Jerry and get the footage that covers the front of the store this morning?"

"Sure thing." He never took his eyes off Grace.

"You okay to get home?"

A slow grin. "I'm sure I can get Gracie here to drop me off on her way home."

"Like hell," she muttered.

The two had a past that Harlan never talked about. All we knew was that he knew her from before. Harlan had grown up in Montana before joining the SEALs, and somehow Grace was a part of that. But the rest of their history was private.

I wasn't about to get in the middle of it. Harlan was an adult, and if he had a problem getting home, he could call one of the other guys.

When I pushed back into the office, Evelyn was still sitting where I'd left her. "Before I get you out of here, we should talk to the police."

Evelyn's head snapped up, eyes blazing. "No."

"Ev—"

"Absolutely not." She was no longer in any kind of daze, now on her feet staring me down. "Do not call them."

I stepped into her space so she had to look up at me. "This is a death threat. It should be reported. Taken seriously."

"You think I don't know that it's serious?" She shook her head. "This has been my life for the past four years. I know it's fucking serious. And I know exactly what the police can do and what they can't. Don't call them."

It hit me in a wave. She'd gone to the police before, and they hadn't helped. Either they hadn't, or they'd made it worse.

This was the strongest that I'd ever seen Evelyn, standing tall and defending herself. I wanted to see her like this all the time. She was so fucking beautiful in every way. I wanted to get my hands on the man who had done this. He didn't deserve to take up one more second of her thoughts.

"All right," I said. "I'll take you home."

On the way out, she grabbed both the ring and the card off the table and brought them with us. Good. We'd need them as proof. Police or no, I was going to make sure Evelyn never had to run again.

Chapter 14

Lucas

Evelyn didn't want to leave her car again, so I followed her back to the ranch. I knew she wanted her car close in case she decided to run, but I wasn't going to fight her on it. But when we got back, I needed her to tell me. She might not have wanted to involve me, but I was involved now. I wanted to be. And I wasn't backing down.

When we pulled up to the house, I followed her onto the porch, and she hesitated. Now that we were alone, things seemed easier. The good kind of tension hummed in the air as I stepped close—not nearly as close as I wanted to be, but closer.

The need to kiss her pulled me forward, but we had to fix things between us first. I was still angry, and she had things she needed to tell me. Otherwise, this wasn't going to work.

"Are you going to let me help you, Ev?"

A shuddering breath. "Yes."

Thank God. "I can't help you if you don't tell me the truth."

Evelyn swallowed. "I know." She pushed into the house, and I followed behind her.

Not stopping, she disappeared into the kitchen. The clink of glass and ice followed. When she came back, there was a glass of alcohol in her hand. Not something that came with the house, so she'd bought it. Or brought it with her.

If she needed alcohol to tell this story—I stifled the thought. Listening was the first task. Just listening.

Evelyn curled up on the couch, and I sat across from her in a separate chair. She needed space to do this—I could tell.

"Okay," she said, not looking at me. She hadn't looked at me once since we entered. "His name is Nathan West. *The* Nathan West."

"Nathan West," I said softly. "As in the son of Patrick West?"

She still didn't look at me, her entire face flushing. "Yes."

Fuck. No wonder she was running. Patrick West was a tech billionaire and the founder of the security software almost everyone used. He and his family were very visible and very rich. So this man had unlimited resources and influence. No wonder she hadn't wanted the police.

"We met in college and dated for two years. At the time, we were miraculously in love. I moved in with him before we graduated. Miami. He was rich and beautiful. A perfect gentleman. So when he proposed, I said yes." She stumbled over her words and took a drink. "There weren't signs of anything else."

I kept my breath even. This was about her. Whatever my reaction was could wait. She needed to get this out.

"We'd been together for years, and everything was fine. Or I thought it was. One day, we went out to lunch or something, shopping maybe? I don't remember at this point. We ran into one of my high school boyfriends. It was one of those things where we realized we were better friends and split, so it was nice to see him again. The conversation didn't last long, maybe ten minutes, and then we went our separate ways. Everything was fine. If anything, Nathan was more attentive and affectionate than he normally was."

Dread pooled in my stomach. Given the scars I'd already seen, I knew where this was heading.

"That night, he . . ." She trailed off and took another drink. "He said that he wanted to try something new. Tie me up and tease me. We'd never done that before but—" Another drink. "We had a good sex life, so I was down to try anything once. I realized something was off when he used metal handcuffs and made them way too tight everywhere. But he turned into a completely different person—I'm sorry." Evelyn got up and went to the kitchen, pouring herself another drink.

She didn't come back. After a couple minutes I followed her and sat at the table. She faced away from me, leaning heavily on the counter. God, I wanted to touch her. Let her lean on me instead. I couldn't imagine what it was like to recall something like this.

All the trauma that I'd been through—it was my fault. Dealing with it when it wasn't your fault? She was stronger than anyone I knew.

"He left me alone, just shackled there. And when he came back, he wasn't the same. I'd never seen him angry, and all of a sudden, he was screaming." She turned and looked at me then. "He told me that I was his alone, and no one else's. He claimed he didn't know that I'd been with anyone else—though it wasn't something that I'd kept a secret—and if he'd known, he would have made it clear earlier.

"I was his until I died. No one else would ever have me. And if I ever tried what I'd done that day again, he'd be kind. He would bury me somewhere beautiful. In a field of flowers, even if I didn't deserve it."

She closed her eyes, and I waited. I would wait all fucking night if she needed me to.

Then she looked at me. "You said you know who they are?"

I nodded. "Yes. I'm familiar."

"Nathan is smart. Incredibly smart. And he had a workshop in our house, so he had everything that he needed. To . . . burn me."

This time I closed my eyes.

"He used my engagement ring," she said. "Marked my arms, hips, and chest. His goal was to make it impossible for anyone to touch me without knowing that I was his."

My hands gripped the chair so hard that the wood creaked. It was the only thing keeping me seated. Anger flowed through me, white-hot and explosive. But like hell was I going to interrupt her while she was this open and this fragile.

She made it sound simple. He'd burned her. The circular scars now made sense. What she didn't say was that it would have taken hours for him to do that. Scars that deep took time. Over and over he would have heated the ring and used it on her.

I'd never seen such an intentional act of hatred.

Her voice was small now. "When he finished, he unchained me. Not that I could move at all. He was smiling when he kissed me and told me that he'd be back later. He called me his fiancée. And he didn't come back.

"In the morning when he still wasn't there, I managed to get myself up. I knew the burns were deep, and I took myself to the emergency room. They reacted exactly like you'd want them to. They were horrified, and the nurse called the police."

Evelyn's voice went cold. "The officer who came to see me was pissed. He talked me into pressing charges even though I was afraid to. After he left to file the charges, I never saw him again."

A curse fell from my lips, and she looked at me, confirmation on her face. "Let me guess," I said, the words rough. "Those charges disappeared?"

"Less than two hours later another cop came back. He said that there were no charges to press. And a doctor came and told me that I couldn't stay there."

I stood, unable to keep still. "He paid them off?"

"I don't have proof."

She wouldn't get it either. The Wests were powerful enough to have that kind of reach. But was it just Nathan with access to his family's money? Or was it his father too?

"Nathan was waiting for me outside the hospital. I was in too much pain to run, even after being treated."

"Evelyn—"

She held up a hand. "He took me back to our house and told me that I clearly hadn't learned the lesson. I tried to fight him—I promise that I tried to fight him."

I crossed the kitchen to her, needing to be close, not sure if she wanted to be touched. Instead, I placed both hands on the counter beside her, leaning until I was looking directly into her eyes. "If anyone's ever made you feel like this was your fault because you couldn't fight him off or didn't believe you, they're *wrong*."

Evelyn's eyes were glassy, and she broke away from my gaze. But she didn't move away. "He did it again. This time covering my back. Didn't untie me for days. I'm not sure how long he had me there."

Closing my eyes, I pushed away from her. I couldn't imagine it, because if I did—I couldn't.

"I didn't run. I couldn't. He told my family that I'd fucked up while cooking and there was a grease fire that spread to my clothes. Melanie—my sister—was the only one who didn't believe it. And she got me out. It took a couple of months for the burns to fully heal, and she worked the whole time. She got me a fake ID. A new place, new car, new job. An email account that only we knew about. And in the meantime, I convinced him that I was happy. That I'd learned my lesson.

"When he stopped being so suspicious, I ran. It took him less than three weeks to find me the first time, and I barely got out. With everything at West Tech he has access to . . . I had to get good at disappearing. After that, the bracelets started."

"Bracelets?"

She walked into her bedroom and came back with a shoebox. I took it from her and opened it. Inside were bracelets. Thirteen of them—I counted. "They have the names of my aliases on them, and a birth and death date. His way of telling me that he's found me and killed another one of my lives."

"It's like the ring."

"Yeah." She shook her head. "But it's never been a ring before. And it's never been my real name. I think . . . I think he really might kill me this time."

"That's not going to happen, Ev." She didn't believe me. I could see it on her face. "I'm not going to let that happen."

No response, but it was a promise whether she believed it or not.

He wasn't going to touch her again.

"Thank you for telling me. I'm so sorry, Ev."

"Why?" She shook her head. "You didn't do this."

"No one should have to go through this. And I hope that I've been doing an okay job of showing you that I care about you."

She looked away. "You have. I . . . don't pretend to know why."

"Yes, you do."

A delicate silence hung in the air between us, fragile as blown glass. It was as close as I'd ever come to telling her I wanted her. All of our cards had to be on the table now.

"What happens now?" she asked.

"I'd like you to stay on the property for now. You're the safest here. Until we can figure out if he's here in person and how he found you."

She nodded. "Okay."

"But to be clear, you're not a prisoner."

A small smile. "If I'd thought that, I would have been gone already."

"Good."

"I think it was the email," she said. "When you saw me at the library, I'd gotten an email from Melanie that just said he knew about the account. If he looked for it, maybe he saw where I logged in from?"

"It's possible." I faced her squarely. "I know you don't want to hear this, but we need to tell the police. I understand your hesitation because of what happened, but the police chief, Charlie, is a friend. He's a good man."

She shut down. Utterly deflated, shoulders drawing in in defeat. "You can't guarantee Nathan won't get to him. Or anyone else in the department. Nathan is charming. Beautiful. And he has all the money in the world. What if it happens again?"

It was a valid point. I didn't know the lengths he would go to yet, and there was reason to be cautious. "What if we tell the chief and only the chief? If someone like Nathan is going to be wandering around Garnet Bend, then he'll want to know." She hesitated. "I promise that I know him well, and I would trust him with my life."

Long seconds passed before she nodded. "Okay, but only him."

"Thank you." I stepped into her orbit, daring now to pull her closer. The anger that was pulsing through me was a living thing. At this monster of a man. At the fact that I could have been working to fix this if I had only known.

Now I knew.

Evelyn's hands curved around my back, holding on to me. Holding her kept me steady. As long as I was holding her, nothing could harm her. And that was the most important thing in my life now.

I wanted to kiss her again, taste that sweetness. But this wasn't the moment. Still, the temptation was overwhelming. "I want to kiss you again, Ev."

She tilted her face up, and she didn't say no. Fucking beautiful.

"But I don't want you to regret it later. And I don't want anything between us to be because of your pain." I pressed my lips to her forehead, and she relaxed like the weight of the world had suddenly fallen off her shoulders.

She'd been holding all of that alone. For years. I held her tighter, happy to take the load from her for a while.

"Will you be all right?"

Her hands tightened. "Can you—will you stay? Just . . . like this. Not for anything else."

"Of course."

Even quieter now, "I don't want to be alone."

What Evelyn didn't know was that I would hold her as

long as she wanted—as long as she needed. She didn't realize that I'd been all in from that first day. It was pure chance that she'd ended up here, and I would believe in fate for the rest of my life after this.

I needed her as much as she needed me.

Evelyn stayed in my arms until she was ready to let go. I didn't know how long we'd stayed like that, but the sun was setting outside.

"I think I need some sleep."

"Yeah," I said. "I'll be on the couch if you need anything."

She blushed, and I pretended not to notice. "Thank you, Lucas."

"Anytime, Evelyn."

She disappeared into the bedroom and closed the door behind her. I retreated to the living room and sat on the couch, dropping my face into my hands. All of that was . . .

I needed to tell Harlan and Daniel. Not the full story, but that I was in deep. I had a feeling they already knew, but I still needed to tell them.

Pulling out my phone, I sent a text to Harlan letting him know that I was out of commission for the night. I wasn't leaving Evelyn alone, and I wasn't inviting people into her house so we could talk. I'd fill them in on the necessary details in the morning.

I kicked off my boots and settled back on the couch. It was a good thing that Evelyn had asked me to stay, because I didn't know how to make myself leave.

Chapter 15

Evelyn

When I woke, it was all at once. No grogginess or hesitation. I was clear, though the light through the windows told me I'd slept late.

Last night was the first time I'd told someone everything. Really *everything*. Not even Melanie knew some of those details, because while I'd been still going through it, I'd been desperate to make it better. To make it seem like I hadn't been completely fooled.

Lucas hadn't looked at me the way I'd feared he might. There was no pity or disgust, only anger at Nathan and the cops who'd made my life hell. The way he'd held me . . .

If I'd opened up to someone like this earlier . . . would things have been better? But at the same time, none of those people were Lucas. Something about him fit me in a way that I'd never expected. And I trusted him.

It was a strange feeling. Years had gone by since I'd trusted anyone. Regardless of the feelings that were growing for him, the fact that he saw through me had started before that.

I slipped out of my room. I hadn't locked the door last night. Not because I'd hoped that Lucas would come in, but because I'd known that he wouldn't without an invitation. That kind of safety was everything.

I peeked my head around the living room door. He was still here, on the couch, his big body crammed into a space that was far too small for him. He was sound asleep.

For a few moments I watched him. I was attracted to him. Deeply. And that feeling was so alien and new that it was terrifying. The way he'd felt when he held me last night, the way he'd dropped everything to come to me when I'd needed it. It was almost too much. And not enough.

I'd very much wanted him to kiss me again, but the fact that he hadn't, made me trust him more.

Ever since Nathan, nothing like this had been an option. I'd never believed the lie that I belonged to him. I was a person—I didn't belong to anyone. But he'd gotten his wish. No one had ever touched me, because I'd known the second someone did and he found out, they would be a target too. I didn't want that for anyone.

But Lucas had stepped past that shield, and he didn't care about the fact that Nathan would come after him. It was a breath of relief to have someone standing with me.

I crossed the room toward him and Lucas opened his eyes, alert, like he hadn't been sleeping at all. But as he saw me, his face melted into a smile, and all those butterflies were back in my stomach. I loved having someone react to me that way, and at the same time the last time I'd felt like this—

I shut the thought down. Lucas was not Nathan.

"Morning," he said.

"Morning," I glanced back at the clock in the kitchen. "It's almost not morning anymore."

"Not surprising. Yesterday was a hell of a day. How are you?"

My toes curled under, and nerves made my fingers flare. "I'm good. I feel okay. Last night . . . was the first time I told someone everything. You're the only one who knows it all."

He looked up at me in the middle of putting on his boots. "I didn't know that."

"Yeah."

Lucas stood. His height was never not surprising. He dwarfed me, but I wasn't afraid of it anymore. "Thank you for trusting me with it."

I nodded.

He reached for me slowly, and I didn't move. Lucas's hands on me were still a revelation, and every time he touched me I got a little more used to the idea of being touched. Of *wanting* to be touched.

"You're one of the bravest people I've ever met, Ev. And I've known a lot of brave people." Lucas pulled me against him, and I relaxed, resting my head on his chest.

"It doesn't feel that way."

"Doesn't mean that it's not true."

We stood there for a few minutes before he pressed a kiss to my forehead. I wanted more than that, but I didn't know how to ask for that either. Yet.

"I need to get over to the stables. If you want to come with me to see the animals, you're welcome to. But take your time. There's no rush."

Immediate terror and dread gripped me. I didn't want to be alone. Because when I was with Lucas I didn't have to think about the fact that Nathan had found me. And it was easier to ignore the urge to *fucking run* that had been burned into me. Literally.

"Can I come now?" I asked. "I'll get ready fast."

Lucas's shoulders relaxed. "Yes. Absolutely. And there's no rush."

I hurried back to my room and dressed, ignoring his order to take my time. I didn't want to keep him, and I was suddenly eager to get out of this house for a bit. I wanted air, to get away from the weight of everything that I'd told him in here.

"Okay, I'm ready."

Lucas's gaze stopped me in my tracks. The way his eyes traced me up and down—even though I was in a long-sleeved T-shirt and jeans—made me shiver with sudden heat. I'd forgotten what it was like to feel wanted. I didn't mind it. At all. But I wasn't ready to admit how much I liked it.

"All right, let's go."

We walked toward the stables. I hadn't really been close to them yet, but I found a spring in my step. "I used to ride horses. When I was younger. I haven't for a long time, but I loved them."

"Really?"

"Yeah."

He sighed. "That's good to know. Unfortunately, the horse you'll see today has been a bit difficult. I can't seem to get through to him that people are worth trusting."

"This is the horse you brought out to the field?"

"It is."

"What's his name?"

Lucas shook his head. "We haven't given him one."

"Maybe that's part of the problem."

He shrugged, smiling. "At this point I'll try anything. You want to name him?"

I smiled back. "Sure."

We reached the paddock, and Lucas brushed his hand down my arm before hopping over the fence. I climbed up onto the first rung of the fence and leaned on it, watching him.

He was beautiful in his element. All power and control, and he was here with me. Protecting, watching, and wanting.

Right here in this moment, I felt free. There was so much wrong, and the weight of Nathan hadn't gone away, but it was easier to set it aside for a while.

Lucas disappeared into the stable. While I was waiting, a woman came up to the fence a few feet away. She appeared out of nowhere, no sound, like a ghost. I'd seen her at a distance around the ranch, doing various tasks, but I didn't know anything about her other than that she worked here.

"Hello," I said.

She smiled but said nothing. Given the way Lucas and the other owners cared about this place, I didn't doubt that she was safe. And even without words, my gut told me that she was a good person. There was no disturbance or tension around her. I'd relied on my gut for years to keep me alive, and I wasn't going to stop now.

Lucas came out of the stable leading the horse, smiled in my direction, and raised his hand in greeting to someone behind me. I turned to find a middle-aged woman approaching. She was beautiful in an effortless way and clearly not dressed for ranch work. I stepped down off the fence as she approached. I recognized her vaguely. She'd been here the day I arrived, before I'd met Lucas. I'd been coming in as she was going out. "Hello, Mara," she said to the other woman.

Mara. I would remember that.

Then she turned to me with a smile. "Hi again. We haven't officially met. I'm Rayne."

"Evelyn." I shook her hand when she offered.

"Oh," her face lit up, "I'd heard someone new was staying at the ranch. I didn't realize that you'd stayed."

My stomach tightened. They'd told her about me? What had they said?

She noted the look on my face. "Don't worry, I don't know anything about you apart from your name. I'm a therapist in Garnet Bend, and I work with Resting Warrior and their clients. I have someone who could benefit from a good therapy horse, so I made arrangements to come see the progress with Lucas."

"Slow progress, I'm afraid," he said, approaching on the other side of the fence. "He's still stubborn."

Rayne looked across the paddock at the horse who was prancing around nervously. "Do you still think he has potential?"

"I do," Lucas said. "I think there's something I'm missing that will unlock his trust, but I haven't found it yet."

They continued to talk about the horse, but I took the opportunity to observe Rayne. A therapist. When Lucas had suggested that I talk to someone, this must have been who he meant. He'd mentioned she was a doctor and everything. She seemed nice and approachable. I'd never thought that I'd be able to talk to anyone about what had happened, but I'd told Lucas everything.

If I really did have PTSD, then maybe it was a good idea. But I was still worried about what would happen if Nathan found her. She didn't live at Resting Warrior and wouldn't be protected in the same way.

"I offered the naming opportunity to Evelyn here.

Have you thought of one?" Lucas's voice brought me back to the present.

I looked over at the horse—a chestnut stallion whose color shone copper like metal in the sun. "Penny," I said, going with instinct. "That's what he looks like when he shines."

"Penny," Rayne said with a smile. "A good name for a horse."

"It is." Lucas smiled.

He moved away, and the chase began. He wasn't actually chasing Penny, just trying to approach slowly. It was a way of pushing his boundaries. Harlan came out of the stable, too, and nodded to Lucas. Together they walked around Penny, the horse not having it even though they weren't doing anything threatening.

I had a flash of memory. Something I hadn't thought about in years. At my stable there had been a horse like this one. Never seemed to want to be with people, but he'd liked me. I'd helped the trainers at the stable tame him. He'd ended up being one of my favorite horses to ride.

"Lucas," I said. "Can I come in?"

He met my eyes, assessing. I felt him weigh the risks before he nodded. "Just let us actually catch him first, all right?"

"Okay."

It took a few minutes for them to get close enough, but they did. As soon as they took the reins I climbed up and over the fence, dropping down. The movement startled Penny, and he reared. They lost their grip on the reins, and Penny charged straight at me.

Adrenaline spiked through my veins and Lucas shouted, but I didn't move. This didn't scare me—I had real monsters in my life.

Penny slowed at the last second, and I caught his reins.

That movement startled him again, but this time it startled him *still*. He huffed out a heavy breath but didn't seem interested in running anymore.

"Hi, Penny," I said softly. "You're okay."

He tossed his head, and I took a step closer.

"I know you're scared, but these are good people. You can let them touch you." Another step closer, and another. He pranced a little, but he didn't pull away like he had with Lucas or Harlan. I kept my voice low and steady. "You don't have to be scared."

I was close enough to touch him now, and I dared to do it. My heart pounded in my ears, my body reacting to the potential danger even if I felt calm. But Penny stayed still while I touched his nose and petted him slowly. "There you go."

He made a low noise and lowered his head for more.

"Well fuck," Lucas said with a laugh. He looked over at Harlan. "Looks like I forgot to try one thing."

Lucas edged closer and immediately Penny's entire stance changed. He was ready to charge away, to run so that Lucas couldn't touch him.

"Will you lead him over to Rayne and Mara?" he asked, backing off.

"Sure."

He followed me without hesitation over to the fence where the two women were. The perfect horse. Rayne smiled and reached over the fence to pet him. "Looks like he has some potential after all. What do you think is the problem?" she called to Lucas.

"I think he's afraid of men. Makes sense, given how he was rescued. But this is something that I can work with." Lucas approached again, but this time he stood directly behind me. It seemed to do the trick, because Penny didn't bolt.

Lucas placed a hand on my lower back, and the casual touch was distracting. But I didn't want him to pull away. "If I stand behind you," he said softly, "can we do a couple of circles?"

I nodded, pulling on the reins and getting Penny back to the center. Lucas stuck close with me, and I understood why. If Lucas could get Penny to associate him with me, he might trust Lucas more. His hands stayed on me as I spun, leading Penny in easy circles around the paddock. I gave him a few commands to speed up or slow down, and he followed them without trouble. A decently trained horse when he wasn't scared out of his mind.

Lucas laughed behind me and leaned down to speak in my ear so he wouldn't spook the horse. "Thank you for exposing the problem."

I smiled. "I've missed this. I—"

"What?"

There were things I hadn't thought about in a long time. That were too painful and too tainted to dive into. My love of animals was one of them. And what I'd hoped to do before I met Nathan. My voice felt thick in my throat and the world blurred with tears that I blinked back. "I'm not ready."

The fingers on my waist tightened. "I'm here when you are."

No questions or ridicule. Just acceptance. If I weren't controlling a horse, I would have leaned back into him. We made a few more circles before Lucas spoke again. "Ready to put him away?"

Chapter 16

Lucas

Evelyn was a natural. Penny—the name suited the horse—was not a small animal, but she had showed absolutely no fear. It was clear that she had experience with horses and led Penny back to his stall in the stables without any fight. Exactly like I'd been trying to do for weeks.

It's something I should have thought of, and definitely something that I would keep in mind in the future. Animals could experience PTSD too. That I'd missed that . . . I needed to pay better attention.

She led him into the stall, pet his nose when he hung his head over, and murmured soft words in his ear. Harlan had followed us into the stable, but I motioned him away. I was trying to convey the words *get the hell out* with my face.

He gave me a knowing look and chuckled. But he went. I would owe him one another time.

"Do you want to see the other animals?" I asked, stepping up behind her so that Penny would see my closeness to her.

"Sure."

Before either of us moved, I reached out my hand and slowly stroked Penny's nose. He skittered, but settled when Ev's hand joined mine. "There you go," I said softly. "I'm not going to hurt you. I promise."

We stepped away, Penny still watching us.

"Seriously, thank you."

"It's not a problem." She smiled softly.

"If you want to help more with him, you're more than welcome."

Evelyn lit up like I'd flicked on a light switch and she'd been in the dark. "Really?"

"Of course," I said. "He obviously likes you, and that was more progress than I've made with him in a month. I could use the help."

She blushed. "Thanks."

We walked outside a little, past the alpacas and sheep, laughing at the one sheep who thought he was an alpaca and followed them around constantly. Alpacas and llamas weren't generally used as service animals for people with PTSD but had been found helpful for people with emotional or learning difficulties, as well as the elderly suffering from dementia.

And they were always a riot to watch. Big and fluffy with the cutest ears.

When we went back into the stable, I led her to the only other horse we had on the property. For now. I was picking up another one tomorrow. "This is Blanche." She was a gentle mare that had taken to training perfectly. "She's going to a rehab center in Arizona at the end of next week."

"Hi, Blanche," Ev said quietly. "How did you all get the idea for this place?"

I scratched the back of my neck and looked away. It wasn't an easy thing to talk about, but after everything that she'd shared with me, it would be hypocritical not trust her. "I told you that all of us were SEALs, but not how we met. When we came back from our various assignments and got out, we all ended up at the same treatment program for PTSD. Government run. The kind of place you get stuck when they have nowhere else to put you."

Evelyn winced. "Doesn't sound fun."

"No," I said, "It wasn't. And we all knew that we weren't getting the help that we needed. Though I give the program credit for getting us to the point where we could admit that we needed help. For men like us, that's hard to do."

Evelyn returned my smile as we stepped out of the barn and into the sun. I headed toward the kennels. I didn't know if she was aware that we kept dogs on the property yet. We kept them pretty locked down because dogs running wild weren't a good thing for people with post-traumatic stress.

"So we talked about it, and together over some drinks we came up with the idea of a safe place for people like us. A place away from everything, where people could recover. A couple of us had had good experiences with animal-led therapy, so we wanted room for that. Help people any way we could.

"Harlan helped us get this property. Liam and I studied how to train animals properly. Now Grant and Noah help find our clients and place our animals. Daniel takes care of the day-to-day tasks, and Jude is our security. He also helps with whatever needs doing."

"That's amazing," Evelyn said. "Really. I feel like most

people would have kept their anger and not wanted to help anyone."

"There's plenty who do. Hopefully, some of them can find their way here. So we decided to do it, but we're not therapists. That's why we work with some local providers. A psychiatrist and physical therapist who are a married couple, and a therapist."

Evelyn smiled. "Dr. Rayne?"

"Yes."

"She introduced herself."

I was careful not to react. The last time I'd suggested talking to someone, it hadn't gone well. Nor should it have. That had been stepping over a line far too soon.

"Who's Mara?" Ev asked. "She was there, Rayne greeted her, but she didn't say anything."

"She's the one who took the job you came here looking for," I said. "But she's very quiet, and she has her reasons."

"Oh." She looked down. It seemed like she wanted to ask more, but there wasn't much more to tell her. Mara was a sweet girl and did her job efficiently and quietly. Any indication that she'd experienced something in the past was just that—an indication. I'd heard her speak maybe three times in the year that she'd worked for us, but she was always ready with a smile.

Evelyn and I were so close together that I could take her hand, and I wanted to. But I wasn't sure where she was at after last night. When she looked up she took a deep breath. "I'm thinking about talking to Dr. Rayne. I know you suggested it, and I . . . was rude. And I still don't know if I'm ready. But I'm thinking about it."

"That's great," I said, the pressure in my chest easing. "And you weren't rude. I shouldn't have pushed you to begin with."

She sighed. "Sometimes I need pushing."

We turned the last corner, and Evelyn stilled. "You have dogs?"

They were all behind a chain-link fence in the large area that we used to train and house them. But on seeing us, they were all barking up against the fence, excited for people. The dogs we trained were all personable—they had to be in order to be therapy dogs—and they loved visitors.

"We have dogs," I said, approaching the gate. "Sit."

The dogs all backed up and sat, allowing Evelyn and me to enter. As soon as the gate closed, they knew they were free, and Evelyn was swarmed. Not in a bad way. These dogs loved people, and for her they were all joy. A dozen wiggling balls of it.

Evelyn laughed, and I froze. Had I heard her laugh before? It was light and free. Beautiful. She sat down, still laughing, allowing the dogs to lick her face and climb into her lap. I think it was the happiest I'd ever seen her.

I burned the image into my brain. Head thrown back, sun shining on dark hair, face scrunched as dogs licked it, and laughing. Evelyn was so fucking beautiful.

She looked at me. "I've never owned a pet. Not since I was really little. I rode horses and stuff, but I always wanted a dog. Nathan didn't like them, and the past few years . . ." She paused. "They wouldn't have been fair to a dog."

"You love animals." It was a fact that would be apparent to anyone watching.

"I do." She hesitated, then stepped away to fill the dogs' bowls with food.

From across the space, I watched her play with them after they ate. They brought her a ball and fell over themselves to get it and bring it back to her. If I hadn't already known, this would have confirmed that Evelyn was a good person. The animals were trained to be sensitive to people's emotions and react accordingly. They all loved her.

Especially Aspen, an English setter that had been here a while. He wasn't playing with the other dogs, instead sticking to Evelyn's side, bumping her leg, and practically sitting on her feet.

A dog like Aspen would be perfect for someone like Evelyn. English setters were gentle, protective, and one of the ideal breeds for therapy. And given what was happening with Nathan, she might appreciate a little backup. I knew that I would feel better if she had one of our dogs watching her back.

I walked over to her, and she smiled at me. It was my goal to have her smiling like this every day. She deserved that. "What do you say you have one of these guys as a buddy for however long you're here?" I avoided setting any kind of end date, because if I was honest with myself, I didn't want her to leave.

"Wait, really?"

"Really."

Tears filled her eyes and she covered her face with her hands. Then she laughed, looking down at Aspen. "I'm not sure this one would let me go anyway."

"Aspen."

She knelt down beside the dog. "Hi, Aspen."

His tail wagged so fast it was nearly a blur, and he sat still while Evelyn hugged him. There wasn't going to be any problem with them settling in together, that was for sure.

When Evelyn stood she looked at me. It was a different kind of look—shy and hopeful, paired with a blush. "Did you—" She looked away for a moment, and it seemed like embarrassment. "Do you still want to kiss me?"

Shock rooted me to the spot for a moment. Was I hallucinating words because I wanted to hear them so badly? No. She was looking at me expectantly, and I stared at her like an idiot. "Yes," I said. "Hell, yes."

The distance between us disappeared in three steps, and then her mouth was under mine. Fuck, she was so sweet, fit exactly against my body like she was meant to be there. I couldn't ignore the deep sense of *rightness* when she was in my arms, those deep instincts that had roared to life when I'd first seen her settling and soothing.

Evelyn opened her mouth to me, and the kiss turned from restrained to fiery in an instant. I couldn't stop the groan that came from me or the need to have her closer. I moved us, guiding her against the wall of the kennel so I could kiss her harder. Deeper. And she kissed me back.

That undid me. It was like she'd unlocked something by trusting me, and for the first time she touched me —*really* touched me. Her hands slid up the front of my shirt and her arms twined around my neck.

She was all delicate curves pressed between me and the wall. The only way we could be closer is if clothes came off, and I wanted that. If she ever trusted me enough for that—

I brought myself back to her lips. Her tongue was still shy, but daring enough to dance with mine. We were in the open. Anyone could walk to the kennel and see us, and I couldn't bring myself to care. I could stay in this moment, kissing Evelyn, forever.

Running my hands down her ribs, I allowed myself to feel her the way I'd thought about. I hooked my fingers into her belt loops on either side the way she'd done to me, thumbs brushing up and feeling skin.

Evelyn gasped and pulled away from the kiss.

Fuck.

Too far, too fast.

"I'm sorry," I said, dropping my hands away from her body and placing them on the wall. "I'm sorry."

She looked at me, lips swollen from our kiss and eyes still glassy with it. Determination entered her gaze, and she pulled me back down to her, kissing me again, harder this time.

I didn't deserve this woman who'd been fighting demons for years and did it even while she kissed me. When I'd told her that she was one of the bravest people I'd ever met, I hadn't been lying.

Evelyn moaned, which broke any control I had over my body. I wanted her. More than wanted. There was an ache in my chest that only she was the answer to.

My phone rang in my pocket, and I let out a curse. Evelyn laughed against my lips. "Ignore it."

I checked the screen and cursed again. "I can't. It's the police chief. I left him a message to get back to me so I could tell him about what happened."

Her eyes went dark. "Yeah."

"I'm sorry," I said again. "Not exactly what I wanted to mention while kissing you."

"To make up for it, you could keep kissing me." She bit her lip, and I think I lost all the blood in my body as it ran south.

One more press of my lips against hers, and I pulled myself away. "I swear to you, Evelyn, there's more where that came from, any time you want it."

She blushed at my words, and I memorized the color on her skin, hoping I would see it again.

Walking away from her was the hardest thing I'd done in a long time.

Chapter 17

Evelyn

It was nearly a day later, and I was still thinking about the kiss.

After I'd brought Aspen and his things back to the Bitterroot House, I'd taken a nap. Aspen had joined me, and it was the best thing I'd ever experienced. I slept so much easier with him there, and I hadn't noticed I'd needed that. Who knew you could be tense while sleeping? But there was a knot between my shoulders that had loosened.

Nathan was still a threat, a very real black cloud on the horizon, but for the first time I had people who had my back. And it felt like a fucking miracle.

But that kiss—my whole body still tingled. It was the absolute best kiss of my life. Aspen hadn't minded the interruption, just sticking to my side as soon as Lucas stepped away to take the call.

I hadn't seen him again yesterday. Not really. Five

minutes in the evening to tell me that he had filled in the police chief and that the chief had agreed to keep it quiet. Lucas apologized about walking away from the kiss and kissed me again before he had to leave for a weekly meeting. Even that little kiss had left me buzzing again.

It was fine, because yesterday was one of the best days I'd had in a long time. And today was giving it a run for its money. I'd slept in later than I had in recent memory with Aspen curled against my side. Then I'd taken a long and luxurious shower before heading out into the afternoon for a walk with him.

The weather was mild and perfect, with a breeze carrying that scent that I couldn't get enough of. Aspen didn't need a leash. He stuck to my side like glue. If he left to investigate something, he was back within a minute. The smile on my face never seemed to slip away.

I sat by the lake and watched the clouds for a long while before going back and playing with the other dogs again. It was wonderful to just *exist*. To do what I wanted and not be consumed by the things that kept me hanging on to the cliff by my fingernails.

Lucas texted me in the afternoon. He'd left to pick up a horse on another ranch a couple of hours away, but he was back now. I was hoping to see him again tonight, because I wasn't done with the way he'd kissed me. I could tell that he was still holding himself back, and I didn't want that anymore.

I wanted all of Lucas. He'd shown me that I could live again, and now I was done with merely surviving. Maybe I'd head over to the lodge and see if he was busy later. Nerves bubbled in my gut at the thought. It felt vulnerable to be that forward, but it was a step I needed to take.

Aspen trotted alongside me as I walked up the lane to the Bitterroot House, panting happily. Something snagged the corner of my eye, and I nearly missed a step up onto the porch. A black rose petal lay on the faded wood. Taking a breath, I willed my heart to stop the pounding that had started. I was just startled. I was fine. A petal had gotten stuck to my clothes when I'd come home from Deja Brew and I hadn't noticed.

But it was the door that made me truly freeze. It was open a fraction, and I'd closed and locked it behind me. I *know* that I had, because I did it every time I left, no matter how short a time.

I pushed the door open—and fell into ice-cold water. I couldn't breathe. Iron fists jammed themselves around my lungs and tried to suffocate me. Black petals were everywhere, ripped off stems that had been left on the floor and scattered through the entire living room. The petals disappeared into the kitchen. No surface was untouched. It looked like ash or charcoal—the remnants of my life burned into ruins.

My feet were glued to the floor. Was he here? How had he gotten in here? The ranch was secure. I *knew* the ranch was secure because Lucas made sure of it. All my safety, the pool of cool water that it had been, was evaporating in front of my eyes. Was Nathan still on the property?

Movement snapped me back into the moment. Aspen was at my side, staring into the house. I'd not seen any aggression in him, but he was bracing himself like he was about to charge, a low growl filling the air.

The sound released me. I turned and sprinted toward the lodge. If Nathan was still inside, speed might be the only advantage I had. Aspen was keeping pace with me, not leaving me alone for a second. Everything seemed too sharp and too bright. My heart raced and my breathing felt tight. I was shaking—I hadn't run like this in years—but I couldn't stop. I would not stop.

I wasn't going to let him take me when I finally had things to live for.

There. The lodge was in focus. A beacon. "Lucas." My voice came out as nothing but a breath. That wasn't going to work. I dug deep and found everything that I had. "Lucas!" I shouted his name at the top of my lungs. And again. A third time.

He came barreling out of the door, eyes wild, and caught me on the stairs as I nearly collapsed. "My house," I managed. "He was in my house."

Lucas didn't wait, setting me on the stairs and running toward where I'd just left. The breath burned in my lungs as I tried to recover from the sprint. I didn't want Lucas over there. If Nathan was in the house waiting for me, he was dangerous. Not for one second did I want Nathan and Lucas in the same room.

But then again, Lucas was dangerous too. A Navy SEAL and big as hell. If I had a choice, I would bet on Lucas any day of the week.

I knew I should get inside, but my limbs shook with the aftermath of adrenaline. My stomach swam, and I felt sick. He was here. He'd gotten *here*. Past everything that was supposed to keep him out. If he could touch me here, what did that mean?

Aspen put his head on my lap, and I held him close. Thank goodness for him. He'd been the one to snap me out of the frozen fear that had held me.

Lucas came back, striding down the road with purpose. His face held the anger of an avenging angel. The fury in his eyes knew no bounds, but it wasn't directed at me. Never at me. His arms were gentle when he picked me up off the stairs and carried me inside. The chair he tucked me into was the same one I'd sat in when I'd come here looking for work.

That was a nice kind of symmetry.

Lucas had his phone out and was speaking too quickly. Snapping orders. I couldn't focus on the words because my head was still spinning. If I'd stayed home this afternoon instead of going out for a walk, would Nathan have killed me?

A chill ran down my spine.

Aspen jumped into my lap, though he was too big for it. It didn't matter, it was exactly what I needed. The comforting weight and warmth of his body helped the world slow down enough that I could breathe.

He whined, laying his head against my chest.

"Hey, boy," I whispered. "Thank you."

"Do it," Lucas said into the phone with enough force to shake the building. "Now."

Lucas came to stand in front of me, and it took him a second to snap out of mission mode. That was okay. I wanted him to be prepared.

"I don't know how they got in, but I'm going to find out, Evelyn. If it was Nathan or someone working for him, it doesn't matter. We're going to find them." He crouched down and put his hand over mine where it rested on Aspen's body. "I can't let you stay in that house anymore. But you can stay with me. I live here on the property, and my house is a fortress. I have a guest room. Will that be all right?"

Cool relief poured down over my head. It was something I hadn't known I needed. Staying near him? Near the only person that still felt like safety? "Yes. Please."

"Okay." He whistled and Aspen scooted off my lap. "We're going there now. I'm taking you out the back door to a car, and you'll duck down in the back seat. I know it seems like a lot, but I don't want to take any chances while we don't have things secured."

I shook my head. "No crazier than the things I've done to run."

His mouth quirked into a smile for a moment. "You'll have to tell me about them sometime."

Lucas extended his hand, and I took it. Then we were moving. I was glad he had a plan, because I didn't, and letting someone else do this part of it was a relief. Exhaustion hit me like a wave.

Tired.

I was so tired of running.

The car waited outside the back door of the lodge— where I'd never been. It was already running, Harlan sitting in the driver's seat. When he saw us, he got out and opened the back door in one fluid movement. Aspen jumped into the back, and I followed.

"Stay down," Lucas said.

I did. I held on to Aspen and made myself as small as possible as Lucas pulled away. We weren't speeding though. That was something I was familiar with. You didn't make anything look out of the ordinary if you could help it. Especially if you didn't know who was watching or where they were watching from.

Even going a normal speed, it was only a few minutes before we pulled to a stop in the shadow of another building. Lucas helped me out of the back seat and walked me through the door Liam held open. The door slammed shut behind us, and Lucas flipped locks that looked like they belonged on a bank vault. He keyed in the code on an alarm panel next to the door. A chirp confirmed the activation.

And then his hands were on me.

Lucas kissed me, hauling me against him like I was the last thing he was going to feel on this earth. This was not a safe kiss. It was hot and desperate. There was more behind this kiss than I'd ever imagined.

This. *This* was Lucas when he wasn't holding back. Full of desperate passion and heat. I wanted him exactly like this. Unafraid, and mine.

I kissed him back.

Aspen was still pressed against my leg, but it didn't matter. I was already lost.

Lucas lifted me off my feet, holding me off the ground while he kissed me deeper. I was so small compared to him, it was nothing. One of his hands sank into my hair, and I shivered.

The stirrings of something deep rose in my gut. Feelings that I'd thought I'd left behind forever. They drew me closer to Lucas. I clung to him like he was an anchor in a storm. But he was the storm too. That anger was directed outward, keeping us in its eye.

"I promise you, Ev," he whispered against my lips. "I swear that I'm going to keep you safe and that this is going to *end* for you. I'm not going to stop until you're free of it."

My feet touched the ground, but I didn't let him pull away. "I believe you."

"I'm so sorry."

I shook my head. "It's not you. It's him. I should have known. He won't stop."

Lucas placed a finger under my chin and raised my gaze to his. "You are not his. You don't belong to anyone."

"I just—" I took a breath. "I don't want to run anymore."

"I'm going to make sure that you don't have to. The other owners are meeting me here to talk about what happened and what can be done. You're welcome to listen, if you want."

That kiss had sizzled my nerves, and I was still a little numb. I nodded.

"Your story is yours, Ev, but I need to tell them something. Which details can I share?"

I swallowed. "You can tell them that he scarred me and claimed me. That he's been stalking me for years. How many identities I've had. That the cops made it worse."

"That's a lot," Lucas said, eyebrows raised.

"Now that I've said all of it out loud, it's easier. Half the reason that I didn't show anyone my scars was the pity. Or the assumption that I was some kind of fool for not seeing it." I searched for that resistance that I'd always found before when considering revealing the truth—and found nothing. "I'm done hiding."

Maybe Nathan had finally broken me and I didn't care anymore. But I was done. I didn't want this. People deserved to know the kind of monster he was, and I knew that no one at Resting Warrior would ever look at me with pity or disgust.

"Thank you," said Lucas.

"All my things are still in the house."

He pulled me deeper into the house, up a set of stairs into a gorgeous and comfy living room. "I sent Harlan to get your things. He'll be here soon."

"Okay." The sun had barely started to set, but I wanted pajamas. Comfort.

"I'll make you some tea."

The kitchen branched off the living room, and I could hear him moving around, but my eyes wouldn't stay still. This was Lucas. His home. Where he spent time when he was alone.

It was sparse but comfortable. Warm woods and leather. A large fireplace dominated the space, and I had a vision of both of us curled up on the couch under a blanket. I blushed at the very idea of it. That image meant a future.

Was I envisioning a future with Lucas?

Those same stirrings rose in my gut again, and I pushed them down. I couldn't think about the future until we'd dealt with the danger that was in the present. Until Nathan was gone, the future was blank. Because he'd made it that way.

Lucas returned from the kitchen with a large mug, a tea bag steeping in it. As he handed it to me, a knock came from behind me. I jumped. The front door.

"It's Harlan," Lucas said softly. But he still checked through the peephole before unlocking the door.

Harlan stepped in quickly so Lucas could shut and lock the door again. They were a well-oiled machine, these men. But Harlan didn't have anything with him, and his face was grave. He spoke softly to Lucas, low enough that I couldn't hear him. But Lucas scrubbed his hands over his face. "Okay. Thanks. Wait here for the others, okay?"

Lucas took the mug from my hands and put it on the coffee table. "Come with me." He took my hand, and we went up another set of stairs. The whole top floor was a bedroom. Lucas's, obviously. But it felt strange to be here. Why? "What's wrong?"

He paused at the top of the stairs, and shook his head, eyes closed. The words came out like they were being yanked out of him. "All your clothes were shredded in the drawers. There was nothing left. The bracelets and ring are gone too. I'm so sorry."

The emotions hit me in the chest. They were just clothes. I'd lost more to Nathan than this. But after every-thing—tears flooded my eyes.

"I'll take care of it in the morning," Lucas said. A drawer scraped. He pulled a pair of flannel pants and a T-shirt out of his dresser. "You can wear these. I know it's not the same."

"Thank you."

He pulled me close and pressed one kiss to my lips. Just long enough to ground me. Remind me that I was here with him. I could survive the loss of clothes. "I'll be downstairs."

It didn't take me long to change. I was practically swimming in the clothes, but they smelled like Lucas, and that was pure comfort. Gentle pine and clean mountain air.

Like Lucas had pulled it out of my head, he had started a fire and held a blanket for me when I returned to the living room. I burrowed underneath it into the armchair, Aspen resting his head on my knee. And I had the mug of tea again.

I liked the heat from the fire, but I also knew that I couldn't be any closer to it than I was. Not right now.

"You know how to treat a girl," I said softly.

Lucas's eyes were filled with pain. "I know how to care for someone with trauma. Because I've been where you are. Nothing helps, but little things matter."

There was a knock on the door, and he kissed my forehead. "We'll be over here. If it's too much, the guest room is directly behind you."

"Okay."

But I didn't want to move. Exhaustion crept up on me. I wanted to hear what they were planning, but I couldn't keep my eyes open. Setting the tea on the table beside me, I stroked Aspen's head, watching as each of Lucas's friends arrived. When the last one came in and the door was locked again, Lucas called the meeting to order.

Chapter 18

Lucas

My body vibrated with poorly contained energy. I was keeping a hold on it. But barely. The devastation on Evelyn's face was enough to turn me into an animal. She was curled up on a chair in the corner with Aspen. Looking in our direction but not at us. Into space. Like every last bit of life had been drained from her eyes.

If I ever put my hands on Nathan West, it would be a struggle not to kill him.

Around the table, my six friends looked at me. A couple of them weren't remotely informed about this. I'd tried to keep Evelyn and her story as private as I could. But now this man had violated our property and her safety. It could not—would not—stand, and I knew they would agree with me.

But as I stood here, I was torn between my desire to *fix* and to *protect* and the desire to carry Evelyn upstairs to my bedroom and lock the door behind us.

"What's going on?" Grant asked.

I swallowed and focused on the group in front of me. "There's been a breach of the property. We don't know who, but it was either a dangerous stalker or someone working on his behalf. They got through the gates and broke into the Bitterroot House with the intent to at least terrify Evelyn, if not worse. We're lucky she was out of the house when they were there."

Harlan looked at me, understanding just how much of my fury I was holding back. "What can you tell us?"

"I'll tell you what Evelyn has given me permission to, starting with the fact that this man is Nathan West."

A low curse came out of Jude. "You're serious?"

"Yes."

Grant shrugged. "What am I missing?"

I took a shaky breath. "Nathan West is the son of billionaire Patrick West, CEO of West Technologies."

"Ah," Grant said, looking gray. "I see."

"Evelyn and Nathan West were engaged. Then he revealed his true colors. Evelyn has permanent scarring from his actions, and he's declared that she's his. Permanently. The cops only made it worse, and she suffered more damage at his hands."

Not one of the men at the table spoke, their faces reflecting varying degrees of nausea and rage.

"She's been running from him for years and has run through multiple false identities trying to hide from him. And the . . . significant fact that she's chosen to let us help her instead of running is not lost on me." I looked over to where she was, eyes now closed in what I hoped was sleep. "She'll be staying here with me for an extra layer of security, since the Bitterroot House is a mess."

Liam grinned at me. A shit-eating grin that grated on

my skin. Really? Right now? I leveled a stare at him until the smile faded and he looked properly chastised.

"Are you all right?" Harlan asked quietly.

"I'm not the person you should be asking that question."

He fixed me with a stare. "But I am asking. Are you okay? To do this? To help her?"

"No, I'm not fucking all right," I said, low and dark. "He's terrified her for years, Harlan. *Years*. And he came into our home to do it again. I want to tear his throat out with my bare hands."

Jude flashed a grim smile. "I'm sure that could be arranged."

Harlan was still assessing me with deadly quiet. Daniel was too. "What do you want to do?"

"First and foremost, we need to make sure that things are secure, and secondly, we need information. Jude, I drove the perimeter the other day and everything looked normal. No spikes in the control room, but that's your specialty. Check everything, lock it down. If you have any extra measures to put into place, now's the time."

He stretched, almost looking eager. "I can do that."

"We need to know if Nathan is here in Garnet Bend or if he's hiring people. He has nearly limitless resources, so we can't discount anything. I know we all have our own contacts, and I don't particularly care about redundancy. Reach out to whoever you can—and more importantly, who you can trust with discretion. Figure out how Nathan discovered that she was here, and what he knows about us."

All around the table their faces were grave. But I didn't doubt them. I could trust every one of these men with my life. And more importantly, Evelyn's life. None of us took this kind of job anymore. But just because we'd left a life of stealth and covert operations behind didn't mean that we'd forgotten any of the lessons we'd learned in that life. Or what had been burned into us.

I winced at my own thoughts. Evelyn had actually *been* burned. "After that," I admitted, "I don't have a plan. We don't have enough information to make one."

"You're right," Harlan said. "We don't know enough. But we're with you. No one attacks us here. No one."

Soft sounds of agreement from around the table.

"Don't hold back," Daniel said, addressing everyone. "Whatever contacts you need, wherever you need to go, do it. I'll move anything we need to around in our schedule here. This takes precedence over anything else."

I nodded my thanks at him.

"I think my first priority is to get eyes on him," I said. "I've never been so sick to my stomach that we don't have cameras in the grounds."

It was a decision that we'd made early on—to only have cameras watching the fence and the gate to protect our clients' privacy. Given all the things that we'd experienced and the vulnerable moments that we'd had to go through in our own recoveries . . . having private moments recorded—even accidentally—would have felt like a violation.

"I'll check every frame we have of the fences. There has to be something," Jude said.

"Make sure you check for manipulation. Tampering. We have to remember who we're dealing with."

He nodded.

"Thank you for helping me with this. I know it's not our normal mode of operation."

Noah cleared his throat. He'd said nothing so far. "You don't need to thank us, Lucas. You'd do the same for any of us."

I would. "Find out what you can in the next day. We'll meet again tomorrow night. Anything important before then, you know where to find me."

The meeting broke up. At this point, we were so comfortable with each other that we didn't really stand on ceremony. I walked them to the door, went out with them, and stood on the porch in the darkness. It seemed like Evelyn was asleep, but I didn't want to freak her out if she was still listening.

"I want extra security," I said. "At the gates and around the house until we catch this fucker."

"No arguments from me," Harlan said. "I don't like the idea of someone being able to do this without us noticing."

"Me either," Jude rumbled. "I'll take care of it."

The rest of them faded away until it was just me, Harlan, and Daniel.

"So much for not getting in too deep," Daniel said with a chuckle.

"I won't apologize for it."

He held up a hand. "I'm not asking you to. I need to ask how deep you are now. How far are you willing to go for this woman?"

There wasn't any judgment in the question. He was asking so that he could know and move accordingly. But still, the answer felt like stripping myself bare. For Evelyn, I would do anything. "All the way."

Daniel and Harlan nodded. "All right," Daniel said. "Then we'll catch the fucker."

"I need to let Grace know about this." Harlan sighed. "She's close enough. He could have crossed her land."

I raised an eyebrow. "I imagine that'll go well."

He smirked. "About as well as last time."

"She ended up giving you a ride home?"

Daniel choked on a laugh. "I'd say she did."

Harlan glared, but didn't disagree.

"I got an eyeful of this one kissing her, until she took the opportunity to slap him so hard his neck almost snapped." Daniel was clearly trying to hold back his mirth.

"It was a misunderstanding," Harlan said.

I shook my head. "What the hell happened between the two of you?"

His face hardened. "A story for a different time."

I nodded. "I'll see you both tomorrow."

"I'll grab Liam, and we'll take the first watch."

"Thanks." Once inside, I locked the door behind me and activated the alarm system. We were as protected as we could make ourselves right now. The only thing that could be done was to wait until we found Nathan. Hopefully, that would be sooner rather than later.

Evelyn was well and truly asleep by the fire, Aspen curled up on her feet. I reached down to pet the dog. "Good boy," I whispered. He licked my hand once in response.

I didn't want her to spend the night in a chair. I eased the blanket aside and lifted her into my arms. Like this, she felt so small. So light. Delicate. Something that needed protection.

But she was strong. Stronger than I was. She'd survived everything this monster had thrown at her so far, and I was going to make sure that she succeeded.

The guest room wasn't far. I carried her into the dark space, lit faintly from the lights in the living room. Evelyn jerked awake as I went to put her on the bed. She struggled for a moment before she realized that it was me. And the way that she relaxed when she did wasn't something I would take for granted.

She looked around. Her voice was laced with sleep. "This isn't your room."

Breath stilled in my chest. "I would never assume that, Evelyn. Staying with me doesn't have to mean anything that you don't want it to."

She twisted in my arms, lifting herself up to kiss me. "Please." Her voice was soft. "Please assume. Don't leave me alone." Another gentle press of her lips. "Please."

I captured her mouth with mine. It was something that I hadn't let myself truly hope for, this time with her. She clung to my neck, fingers digging into my shirt, desperation leaking through her fingers. I turned and carried her up the stairs to my bedroom.

Chapter 19

Evelyn

For the second time today, I was in Lucas's bedroom. But this was different. This time, soft darkness wrapped around us, and I could feel Lucas's heart pounding as hard as mine was. He let me slide to my feet before we reached the bed, but his hands didn't leave me.

Light still poured up from the stairs and through the windows from the floodlights outside. Enough light that I could see him, and enough darkness to make me feel bold.

"Evelyn," he said, "whatever happens, it needs to be what *you* want."

I touched him, reaching out and drawing my fingers up his chest, and he stilled. "This afternoon, before I found the house," I managed to say. "I was thinking about you. About the way you'd kissed me, and how I wanted more."

I was glad the semidarkness kept him from seeing my blush. "I was going to try to find you and see if you were busy. I had hoped—" My voice cut off. "I don't know what

152

I hoped. But it's not because of what happened today. I'm not . . . I'm not using you."

Lucas's gentle hands drew up my arms and curled around my neck. His thumbs tilted my jaw up so I looked at him. "The thought didn't cross my mind. But I'm glad you told me."

I released a shuddering breath. Just because it was something I wanted didn't mean it was all going to be easy. "I don't know how to do this anymore. But I do want you."

Slowly, Lucas leaned down and pressed his forehead against mine. "I don't care what we're doing. If you need to stop, we *stop*."

I loved him for that. But as he kissed me, heat building under my skin, I couldn't imagine this man doing anything that would make me want to stop. Lucas was different. My soul recognized it. Reveled in it. This man would never hurt me.

He lifted me into his arms again, this time laying me down on the bed. The kiss was familiar, bordering on the edges of what we'd already touched. He was holding back. Going slow. For me.

I opened my mouth to him and invited him in. Traced his tongue with mine in a way that sent heat shivering down my limbs. I'd pulled away when he touched my skin before, but I was ready now. Still, I broke our kiss apart when his fingers crept under my borrowed shirt. "Lucas, you need to know that what you're going to see isn't pretty."

Nathan had left scars. Patterns that, like the man, had no rhyme nor reason. I never looked in the mirror without clothes anymore. I didn't want to see what he'd destroyed. Ruined.

Lucas lifted the T-shirt away from my skin, working it up and over my head before tossing it aside. His expression didn't change as he slipped the straps of my bra down my arms—slipped his hands underneath me to unhook it. That ended up on the floor too. And then he was looking at me.

I don't think I'd ever been looked at like that before. He was seeing *me*. Like I hadn't been seen since this happened. But the scars . . .

Lucas's face was troubled as he drew a finger across some of the marks on my skin. I couldn't look at him, shame and fear rising up to swallow me. It burned in my chest, a ball of hot metal. Nathan had gotten what he wanted. I was untouchable to everyone. Because of him.

Emotion welled up, pain blooming in my chest. I closed my eyes, bracing myself for the moment when Lucas gave me back the clothes and sent me away.

"Evelyn," he said. I shook my head. "Evelyn, look at me."

There were tears in my eyes when I did. I couldn't make them stop.

Lucas's eyes were fierce in the near dark. No fear or hesitation on his face. Only utter belief in what he said next. "There is no part of you that's not beautiful to me." He set his lips to my skin over a line of scars. "These make you who you are, and are a reminder that you survived him. You're *alive*."

He continued to kiss those scars, moving his mouth over them until he reached the one at the peak of my breast. His tongue traced over it, lips curling around it, letting it harden under his lips until it nearly ached.

The gentle, lazy teasing poured pure heat through me. It had been so long, that the simple contact made me wet —made me want more.

"Your scars," he said, lifting his mouth from my skin for a moment, "are not something you should be ashamed of." His voice was soft, a whisper not meant to break the moment. "And I will spend as many hours as I can in this bed proving it, if that's what you need."

I reached for him, running my fingers through his hair. "I just need you."

"You have me."

My whole body shuddered. Lucas touched me with a tenderness that reached all the way to my soul. He took his time, brushing his lips over my skin and taking care to touch each line of scars. His hands stroked down my arms. Across my ribs. Slow and soothing until my body relaxed under his hands.

I hadn't realized the tension that had crept in. But now that it was gone, I took a deep breath. "I'm sorry."

"For what?"

"I—"

Lucas returned to me, big body looming in the darkness, face close to mine. He was everywhere. Surrounding me. And that was *good*. I was safe here.

"You never have to apologize to me for this." His voice was gentle, breath brushing my ear. "That you're letting me touch you at all is a fucking honor."

I realized then that I hadn't really touched him. He'd touched me—I was letting him touch me. But I wanted that too. Reaching out, I pressed my palm to his cheek, ran my fingers through his hair. "I want to see you."

Lucas shifted away, pulling his shirt over his head and revealing . . . everything. The body I'd found so overwhelming when I'd first seen him was even more overwhelming now. His entire torso was packed with muscle, built with a lifetime of military service and now work on the ranch.

He was beautiful.

Looking down at me, he searched my face. "Are you okay?"

"Yeah." I was a little breathless, being so close to him. He was raising feelings that had been dormant forever. I *wanted*.

A hand cupped my face. "If you need to stop, anytime, I will." Another reassurance. I nodded, but he didn't let go. "I have only one request."

I raised my eyes to his in question.

"Let me take care of you, Evelyn. Let it just be the two of us in here. Right now, nothing exists outside of this room."

He was right. I needed that. My scars were a part of me, and him seeing them . . . accepting them. That was everything. Enough of my life had been taken by the man that had given them to me. Tonight I would not even think his name.

"Just you and me," I breathed.

Lucas's mouth dropped to my skin once more, resuming the path that he'd started to draw. Goose bumps formed under his hands. His lips. Pleasure and heat, twisting and yearning. *Need* that rose to meet his touch. My eyes closed, enjoying the feel of him memorizing me.

That's what it felt like he was doing—memorizing every inch of me with tongue and fingers until he'd drawn an entire map. When he reached the waistband of his too-big sweatpants, I hesitated. The scars below the belt weren't any different, but I still cringed at the idea of him seeing them.

He hesitated too, and I knew he was waiting for me to tell him no.

I didn't.

Big, strong hands slid down my hips, taking the fabric with it. My underwear. Everything was gone, and I shivered. Lucas's hands moved back up my legs. I loved the warmth of his hands, the way he was taking me in. There was no hesitation or judgment—just a hunger on his face that made my breath short.

"I know it's only the two of us," I said. "I just—"

He pressed a kiss to my stomach. Slow. Drifting deliberately lower.

"You're the first one since . . . everything happened."

"Thank you," he whispered. "For trusting me with that."

He slipped between my legs, and that was the last thought I had about anything else other than the man touching me and his tongue. Slow. Luxurious. Pure pleasure. The shock that he would do that at all kept me from crying out—

I slammed the thought to a stop. It didn't matter that *he* hadn't liked doing that or that he'd only done it when I'd begged. All that mattered was that Lucas groaned as he licked into me, hands gathering me closer to him like I was a feast.

"I—"

Words were on the tip of my tongue, but I didn't know *what* words. I just needed to speak. "Are you sure?" The words were less than a breath and barely a question.

Lucas lifted his head for a moment. "I tried not to think of you like this. With everything you'd gone through, it felt like too much. Too far and not fair to you. But there were times I couldn't stop." A long, slow stroke of his tongue accompanied the words, and my whole body shuddered. "If you're asking if I'm sure that I want to do this," another slow caress, "then yes. I am very, *very* sure."

Anything I might have said in response evaporated into mist. He memorized me with his tongue and his lips, savoring every part of me. He made small sounds of encouragement when I shook and arched, repeating those movements over and over until pleasure unfurled inside me, rising in a wave.

It was a bright star of sensation—a nova. A flare. It flashed through me like an explosion and vanished as quickly, leaving me breathless.

I had not thought about having an orgasm in a long time. There were . . . times that I had tried. And each of those times I'd been overcome with fear and shame and the feeling of invisible eyes stalking me. Eventually, I'd given up.

"I was worried," I breathed. "That I couldn't anymore."

Lucas smiled against me, not bothering to speak. I expected him to pull away. To release his lips from my skin and move on to other things.

He didn't.

I reached for him out of instinct, fingers finding his hair. Holding on. Wordlessly asking for more of that pleasure that he offered. Lucas obliged. He slid his tongue along my entrance. Slipped it inside me until I couldn't hold back my voice.

He broke through my hesitation and my shame and the parts of me that questioned this. He sealed his mouth over me. Long, sure strokes took me higher, built on the pleasure I'd already received and expanded it. It ran through my body like electricity, stunning me. It took my control away and shivered through every cell of my body until I was panting and spent. Pleasure broke over me like a wave as Lucas kept using his tongue.

I was shaking when he pulled away. Breathless. He crawled back up my body until his eyes were level with mine, and I gripped his arms. After that pleasure, it felt different between us. We were closer.

"How do you feel?"

My whole body flushed in the dark. "You want to talk about it?"

Lucas brushed his lips along my jaw. Down my neck and across my shoulder. "We don't have to. But I want to know what you like. What you don't like. What you're holding back."

"Why?" It came out as a strangled whisper. This already seemed . . . impossible. Beautiful. And I—

I didn't feel like I deserved it.

The guilt that clung to my insides shriveled under my attention. This wasn't something that I needed to feel guilty about. Being with Lucas was my choice. I wanted him. And he wanted me.

Taking a shaky breath, I reached out and looped my arms around his neck. "I liked that. A lot."

He made a low sound in his throat before his lips moved to my ear. "Good. Because now that I've tasted you, I'm going to want to do that more often."

My whole body shivered, nipples hardening, my thighs pressing together in response.

Lucas laughed softly. "Do you want to stop?"

"*No.*" The word flew from my lips.

He grinned. "Then I'll be right back."

I watched him as he got off the bed, shedding his pants and retrieving a condom from his bedside table. I couldn't stop staring at him. Lucas was big. Bigger than . . .

Bigger than anyone I'd been with. He saw the look on my face when he returned to the bed and smiled. "I don't think you know how beautiful you are."

I blushed, though hopefully he couldn't see it in the dim light. "That's not what I thought you were going to say."

He smirked, eyes dancing. "I know what you thought I was going to say, and we'll go slow."

Lucas took his time, stroking his hands up and down my body, warming my skin until I relaxed again. I lost my breath when he settled between my legs, pressed himself against me. This was real.

I lost myself in his kiss, distracted, overwhelmed, and ready. He pushed in and I gasped. Closed my eyes. He felt so good, my body gripping him like it would never let him go. Lucas paused, but I grasped his shoulders. There were scars under my fingers not so different than mine. "Don't stop," I breathed. "Don't stop."

He didn't. All the way in, inch by inch. Until he was seated so deeply within me that I'd never felt so full. Until I never wanted to feel anything less than this.

Lucas kissed me, long and slow and deep. This was real. We were both still, holding our breath. He was waiting until my body eased—got used to his sheer size. Tiny movements of his hips brushed me, gliding, shooting sparks under my skin and foreshadowing what was about to happen.

I'd never felt anything like this. This was more than pleasure; it was closeness. The way Lucas was aware of every movement—the way he was focused more on me than he was on himself.

I didn't dare think about the depth of the emotion in every movement of his lips. Of his fingers. Or the mirroring emotion that lurked under my skin not ready for words.

"You're all right?" He moved his hips harder, and I gasped.

"Yes. I—yes."

He started slow, rolling his hips as I adjusted to him. That elusive feeling curled up and through me, stretching inside me like it was waking up. All of this was familiar, and also brand new. Embers flickered under my skin with every smooth movement.

"Lucas," I breathed. He slowed to a stop, but I reached up and took his face in my hands. "I want all of you. Don't hold back."

For a breath, he studied my face, and then his mouth came down on mine. Hard. The careful control he'd shown cracked, and everything was unleashed. He matched every driving thrust with a brush of his lips. His tongue.

Each time he drove into me, that shining spark of light got a little brighter. Sharper. Pleasure built until I gasped for breath. We both were.

Lucas pulled my legs up, wrapping them around his hips so he could plunge deeper. Harder. He buried himself inside me again and again, fractured light shining behind my eyes.

I panted for breath, hanging on to that shining flame of pleasure, holding it back and making it last.

"Don't you dare hold back either," he said with a groan.

But I did. The building pleasure was a golden light painting my skin, and I wanted to bathe in it. Drown in it. I never wanted this moment to end.

I held back until the last possible moment, kissing Lucas as hard as I dared, wrapping myself around him until I wasn't sure where we began or ended. Harder. Faster. And when I couldn't hold back for one more second, pleasure shattered through me like thunder.

My voice was lost in his kiss, ripped out of me by sheer force. Nothing but silvery ecstasy traced down my limbs, a sharp edge plunging deep because he didn't stop. I was carried on the wave of bliss, wave after wave of light shining behind my eyes.

Lucas drove into me, rhythm going erratic as he plunged deep again. And again. And a third time, burying himself to the hilt and holding himself there, shuddering with his own pleasure.

We hung in the moment together. For the moment, there really was nothing else but him and me, together. I would always remember these seconds and how long they seemed to last.

Our breaths were ragged in the dark, shared between us as we came to stillness. Peace and exhaustion seeped through me, and I laughed.

Lucas smirked. "You know most men might be worried if a woman laughed after that."

I shook my head. "No, it's just that . . . I feel peaceful. Calm. And after *that*, it seemed funny."

He laughed too. A dark caress that whispered over my skin. "Don't go anywhere," he murmured, pulling away and stepping into the adjoining bathroom. In moments he was with me again, easing us both under the blankets and pulling me into his chest. I was wrapped up in his warmth.

My eyes closed, pleasant darkness sweeping in. I would be asleep soon, but I didn't want to be. If I slept, we would have to go back to the real world. It wouldn't just be the two of us in this room, and I wanted the refuge that we'd created here.

Lucas pressed a kiss to my hair, lifted it off my neck so he could kiss me there too. His hands, where they wrapped around me, stroked down my back. Where the worst of the scars were. I could feel the ridges under his fingers. I pressed my head closer to his chest, not wanting to think about it.

"You're okay," he breathed to me. "You're okay."

"I am, I just—" I sighed. "I don't want to always think about it."

He rolled onto his back and took me with him so I was draped over his chest. His heart beat steadily under my ear. "You won't always."

"How do you know?"

A slow stroke of his hand down the marred skin again. "Because it's the first time you've let anyone touch them. It will fade more when you're used to it."

"Maybe."

"I'm sure of it," he whispered. "And I'll gladly volunteer to be the person that helps you get used to that."

"You want to spend time touching my scars?"

He chuckled. "I want to spend time touching *you*. In any way and every way possible."

My cheeks heated.

Sleep was rising quickly, and I tried to hold on to the moment, burning the settled feeling—the peace—into my brain. "Lucas," I whispered.

"Yes?"

"Thank you."

I fell asleep with a smile on my face.

Chapter 20

Evelyn

The large windows in Lucas's room let the light in early. From the pale shade of the sky, I knew that the sun was barely peeking over the horizon. I could close my eyes and fade back to sleep, but I didn't want to. This feeling—I hadn't felt like this for longer than I could remember.

I felt peaceful. The same peace that had found me last night. Like I was in my own skin for the first time in years. Lucas was . . . absolutely amazing. There were no regrets or doubts lingering in my head. Just cloudy, dazed happiness.

Lucas's arm was slung over my waist, his full warmth pressed up behind me. The sleep had been as amazing as the sex. Like the way I'd slept with Aspen at my side, but more complete. How long had it been since I'd been fully rested?

I took a huge, full breath, turning to face him. My aim

was to watch him sleep the way I had that time he'd been on my couch, but closer. Except that like the night he'd slept over, Lucas's eyes had opened the moment I faced him.

"How do you do that?"

"What?"

I shook my head. "Manage to be awake the second I move."

He chuckled. "A lot of time spent in places where needing to be awake quickly was a necessity."

"Oh." Not exactly a fun answer.

Lucas leaned in. "Good morning."

"Morning," I managed before he kissed me. And this wasn't a hesitant, delicate kiss. This was a kiss of new intimacy. Deeper, harder. Just like what I could feel against my leg.

He shifted, rolling over so he could look down at me, only a little of his weight on me. I traced the lines of his face, down his nose and across the strong lines of his jaw, now covered in stubble. His lips.

Lucas's brown eyes were filled with warmth. The color of summer woods and chocolate syrup. Like roasting chestnuts and flickering fire. So many shades of color up close. I could stare into them forever and get lost.

His mouth tugged up into a smile. "How are you feeling?"

He wasn't asking how I'd slept, but about him. About us. "I feel good." I couldn't keep the mirroring smile off my face. "I'm nervous, of course, but it was good. Being with you. The sex was better than good."

Another short laugh. "Glad to hear it. No regrets?"

"None."

"Thank God," he said before he kissed me again, his hand slipping down my naked body under the blanket.

Now that I knew what he felt like—what he could make me feel—it was a purely chemical reaction. My back arched into his hand and a moan slipped from my throat. I knew right then that I would stay all day in this bed with him if he asked me.

But there were questions I had. Things I hadn't been ready to ask, but now . . . I could ask him anything. Or I hoped I could. I broke away from the kiss and looked up at him.

"What is it?"

"Can I ask you something?"

Lucas nodded. "Of course."

"When you were trying to convince me to stay, you told me that—" I swallowed. "That you knew what it was like to look over your shoulder. What does that mean?"

His eyes shuttered, and he closed his eyes. "My father was an asshole," he said quietly. "Fucking abusive prick. He beat my mother regularly. I only escaped the worst of it because I was a boy and my mother tried to shield me. But in her . . . I saw all the things that I saw in you that first day. The way your eyes looked. The fidgeting. All of it.

"When I got old enough to stand up to him, I took more of his anger, and he learned that he had to surprise me in order for it to work."

Oh. That's why he knew what it felt like. Why he saw far too much too soon. "Is that why you wanted to help me?"

"Partly."

"What's the other part?"

Lucas blinked again, eyes going distant. He wasn't fully here anymore, dragged into a memory that affected him more deeply than his childhood. I knew in my gut that this was the harder story to share. The words came slower, every one laced with long-buried emotion. His fingers

166

tightened on my hip, and he leaned down to press his fore-head to my shoulder—and to kiss the place where it met my neck.

"I lost someone. A teammate. We were pinned down, and he was wounded. He'd been shot in an ambush we'd walked right into. We should have known. I should have —" His words broke off. He finally pulled back enough for me to see, and his gaze was full of misery. "I carried him. We were so deep in shit where we shouldn't have been, but I carried him. They shot me too. Not enough to keep me from walking and fighting like hell to get us both out. But when we made it back . . ."

He trailed off, and I guessed the rest, though I waited for him to say it. Reaching up, I smoothed my hands over his shoulders, feeling the scars I'd felt last night.

Lucas looked at me and nodded. That's what these were from. That day, when he'd carried his friend.

"When we reached our base, he was dead. I was too late." He closed his eyes.

"You didn't kill him," I said softly.

"I know. I've . . . had a long time to go over everything. Process it. I know it wasn't my fault, but I know it will never feel that way. I was too late to save him. And—"

He kissed me hard, covering my body with his own. Our fingers tangled together, and I savored the feeling of his skin on mine. It was a luxury I'd never imagined having again. I couldn't identify the emotions on his face when he broke away. "I didn't want to be too late to save you."

A tiny gasp caught in my throat. My chest ached for him, for what he'd been through. I recognized the haunting in his eyes. It was the same haunted gaze that I saw in the mirror every day.

I slid my hand back down, laid it over his heart. "You aren't. You weren't. You did save me."

Lucas's eyes went dark. "Not yet."

"No," I said, holding on to him. He had to know. "You pulled me out when I was drowning when I didn't think I'd ever come back up." My voice dropped to a whisper. "When I wasn't sure that I wanted to."

His mouth on mine was the only answer he gave. It was the only one that I needed. There were no lies in what I'd said.

I lost myself in him for a while, and he in me. We were a tangle of limbs and hands, shuddering breaths and desperate moans as the sun brightened the sky.

Clever fingers moved lower, and lower still, stroking into me, moving until he found a spot that drew cries from my lips. And then he didn't hold back, using that spot to bring me to pleasure, watching my face every moment. Like he was studying me for every reaction, every shudder and writhing movement.

"I love watching you," he whispered.

I flushed what had to be a deep shade of red to bring that smile to his eyes. "Why?"

Instead of a verbal answer, he spoke with his hand once more. Pleasure spiraled straight out from it until I was writhing, shuddering on his fingers, breathing *yes* and *more*.

"Because I like making you feel good," he finally said. "And because watching you come is so fucking hot that I can't breathe."

The haze of the orgasm still clouded my mind, but I felt him, hard and pressed against my hip. But when I reached for him, he pulled slightly away. "You won't let me return the favor?" I asked.

"Not today."

"Why?" For a second, worry barged into my mind. Was there something wrong? Had I done something?

He stopped the thought in its tracks. "Nothing is

wrong. You have no fucking idea how much I'd like your hands on me."

"Then why?"

"Because." He smiled. "Not everything is an even exchange. It doesn't have to be. And you never, *ever* owe me for pleasure that I choose to give you."

I blushed again. That hadn't been my conscious thought, but now that he'd said it, that *had* been in my head. An apology was on my lips, but I pulled it back. He wouldn't want that. "Okay."

He settled beside me, gathering me close. It was still early, and it was nice to relax in his arms. But it was day now, and it couldn't just be the two of us anymore. Not with what was waiting for us outside these walls.

"What do we do now?"

"Everyone is reaching out for information. We have contacts, sources that civilians might not have access to. We're going to get eyes on Nathan, figure out where he is exactly, and move from there. It's a battle of information first."

"Anything I can do?"

He kissed my temple. "Is there anything that you haven't told me about Nathan, anything you think might be useful? Whether it relates directly to your relationship or not—it all could help."

"I don't know. Other than the fact that he's a genius. Not only that, but he's determined. When he wants something, he gets it. Either he buys what he wants, or he finds a way to make it happen. Please don't underestimate him."

"I won't." Lucas's voice was dark. "I'm as stubborn as he is, and I have far better motivation than he does."

"Oh?"

His whisper shivered down my spine. "Not fucking losing you."

I curled closer to his chest.

"I'm not going to let him near you, Ev. Security is going to be high. I will be with you as much as I can. You won't be alone until this is over."

I nodded. "Yeah, I know. Thank you."

Nerves still swam in my gut. It was hard to believe that after all the times Nathan had chased me that this time would be different, even with allies. But I had to try.

"Do you trust me?" Lucas asked.

"I do." The answer came immediately and without question. I did trust Lucas, and I knew that he would do whatever he had to do to keep me safe, even if that meant throwing his own body between Nathan and me.

"Good."

I sat up, blinking as light from the windows hit my eyes, and I realized that I still had no clothes. Lucas realized the same time I did. "I'll call Lena," he said, opening some drawers and pulling out fresh clothes for him and a new pair of too-big clothes for me. "We'll stay here until she can bring you some things."

"What about everyone else? Don't you have to go find out what's happening?"

Lucas came back to the bed. I was very aware that I was still naked, the sheets pooling around my hips. He was naked too, and in the morning light his body was a masterpiece. A living sculpture of muscle. Light and shadow painted him beautifully.

He leaned down and kissed me. "You are priority number one right now. Everyone on this ranch is focused on finding that asshole and making sure you never have to think his name again. If we need to talk to them, they can come to us."

After so many years trying to hide—never drawing attention to myself, never stepping out of the shadows—

being the center of focus was overwhelming. But even with the nerves swirling in my stomach, I felt calm. There wasn't irrational panic or dread or phantom iron fists crushing my lungs.

I nodded, embracing the steadiness that Lucas was giving me. Okay. I put on the temporary clothes, and together we went downstairs to take the lay of the land.

Chapter 21

Lucas

Three days, and things were fine.

And at the same time, they were very much not fine.

Each morning, a bouquet of black roses had appeared somewhere along the perimeter fence, and each morning, there was a brute force attack on our security that altered the security footage. It was skilled and fast, and so slick that the things Jude kept putting in place weren't enough to stop it.

Evelyn knew about the flowers. She didn't know about the attempt to take down the electric fence that Jude had been able to stop. Barely.

The three nights, she'd slept in my bed. After the first time, it was like there wasn't even a question. I had asked if she wanted her own space, and her answer had been to wrap her arms around me and tilt her mouth up to mine. And that was that.

The clothes that Lena and Grace brought for her were in my room along with the few things that had survived Nathan's destruction. Her toothbrush was on my sink, and her towel hung next to mine. I couldn't ignore the way she was already folded into my life like she belonged there, that sense of rightness in my bones whenever I walked up the stairs and saw her in my space. Our space.

I'd never realized how lonely the house felt until I was sharing it with someone.

There was no way I was about to lose that.

I scrubbed my hands over my face as I walked toward the main house. There wasn't any direct evidence that Nathan was here in person. We had people walking the perimeter, but we couldn't be everywhere at once. With the attacks on the cameras, we didn't have proof.

The florist in town—Maria, a sweet, charming woman who everyone loved—swore that she hadn't sold any black roses in months. She didn't keep them stocked right now and only ordered them later in the summer, closer to Halloween.

Every contact that we'd tried, every favor that we'd called in, had mysteriously come up with nothing. In front of Evelyn I was calm and hopeful. But inside I was getting more and more frustrated. No one in the world was that clean. Especially someone from a family like the Wests. It wasn't always true, but in my experience, the more money someone had at their disposal, the more secrets they had to bury.

Which only left the conclusion that Nathan was paying a lot of money to cover his tracks, or he was being protected by someone incredibly powerful. Maybe both.

I looked back toward the stable. This was the first time I'd been separated from Evelyn since that first night together, and already I felt an itch under my skin. She was with Harlan and Jude, working with Penny.

That horse fucking loved her already. He was the happiest he'd ever been when we got there today, and that was fantastic. With her help, I was hoping we could turn him into a therapy horse after all. But that also depended on Evelyn being safe enough to continue working with him.

Harlan and Jude knew what was at stake. They would keep her safe. I *knew* that with every bone in my body. It didn't stop my instincts from screaming at me to turn around and go back. To haul her into my arms, or just be in her proximity. To protect what was mine.

I stopped in my tracks. Evelyn wasn't mine. No matter how much it felt that way. I refused to think like that. I understood the impulse, but I was going to reject anything that made me like *him*. Starting with the knowledge that Evelyn was her own person, and the fact that she chose to be with me was a fucking gift. One she could walk away from any time she felt like it.

One deep breath. And then another. The urge to turn around receded, and I kept walking. It wasn't only protective instincts; it was my past. Old wounds rearing their head. If something happened to her and I wasn't there. If I was too late—

I cut the thought off.

No.

This wasn't the time for those thoughts. Dwelling on the possibility of something going wrong would only distract me if something *actually* happened. I'd made a call to Dr. Rayne with the intent of asking her to come over in case Ev decided she wanted to talk. But that call had turned into me checking in with the psychiatrist myself.

I wasn't doing as well as I wanted to be. I would deal

with it when this was through. Rayne would nail my ass to the wall if I didn't. Hell, any of the guys would. They'd been where I was, and they knew the signs. One way or another, I was going to have to face my demons again.

Daniel was waiting in the security office for me, and I'd hoped he'd have good news for me. But his face wasn't promising. "Nothing?"

He shook his head. "Nathan West is a ghost. Spook level. The only time I've ever seen this *lack* of information is when they're trying to make someone disappear completely."

"Fuck." I shook my head. "Do you have any idea who's protecting him?"

Daniel shrugged. "His father is a billionaire and West Technologies holds more government contracts than any other company out there. If I were a betting man, I'd say he has more than one person protecting him. There are likely multiple interested parties making sure that the West family appears squeaky clean, no matter what they've done."

"Is there any way that could be changed?"

"I wish the answer was yes, but I doubt it. You know I don't mean it this way, but when you're comparing hundreds of millions in military technology contracts to the life of one woman, you're not going to get very far."

The insinuation burned under my skin, but he was right. Especially if we couldn't identify the people protecting him and figure out a way to put pressure on them. I'd asked Daniel to look into a few things for me so that I could stay with Evelyn more. That was only one of them.

"Anything on the cops?"

He shrugged. "No. There's no record of any complaint. The hospital doesn't have any record of her admittance. Evelyn has just as few records as Nathan. All normal until four years ago. Then nothing. Like she vanished."

"She did."

"Yeah," he said with a nod.

I sat down in one of the chairs and leaned my elbows on my knees. "So what do we do? He's circling us. And neither we nor Evelyn can stay in limbo forever."

The guys were willing to do whatever it took, but that still meant pulling long hours and extra work. It was fine for now, but we were all human, and it wouldn't take long for us all to be exhausted. That was a worst-case scenario. Exhaustion led to mistakes, and that was something we couldn't afford.

"You're not going to like it."

"Probably not."

Daniel crossed his arms. "If we can't find him, we need to bring him to us."

"You're right," I said. "I don't like that."

My friend chuckled. "I've got the basic outline of something. Maybe it'll work, maybe it won't, but either way it might give us more information."

"Okay," I leaned back, "hit me with it."

"He destroyed her clothes—or whoever he has working for him destroyed them. Aside from one hell of a statement, that could be his attempt to do the same thing. Draw her out."

"Could be." I wasn't sure if that was Nathan's style, but given the erratic nature of what he'd done over time, I wouldn't put it past him.

"So," Daniel said, "a simple trap. A phone call that's lightly encrypted, so it's not obvious that it's a trap, but easy enough for whoever's doing their hacking to intercept and listen to."

We'd been sticking to in-person conversations as much as possible, and Jude had swept the entire ranch for bugs just in case.

"We'll make it seem like she's going shopping for a replacement wardrobe in Missoula. That she'll be accompanied, but that we're too nervous about whatever he's going to do to leave the ranch unattended. Hopefully it will create the appearance of vulnerability. With his level of obsession, it will be too good to resist."

I hated it, but it was a good plan. "And where will Evelyn actually be during this? She can't be anywhere near the trap, Daniel. It's too dangerous for her."

He was quiet, and I could practically hear his urge to ask me more, but he didn't. They all knew better. It would have to be Evelyn who shared any more intimate details than what she'd already surrendered. "You can take her to the high woods."

I hadn't actually thought about that. The high woods was a property in the mountains an hour to the north. We owned it outright and kept the perimeter as secure as we did at the ranch. We'd have to do a sweep before we went, but it would certainly be out of the way. We used it if we needed to get away and camp alone, or bone up on any of the older training that we used to do.

And of course, we'd kept it off any official documents. Because we were that paranoid. God, I was glad that we were. If Nathan knew about that property, then there was absolutely nothing he *didn't* know.

"And what's the idea in Missoula? See if he shows up?"

Daniel nodded. "Maybe we'll see if he's here in person or if he's using a proxy. At the very least, that will be more than we know now."

"How fast can we set it up?"

"Already working on it," he said with a grim smile. "I

sent Grant up to the high woods this morning. He's making sure everything is good. Jude has the encryption ready to go whenever. You have to ask Evelyn if she's okay playing bait, even though she'll be nowhere near it."

"Yeah," I said. "I think she'll be fine with it, but I'll make sure."

"As soon as you find out, let me know. The sooner we can do this, the better."

I stood up and walked out, relief entering my body knowing that I was going back to her. The idea that we were giving Nathan what he wanted—even though it was fake—made me ill. I could imagine the sick glee he'd feel thinking that he had a shot at taking her back, and I felt cold in spite of the summer heat.

Never. He would not take her. Not while I was still breathing.

Evelyn's laughter came from around the corner, and the smile that came couldn't be stopped. I wanted to hear that laughter every day. She deserved that.

Jude and Harlan were standing on opposite sides of the paddock. They were smiling, but I knew them well enough to know that they were on alert and aware of everything around them as well. Harlan met my eyes around the corner and nodded. In the center, Evelyn was leading Penny around in circles, and the horse was actually trying to catch her. He was a completely different creature in her presence.

I wished I'd been able to see her before all of this. She clearly had a love of animals and was a natural from whatever experience she'd had before her life had fallen apart. What would her life have been like if she'd never met Nathan? Where would she be now?

She turned and spotted me, eyes lighting up so brightly that it made my chest ache. I didn't deserve that kind of reaction, but no matter how long I knew her, I would not take it for granted nor forget that it was precious.

Evelyn led Penny over to the fence to meet me, and Penny saw me. He slowed and resisted, but he still came. His skittishness wouldn't disappear overnight. "Hello," I said in the voice I used with animals. It was for both of them.

"Hello," she said, climbing the first rung of the fence so she could lean over and kiss me. For a second, I froze. It was unexpected, and in front of Harlan and Jude. And in the next second I wrapped my hand behind her neck and pulled her closer.

I wasn't going to waste a second with her, and if everyone didn't already know, then I didn't care about the confirmation. Her cheeks were pink when she pulled away. "Too much?"

"Never."

She bit her lip, but she was smiling. "How did it go?"

"About as well as it could have, I suppose."

Some of the light in her eyes died, and it killed me. "What happened?"

I sighed. "How do you feel about getting off the ranch for a little while?"

Chapter 22

Evelyn

I took a deep breath as we pulled out of the gate of the ranch. Anxiety burned in my lungs. Not for me, but for the people who were springing this trap on my behalf. Everyone had told me about a hundred times that there wasn't any danger to them, but I wasn't fully convinced. I didn't think they were lying, but any situation involving Nathan in any way was more dangerous than they could anticipate.

Aspen's head was in my lap where he sat between Lucas and me. He hadn't left my side. Whenever he could, he was next to me or lying on me. This dog understood something wasn't right, and it made me feel better.

The only times Aspen hadn't been with me was when Lucas had stepped in. To sweep me upstairs into his bedroom. Or into the shower. When he was loving me. Like Aspen knew that I was safe with him.

Lucas reached across the cab and took my hand,

weaving our fingers together without taking his eyes off the road. "You okay?"

I blew out a breath. "Not really."

"It will be fine."

Pressing my lips together, I said nothing. I wasn't going to declare that things would be okay until I actually knew that they were. And we wouldn't know until tomorrow.

"Did you know that this whole place was a glacier?" he asked. "Huge. It's what made the mountains what they are now. However, long ago this would have been all underwater."

"Really?" It was interesting, and I looked out the window at the towering mountains on our right. But my mind strayed a few hours south to the small city where our friends were driving and setting up the bait.

Honestly, I wasn't sure that it was going to work. Nathan was smart enough to see a trap like that coming. But then again, he seemed to be getting more desperate, and they were right—if he was unhinged enough to want me by any means possible, this would be perfect.

"They'll be okay," Lucas murmured.

"I know . . . I just—yeah."

They'd talked me through the plan a couple of times before having me call Lena and make plans like we were actually going to Missoula. Then after, Jude had gone in person to tell her why, not wanting to risk a secondary call to explain the trap no matter how much he'd beefed up the encryption.

Everybody was doing all of this for me, and they didn't even know me. Why? We couldn't do this forever. Eventually we'd either have to find Nathan, or I would have to leave. That was the end of the story. Because Resting Warrior's family and friends couldn't become my bodyguards for the rest of my life.

Lucas's thumb brushed across the back of my hand. "What's going on in there?"

"Just thinking about how this can't last."

"What can't?"

I shrugged. "What you're all doing. Nathan can play cat and mouse with us as long as he wants, and all of you can't protect me forever."

Lucas's smile turned grim. "It won't come to that."

"How do you know?"

"Because you're not playing on his terms anymore. For years he would chase you, and you'd run. You were alone and there was nothing standing in his way. He was circling you like prey. And now you're not doing that. You have allies and barriers to stop him from getting to you. That's going to drive him crazy. From everything you've told me, he's a guy who wants things his way. The more he *doesn't* get them? The angrier he'll get. I know that doesn't sound like a good thing for us, but it is."

"Why?"

He squeezed my hand. "Because angry people make mistakes. Sometime soon, he's going to make one. So even if he realizes that the phone call was a setup, it worked. Because he'll realize that we're playing him. All we need for him to do is show his hand."

I chewed on my lip. But the anxiety I felt now was different from the outright terror that I usually felt around anything regarding Nathan. That was an improvement, at least.

Lucas took his eyes off the road for a second and looked at me. That look—I would never get tired of it. Like he saw me for who I was, wholly and completely. His eyes skimmed me before they looked back to the road, and his face was full of amusement.

"When I first saw you, I wondered if that was your natural color, but I didn't know that you're blonde."

I startled for a second, then pulled down the mirror on the sun shield. Sure enough, the barest hints of my roots were showing. I hadn't dyed my hair in a while. "Yeah, it seemed like a good idea when I was first running because I was naïve enough to think that making myself look different would keep him from finding me. But I kept doing it because I like it. It makes me feel like a different person than the one who fell for him. At least a little bit."

"It's not naïve. It was all you knew at the time."

My heart stilled in my chest for a moment. "Do you want me to change it back? Be more natural?"

I knew Lucas wasn't Nathan. He was the furthest thing from it. But I couldn't get the echoes of Nathan's words out of my head. *The more natural the better.*

Lucas frowned, but I knew it wasn't directed at me. That was the kind of expression he made when something occurred to him about my past. Slowly, he pulled over to the side of the road. We were on a highway, and we hadn't seen a car for miles. "I want to look at you when I say this," he said in explanation. "And I'd rather us not crash when we're doing this to save your life."

I smiled at that, but my heart was still pounding. "Okay?"

Putting the truck in park, he scooted closer to me—as close as Aspen would allow—and reached out. He took my face in his hands. "I've told you this before, but it bears repeating. Ev, I think you are beautiful. All of you, even the parts that might make you uncomfortable. And that has nothing to do with what color your hair is. You could dye your hair pumpkin orange, and you would still be beautiful."

My gaze slid away from him, this moment suddenly too

real and too vulnerable. I didn't want to cry, but tears pricked my eyes anyway.

"If I ever told you that you needed to dye your hair a certain color, or that you needed to be 'more natural,' the guys would take me out behind the lodge and kick my ass. And they would be right to do it. All I care about is that *you're* happy. If that means being a brunette for the rest of your life? I would never stop that. You want to dye your hair something different every week? You can do that too."

I took a shuddering breath. "Okay."

"And I'll tell you that you're beautiful as many times as you need to hear it." He leaned over Aspen's body to brush my lips with his. "Because I know what it's like not to believe things."

We pulled back onto the road, and my hand remained in his. "What didn't you believe?"

"That it wasn't my fault." He was speaking about the teammate he'd lost. "Some days I still don't believe it. So I know that it takes time not to fall into thought patterns that have been there for years. It's the way our minds work."

There wasn't any judgment in his voice, just fact. He'd been through his own trauma and lived. I was trying. We were quite a pair.

We spent the rest of the drive in comfortable silence as the mountains and trees whirred by. Before long, we were off the main roads, driving on a nearly hidden road. The only way that you'd know this was here was if you were already aware of it or if you were combing the mountains for something like it.

"This property is something we keep for training if we take an outside job," Lucas said, "or if one of us has a need to get away, not unlike what we're doing. Grant came up here yesterday to make sure that everything is secure. We keep the same kind of perimeter up here as we do at the ranch, and it's not on any records connected to Resting Warrior. We paid for it in cash."

I nodded. He hadn't told me where we were going before out of an abundance of caution, but I understood why he was telling me now. "Nathan won't be able to find it."

"If he does, then," Lucas shook his head, "I would be very surprised."

And Lucas wasn't a man who was surprised often.

We drove between two high walls of rock, so close it looked like the truck might not fit before we slithered through. And certainly, it was a one-way trip.

The gate that met us wasn't unlike the one at the ranch. High, tall, imposing, and obviously electrified. There wasn't enough room for us to get out to open the gate, but we didn't need to. Lucas pulled out his phone and opened an app I didn't recognize, and after he entered a long code, the gate rolled aside for us and shut as soon as we were past.

And beyond the gate . . . it was like we were in another world. Pine woods stretched out on either side in this little, hidden valley, and straight down the road in front of us was a lake. It was perfectly smooth, reflecting the mountains back at me. We were away from everyone and everything, and I loved it.

"This is beautiful."

"It is," he said.

We pulled up to the lake, the trees falling away from the rocky shore, and Lucas grinned. "I'm going to get our tent all set up. But first—" He cut the engine and jumped out of the cab, Aspen scrambling to follow. "I'm going for a swim."

I didn't have a chance to get out the door before he was stripping off his shirt and tossing it on the ground. His jeans hit the rocky shore and soon enough he was naked, splashing into the clear water of the lake. Ripples moved outward from him, marring the entire surface.

It was one hell of a view. Lucas was perfect. Sculpted muscle over more sculpted muscle painted with water and afternoon sunlight. Aspen ran along the shore, happy and splashing. The fact that he wasn't still sitting beside me—he knew that it was safe.

I made my way out of the truck and down to the shore. "How's the water?"

"Cold," he admitted with a grin. "But refreshing. Want to join me?"

"Umm . . ." I hesitated. Part of me wanted to be in that water with him and just be free. The other part of me was choking on the idea of my scars in daylight. I knew that Lucas didn't care about them. That he saw past them. But having him see them in intimate darkness or the shower was very different from under an open sky in the middle of the day.

Lucas raised an eyebrow. "Do I need to carry you in here?"

"I didn't bring a bathing suit," I said lamely. "I don't even have a bathing suit."

"Clearly," he smirked, gesturing around us, "that's not a problem."

"I—"

Lucas came out of the water to me, and I was spellbound. It was a bit like watching one of those perfume commercials that played in black and white, the perfect man walking out of the crashing sea while epic music played and close-ups cut in. There was nothing that cut away from Lucas, and my breath was suddenly short. Not because I was afraid, but because *he* took my breath away.

He stood before me, and Aspen wound around our feet, tail wagging crazily. "What's going on?"

After everything he knew and what I'd told him, I couldn't lie. And I also knew that he wouldn't judge or care about my scars. "It's different. Out here."

"What is?"

I wrapped my arms around myself, and his eyes fell on my long sleeves. Understanding infused his gaze. He stepped in close to me. "Do you like it here?"

The mountains towered next to us in perfect crispness, the shadows already lengthening as it grew later in the afternoon. The air was cool and sweet, and flowers dotted the ground under the shade of the pines. Across the lake were several giant boulders I could imagine lying on after a swim to soak up the sun.

It was beautiful. It was paradise.

"Yes," I said honestly.

"We're alone here like when we're in our bedroom. And I promise that when we come here in the future—and we will—it will always just be you and me. Nothing else is allowed here. No fear. Nothing from either of our pasts. Just us." His hands slid down my shoulders and over my arms.

"That doesn't make it go away."

He nodded. "It doesn't. But we can try for a bit, right?"

That look again. The one that told me that I was everything. For that look, I could try. "Okay."

Lucas smiled. "Okay."

He undressed me, tossing my clothes next to his on the shore, and when that was done, he swept me up into his arms and carried me into the water.

"*Oh my God*, that's cold," I said, clinging to him harder.

"I warned you."

"I wasn't imagining it quite like this."

Lucas's lips warmed my temple. "It's refreshing."

"Masochist," I whispered under my breath.

With a laugh, he dropped my legs into the water and I squealed, the sound echoing off the mountains. "Lucas!"

He wrapped his arms around me and turned me to face the mountains. His body molded to my back—the part of me that made me sick and anxious. Now it was pressed against him. He was the only one who knew, even though we were alone.

And nothing happened.

The mountains didn't crumble down, and I didn't fall apart. I took one breath, and then another, the tension easing out of me until I could lean my head back onto his chest and look at the sky.

Lucas kissed my shoulder. The simple gesture made my stomach drop. We were alone. I felt that, and I didn't doubt it. But all the same, I couldn't stop the thoughts. Not once when I had been with Nathan—before he'd shown me who he really was—not once would he have done something as simple as kiss my shoulder.

Looking back on the things that I had thought were sweet and signs of love . . . weren't. They were the bare bones of it interpreted by someone young and infatuated. I didn't blame the girl that I'd been. I couldn't take anything back. But now this feeling—I would never mistake it again.

I wasn't ready for the thoughts that followed. I pushed them back, instead turning to Lucas and exposing my scars to the air. I didn't feel cold anymore. "We get to come here again?"

"Of course," he said. "I'm going to make sure you're safe. And after we do, we can come here as much as you like."

I smiled. "I like that idea."

He carried me out of the water and followed up on his

promise to pitch our tent. His jeans were slung low on his hips, and he didn't bother to put his shirt back on. Sitting on the shore watching him, I wasn't complaining at all. It was a luxury to have the space to breathe and watch him do this without fear.

Our tent. Just one for the two of us. I was equally aware that he had said *our bedroom*. He considered us a unit. Together. I could never have imagined how much I'd needed that.

"It's smaller than I imagined," I said, looking at the tent.

Lucas grinned over his shoulder. "All part of the plan."

"What plan?"

"The one where we have to use body heat to keep warm."

I laughed, and Aspen came running back from where he was digging in the shallows, panting, tail wagging, equally happy. This was what I wanted from my life—effortless happiness.

Lucas spent the rest of the day distracting me, and I let him. He cooked us dinner over the fire while I played with Aspen, throwing a stick into the water and down the shore for him to run and fetch until he fell asleep, exhausted.

"Oh to be a dog," I said, looking at him passed out near us as we finished dinner.

Lucas chuckled. "It does seem like a pretty good life."

The fire was dying low now, and I licked the remnants of marshmallow from my fingers. Lucas had thought of everything—including bringing supplies for s'mores. "I honestly don't think I've had a s'more since I was in the Girl Scouts."

"That's a tragedy."

"I imagine they're probably a big thing here in Montana."

Lucas shrugged. "No more than anywhere else I don't think, but since we go camping more often and have more campfires, we have more opportunities."

"That's fair."

He set aside the stick he'd been using to roast his marshmallows, and the way his gaze shifted, my stomach dropped. "Come here."

The words were gentle, less of a command than a request, and I went. He was sitting on a blanket, and I'd barely reached him when he caught me around the waist and spread us both out on it. "Remember when I said that the mountains were the best place for the stars?"

I nodded.

"We're still not as high as we could be, but this is a pretty good place."

With the fire so low, it was easy to see what he meant. The sky was filled with more stars than I'd ever imagined existed. It was hard to think that anyone could come here and see this and ever be content going back to a world without stars.

"What are you thinking?" Lucas leaned toward me, his lips teasing my neck.

I tilted my head so he had more skin to play with and smiled. "I'm thinking that it's impossible to see something this beautiful and live anywhere else after."

Lucas raised his head and looked at me. The low, flickering firelight showed me the intensity and hope in his gaze. He wanted this to be my place. I knew that.

He undressed me, but this time it wasn't like before when he'd wanted to get me into the water. This time it was with reverence, his attention focused on every piece of me he revealed.

Lucas overwhelmed me with attention, and by the time I was naked underneath him, I was already writhing with need for him. He'd thought about this too, and he had condoms. I smirked at the box that spilled out of his bag. "A whole box? That's a little ambitious."

"When it comes to you, it's not." He didn't look like he was remotely kidding.

I reached between us, stroking along his length. In the nights we'd shared, I'd explored him more, but I still wasn't over the wonder of his body. It never failed to amaze me. Every time I laid eyes on him, I thought him handsome, and in the firelight was no exception.

Sharp, dark shadows played across his features, drawing them out and making the pure emotion in his gaze stand out. I started to wiggle down beneath him, so I could taste him, and he stopped me.

"I need to see you."

"You'll be able to see me perfectly fine," I said with a grin.

A faint reflection of my own smile. "You know what I mean."

Lucas kissed me slowly, easing my legs apart and settling between them. There wasn't any more teasing or denying, it was just . . . us. I gasped when he pushed into me.

Because of the past few days, I wasn't a stranger to sex anymore. But this felt different. Lucas pressed deep, and deeper, until we were one and the same. His face was in silhouette above me against the canvas of infinite stars, and everything seemed like *more*.

His lips met mine, and we were suspended in a moment that lasted forever. And I knew, though I wasn't ready for it, that the moment was changing us. Like the first time I'd let him hold me, it was a moment we could not come back from.

But then again, knowing Lucas, there would never be any going back.

When we moved, we moved together.

Pleasure unfurled inside me like a wave. Like a rising tide. It moved through us together, rising and cresting until the wave broke over us together, the only witnesses the stars and mountains.

Lucas pressed his forehead to mine, our breaths mingling. There weren't any words to say, and anything would break the spell we'd woven. Instead, Lucas pulled back, lifted me from the blanket, and carried me into the tent he'd pitched—into warmth and softness and more delicious pleasure.

In this moment, it was easy not to think about anything but him and me, and the idea that we might always have something like this.

Chapter 23

Lucas

A s we rode over ranchland, nothing was out of place, and the prickle of tension under my skin eased. There was nothing, but it felt like there was always something lately.

Nathan hadn't taken the bait.

Not only that, but there weren't any signs of him anywhere. They'd set the trap perfectly in Missoula, but nothing suspicious had happened, or any response at all. Perhaps Nathan hadn't been able to get there in time. Perhaps he wasn't in the state and had hired someone to do his dirty work.

The anonymous attacks on our security system continued, but the flower deliveries had ceased. I'd tried to loosen things enough to make Evelyn feel like she was safe and that she wasn't a prisoner while not dropping my guard. That was the only thing I was sure of: Nathan had not given up.

He'd retreated.

The absence of his obvious presence was possibly more dangerous.

It had been ten days of nothing, and the more time passed, the more tense I became, though I tried not to show it. I'd accompanied Evelyn to Deja Brew a couple days. She'd wanted to see Lena and work, and she'd understood why I wasn't willing to let her go alone.

Other than the impending threat, these past ten days had been . . . amazing. For obvious reasons, Ev hadn't moved out of my house. Not only was there the danger to consider, but I didn't want her to leave.

I was falling for her. Hard.

Every moment with Evelyn was a revelation. I loved learning who she was and what made her feel good. I loved watching her blossom into herself more—someone who was less anxious and full of fear. I loved, too, seeing the moments when she was afraid so that I could be there for her. She didn't have to face anything alone.

Something had changed between us at the high woods. We didn't talk about it, but it sang between us with silent certainty. There was a steadiness to this force pulling us together now, and I would thank the universe forever that I hadn't ignored my instincts.

Evelyn had started helping us regularly with the animals, too, and was a natural. A couple of days ago, she'd finally opened that door, telling me that she'd intended to go into a field with animals—training or veterinary science, she hadn't decided—before she'd met Nathan. After, he'd convinced her that she didn't need to have a career because he had all the money in the world, and he would take care of her.

Young and in love, she'd believed him.

If she wanted to do that with her life, I wouldn't stop her. I would help her any way that I could.

"Hey," Evelyn called. She brought Dove, one of the mares that we kept on the ranch, to a stop and dismounted. Not a therapy animal, just a sweet horse. I was riding Storm, a stallion we kept.

This was a part of the ranch that we rarely visited day to day. The large, open part that we hadn't done anything with. Yet. It was a beautiful green space with scattered trees and a few lake-fed streams. Part of me wanted us to keep it like this, pristine and untouched.

Dove drank from one of the streams, and Evelyn stood petting her neck.

"Hey," I called back. We hadn't spoken in a while, just enjoying the day.

"You okay?" she asked as I swung off Storm's back and walked over to her.

I nodded. "Of course." When she looked at me, I sighed. "No. I'm always on edge, waiting for the next thing to happen."

"Me too," she admitted. "But at the very least, I don't think there's much chance of Nathan sneaking up on us out here."

Evelyn was right about that. Out here we could see all around us, and there wasn't enough cover for anyone to surprise us. We'd kept it that way intentionally. The woods had been much thicker when we'd bought the property. "That's true."

She looked at me with a small gleam in her eye. "It's beautiful out here too. Like the lake."

I raised an eyebrow, and I couldn't stop the smile that came to me. It would always be one of my favorite memories, and I couldn't wait to take Evelyn back there. But we could recreate some of that magic here, if we wanted. "The lake, huh?"

Her cheeks tinged pink, and she looked at the ground. I took Dove's reins along with Storm's and looped them over a nearby branch before I pulled her away. The tree that I picked stood alone. I wasn't going to put her in danger.

But as I backed her up against the tree, I savored the fact that I could have these moments with her. The longer I spent with Evelyn, the more she meant to me. She was already smiling when I leaned down to kiss her.

That was one of my favorite parts of this, seeing her open up and learn that love and pleasure didn't have to hurt.

Her lips parted under mine, and I took the time to run my hands along her ribs. She was beautiful and strong, and I couldn't get enough of her. Every moment we were alone, I thought about doing this, and though it wasn't the primary reason I didn't want her to move out of my house, I would miss this if she left. And I couldn't wait for the day when we could do this freely, with nothing hanging over our heads.

But we were completely alone. So I let my hands creep up under her shirt, and I pressed myself against her so that she could feel how hard I was. Evelyn gasped. "Here?"

"Everywhere," I whispered against her lips. "There's nowhere that I wouldn't take you."

Her body arched into me in response, but her eyes flicked around us. Nervous. Though we were safe, there wasn't an absolute guarantee that we were alone like there had been at the lake.

"Too open?"

She bit her lip. "Is that okay?"

"Of course it is," I said, kissing her forehead. "I'll have

to remember to finish this the next time we go back to the lake. There are plenty of trees out there that will do just as well. And in the meantime, our bed might be lonely."

Her blush deepened as I pulled her back to the horses. I loved that reaction as long as she wasn't truly embarrassed. Right now, she wasn't.

We rode back to the stables. Tonight was a community dinner that we both planned to help with, and we needed to get stuff from the house first. Though we had enough time to make our bed very *not* lonely. But when we approached the stable, Daniel, Harlan, and Jude were all waiting for us. That wasn't good.

My stomach dropped, and my senses went wide, searching for anything that I'd missed. The only reason I didn't speed up to meet them was that I was keeping pace with Ev, and I wasn't about to leave her alone.

Their faces were grim. They weren't meeting us out here to invite us to a party. I rode up and dismounted. "What happened?"

Harlan nodded to Evelyn. "Get her off the horse first."

The words were quiet and firm. My eyebrows rose, but I nodded, helping her down off Dove as she slowed to a stop. I felt her hesitation. She knew as well as I did that this kind of welcoming party wasn't good.

Jude took the horses from us, his eyes roving over the both of us like he was making sure we were whole before disappearing into the stables.

"What's going on?"

Daniel handed me two white envelopes. These weren't normal letters, they were thick stationery, like formal invitations for a wedding. My name was printed in calligraphy on one, and Evelyn's was printed on the other. No addresses. "They were delivered today. By hand, as far as I can tell."

"You know what's in them?"

Harlan nodded. "Everyone got them. The seven of us, Evelyn, Lena, Grace."

Evelyn appeared at my side. "What is it?"

"I don't know," I admitted. She saw the envelope with her name and took it from me. "Ev—"

But she was already tearing it open. I rushed to get mine open too. My instinct was right. It was like a wedding invitation, but it wasn't for a wedding.

White cardstock and curling black script matched the envelope.

I*n memoriam*
   You're invited to the celebration of life and interment of Evelyn Jessica Taylor.

T he date was one week from today with a time and address.

My head whipped to Evelyn, and she was white as the card she was holding, back in the shell she'd been in when she'd arrived. This was an invitation to a funeral *for her*. A death threat.

Not a threat. A promise.

"What's at this address?" I asked.

Harlan shrugged. "Nothing. Or at least there's not supposed to be anything there. It's the side of an old road outside of town. We were waiting for you before checking it out."

"I'm going with you," I said before approaching Evelyn. She didn't move as I held her. Stiff. Lifeless. She was trembling. "This will not happen," I told her softly.

"He cannot have you. He does not own you. I will not let him take your life, do you understand?"

She didn't move or speak, just leaned a little closer. The only acknowledgment that she'd heard me.

"I think you should stay here," I said then. "You won't be alone. But we don't know what might be there."

"No."

"Evelyn."

Her face snapped up to mine. "No. Nathan is coming after *me*. I'm going to see what the hell this is."

Every instinct in me screamed to hide her away. To keep her safe. To not expose her to the danger. But she was right—this was her life, and she deserved to know. "Okay. Will you let us sweep it first to make sure there's nothing waiting for you?"

She nodded once.

My breath eased a tiny bit at that. "All right," I said then, looking at the others. "Let's go."

We left Grant and Noah at the ranch to watch things, and the rest of us piled into cars. The address wasn't far, less than twenty minutes from the ranch, but away from town. Isolated. I couldn't think of a time I'd been out on these particular roads in the past couple of years.

I didn't take my hands off Evelyn the entire time, and she didn't bother to pull away. She was practically in my lap, and I couldn't stop moving my hands over her to convince both her and myself that she was real and here and safe. Dangerous emotions—panic, anger, and determination—compressed into something sharp: cold as ice and hard as steel.

It was developing in my friends as well. This kind of onslaught was on a whole different level, and though they didn't know Evelyn as well as I did, they knew she didn't deserve this. No one did. And this made it more than personal.

We pulled up to the address, and Harlan was correct. It was no more than a dirt drive and some trees on the side of the road. Liam stayed with Evelyn and me while the others went ahead. It was only minutes before they returned, but as soon as I saw their faces and their body language, I knew it wasn't good.

Harlan just looked at me as he opened the door for us, eyes hard, warning me.

I didn't let go of Evelyn's hand as we walked past the cluster of pine trees that blocked whatever they'd found.

It was a graveyard, a wrought-iron fence surrounding a plot with neat rows of identical gravestones. I'd never known there was a graveyard here, and I suppose this was an apt place to send someone for a fake funeral.

We walked closer to the stones, and the markers weren't normal ones. They weren't decorative at all, and they were all identical in style. Names, with a specific birth date and death date. The first couple that we passed I noticed weren't far apart. Like whoever was buried there was a child.

It took me a second to realize that Evelyn was no longer moving. She stood stock still in front of that first marker, her hand nearly crushing mine. Her face was so pale and stricken I worried that she was about to faint, and moved closer. "Evelyn?"

"No." The word was so small and anguished, I didn't understand.

Then she was moving too quickly. To the next stone and the next, her breathing growing too fast, eyes wild with panic. What was I missing here? What did she see that I didn't?

I looked around the small yard as she tore away from

me, counting the stones. Three neat rows of five, and two in the middle were empty. Thirteen graves. Thirteen. The same number of false identities that Evelyn had been forced to make.

Fuck.

I looked at the first stone again. Four years ago was the birth, and not long after, the death. It was an effort not to run over to the last one in the sequence, but I knew what I would see. The death date was barely a month ago. Evelyn's previous identity—the one she had burned in order to come here.

This wasn't a graveyard that Nathan had found and repurposed. This was a graveyard that he had *created*. The entire graveyard was made for her. Because of her. This was what he'd been doing in this period of silence.

Joining Evelyn in the center of the graveyard, I took her into my arms. I needed to get her out of here. Right now. "Let's go. You don't need to see this. Or be here."

"Look," she said quietly.

We were standing in front of the two empty graves, already dug. The first stone was a single word. *Thief.*

And the second stone said *Evelyn Taylor*. With her real birthday, and a blank death date. She was perfectly still in my arms and didn't move when I tried to pull her away. Nor did she react when I lifted her into my arms and carried her back to the cars.

The guys were ready and waiting, and the door had barely closed behind us before I barked at them to go. I would fill them in on the true meaning of those graves soon, but an open grave with her name on it was enough for them to understand the seriousness of the situation. And I had no doubt that they'd made the other important connection—the open grave marked *Thief?* That was for me.

Nathan thought that Evelyn was his property. He'd told her as much. By touching her and being with her, I'd stolen her. I didn't care. He could come for me all he liked. I wasn't going to let him touch her.

They drove us back to my house, and Jude whispered that he was going to secure the ranch. Full lockdown again. I nodded. Evelyn came first. Then a new plan. My brothers-in-arms could handle the defenses while I made sure that the most important person in my life didn't fall apart.

She didn't move until we got into the house. And it was a relief to see her come back. Evelyn had retreated so deep inside herself that I hadn't been sure that she *would* come back. But her eyes were filled with black misery when she looked at me. "I have to run, Lucas."

I shook my head. "You don't."

Suddenly her eyes were filled with tears. "I have to leave. He's going to kill both of us if I stay. Maybe more than us. He's not going to stop, and I can't let you die—I *can't.* I have to go."

She'd moved into the center of the room and in three steps she was back in my arms. I made her look at me, guiding her gaze to mine. Fury vibrated under my skin at this man who'd taken everything from her and was still taking more. "I am not running," I said softly. I let her see every ounce of determination that was in me. "I am not afraid of him."

"I am," she said, tears spilling over. "I don't want to be, but I am, Lucas. I don't want to die. I don't want you or anyone else here to die because of me."

"You're not going to die." In my voice, I could hear the rawness of those emotions that were still hardening. "You are *not* going to die."

"Lucas—"

I pulled her close and wrapped her up in my arms. "He

can't have you. You are not his." Those words were ones I'd said before. I made them a vow this time. "We are going to end this. And you are going to have a life that is more than fear. I promised you that, and it's still true."

Tears still ran down her cheeks, and I brushed them away. There was so much pain and fear there, and I couldn't take it away. If I could carry it all for her, I would. "Do you believe me?"

A small, broken sound. "I believe that you'll try."

"That's all I can ask." If our positions were reversed, I wouldn't have much faith either.

Like the first time that she'd been in this house, I lifted her into my arms and carried her upstairs. This was our home now, for as long as she wanted to share it with me. She didn't resist, her strength gone. I stopped to remove our shoes before cradling her in our bed and holding her.

We'd left Aspen here while we were riding, and he was already on the end of the bed. I would thank God for the rest of my life for that dog's intuitive nature. As soon as Evelyn hit the covers, he curled next to her on her other side. We surrounded her, and soon enough her breath smoothed out into long, even breaths, safe in the protection of sleep.

I swallowed down my own emotions, shuddering with my own fear. I hadn't lied to her—I wasn't afraid of Nathan. If and when the time came to face him, I could handle him. I feared losing her, and more, I feared not being there when she needed me the most. History repeating itself. Being too late.

Right now she was safe, and in my arms. For the moment, that was all I had, and I resolved not to waste a moment.

Chapter 24

Lucas

Evelyn rested in my arms, utterly asleep. I didn't think that she'd slept so soundly since she'd started staying with me. Her mind was protecting itself from this new reality: Nathan was still here and close enough to reach us. He was absolutely determined to kill her.

And me, it seemed.

We hadn't undressed to get into bed. Comforting her, making sure she felt safe had been more important. So my phone was still in my pocket when it vibrated against my hip.

A text from Harlan.

We need you here. Grant and Noah are on their way to guard the house.

. . .

Everything in me bristled. I didn't want to leave her alone, especially when she was sleeping. But they were right. We had to move. Now.

Gently, I pulled away from her, making sure that Aspen was still curled up close. I left a quick note explaining that I was at the lodge, and that both Grant and Liam were outside the door if she needed them. And finally, I couldn't resist leaning down to press my lips against her temple.

Evelyn didn't stir. Good. Hopefully, she wouldn't know that I'd been gone by the time I got back.

Noah stood on the porch when I came out. I locked the door behind me. "You all right?"

He was a good guy and had been through more trauma than most people would ever know. I could trust him with my life, and Evelyn's life. He would rather die than let anyone through. More importantly, I knew that if he was asking me, that he really wanted to know.

"I'm not," I said.

He nodded. "Get over there, then."

"Is me being over there going to make me feel better."

"Probably not." His eyes flashed. "But you'll feel more stable if you're doing something."

That was the truth. Being helpless was the worst feeling. Especially when the danger was so real and so close. I waved to Noah as I jogged down the steps. It wasn't that far to the lodge, but I jumped into my truck anyway.

Everyone was clustered around the monitors looking at security footage when I walked in. Ours, and it looked like Jude had the town's cameras patched into our system now. "I'm here."

"Good," Harlan said without turning around. "Police chief told us that he's seen someone matching Nathan's description around town, but we haven't seen him on any cameras anywhere. Also got reports of a cabin about forty miles out that's abandoned, but people have seen lights."

"He's not anywhere?" I looked at the feeds, and Jude was looking too. Arms crossed and frowning.

"No," he said. "I've got facial recognition running, so if he does hit a camera, we'll know it."

"If they don't alter the footage first," Daniel muttered.

Jude swore under his breath. He wasn't happy that they were able to do that, or about his inability to find the digital loophole that allowed them access to the cameras when they were blocked from everyone else.

"He's slippery," Jude finally said. "There aren't enough cameras in town to actually cover everything. He knows where they are and is avoiding them, if he's here."

"If he's here," I said, my frustration like sandpaper under my skin.

Liam paced along the back wall. "Everything he's done. He wants us to know that he's here, but he hasn't shown himself. It's like he wants to be a very present ghost. Why?"

I turned away from the monitors and leaned my hands on the table. Liam was right. What was going on here? I was the only one in this room who knew everything, so it was me who had to put the clues together.

Nathan was possessive. He considered Ev his because they'd been engaged. Hell, he'd used her engagement ring to scar her. Then he'd made a promise about where he'd bury her. I wasn't sure I was right, but it was worth a shot. "He's really caught up in the idea of people not breaking their word. He still thinks of Evelyn as his fiancée. Nathan made promises to her about what he'd do to her if she crossed him. All this time, when she's been alone, maybe he's been giving her chances, or what he thinks are chances, to come back to him so he didn't have to follow through. But now she's here, and she's . . . with me." I swallowed. "The final betrayal. Her actually being with someone else. It's what started this in the first place, and so he's finished giving her chances. Hence the deadline."

"Could be," Liam said. "This guy is a piece of work."

"Tell me about it." I almost choked on the words. They didn't know the extent of Evelyn's scars or the fears that she carried. She thought she was going to die, or cause someone else's death. I knew that weight, and it was a horrible way to live.

"Well," Jude said, "one of the reasons we pulled you away from Evelyn was that we've had a breakthrough."

I turned to him. "Why wasn't that the first thing you told me?"

He stared at me. Because when it came to Evelyn, they already knew I tended to go in guns blazing, and they needed me in a calmer, more rational, more clinical state of mind. Which I now was. "What is it?"

"One of my contacts. More like a last resort. He's deep enough that I can't say shit about him. But after way too much digging—West is definitely being protected—he found this." He handed me a sticky note with a phone number on it. "It's older, so we don't know if it's still his phone. But if it is, we can track it."

Fuck. Relief and anger flowed through me all at once. Like breaking through the water's surface and getting that first sweet hit of oxygen. "We gonna call it?"

Jude nodded and tossed me a phone that was connected to the security setup. "All ready to track it. If it's him. He's going to have encryption, so you need to give me time."

I almost laughed. The old "keep them talking" thing that happened on movies and TV wasn't the way you tracked phones in the digital world. But he was being protected, which meant we couldn't just bounce his signal off the nearest satellite. Jude was going to have to hack it, or try. "Got it."

For a moment, I centered myself. If this was him, I had to keep myself steady. I couldn't lose my temper. I couldn't show him any emotion. He couldn't know that he was under my skin. I couldn't give him any kind of advantage over me.

I dialed the number and switched the call to speaker before setting the phone on the table. It didn't ring a full cycle before it clicked on. "Nathan West."

His voice sounded much like I'd imagined it would. Like someone who could be charming, charismatic, and make you think the world of him. He sounded like a person who'd never been told no. I glanced over at Jude, who was typing quickly.

"Hello?" Nathan said. "Who is this?"

"The thief." The atmosphere went taut. The call didn't end though. I had to keep him here. "I'm calling to ask you what you want."

"You know what I want." The words were soft and smooth. Not incriminating, a simple confirmation.

We were talking to him. It didn't seem real, after him being a ghost for so long. I took a deep breath and looked around at the others. They nodded. I took another breath and focused on the phone and on keeping my voice level.

"Whatever you have planned, Nathan, it's not going to happen."

Silence.

"You need to get out of here," I said evenly. "Leave Garnet Bend while you still can."

Another silence.

"I'm suggesting that for your own good, because if you touch Evelyn—if you touch any one of us—all bets are off.

Nothing will stop us from finding you, and we are not people who go back on our word."

I used that phrasing intentionally. If that was what was really important to him, then I was speaking his language.

For long moments, there was nothing but the soft sound of Jude's typing. Then Nathan spoke. And every word was dripping with delight. I could hear him smiling. "See you at the funeral."

The line went dead, and I let out a curse. "Did you get it?"

"Not quite. General area only."

I snatched the phone off the table and hit redial. Nothing. Not even a ring. The number had been disconnected. "Fuck."

"He's here," Jude said. "Couldn't pinpoint it, but the signal was close enough. He's local."

"Is there anything that will help us find him? If he's here, I want to go find him and nail his ass to the wall. We've sat here and waited long enough."

A dangerous quiet blanketed the room. "You're not going anywhere," Daniel finally said. "Not when he's gunning for you as hard as Evelyn."

I glared at my friend, but he stared me down. There wasn't going to be any changing his mind, and I didn't have to ask the others to know they agreed.

"Jude, Liam, go check out the cabin that Charlie told us about," Daniel said. "Make sure you're not seen if he's there. If the signal is close, it may not be a coincidence."

The police chief was doing us a solid, and I needed to thank him. But I wanted to go. I *needed* to see if he was there. "I'm going too."

"No." Harlan's voice brooked no argument. "Sit down."

Anger spiked. The seven of us were equals. We'd made

that agreement when we started this place. Each one of us had our roles and specialties, but no one had more power than another, and when one of us was out of line, we were allowed to call them out.

Jude and Liam left, and I was still standing. My own stubbornness wasn't going to allow me to sit right now. I wasn't going to do what I was told. "If this is going to be another conversation asking me how deep in I am, you can save it."

"It's not," Daniel said. "But we need to know if you can handle this."

"What is that supposed to mean?"

Harlan's face was hard. I'd seen that face before. It was unyielding. I was going to hear what he had to say whether I liked it or not. "We mean we want to know how much of this is because you're terrified you'll fail to save another person and how much is because you're in love with Evelyn."

The breath went out of my lungs.

In love with her.

Was I in love with her?

I'd already admitted to myself that I was falling, but it honestly hadn't occurred to me that I was already there. But I was. Holy fuck, I was so in love with Evelyn. Hearing the words out loud made it click like a key in a lock. But I wasn't ready to say it. Because the other part of that question was real too. I was terrified. No matter how much I'd worked through my shit, I wasn't sure that something like this would ever lose its power. And if I said out loud that I was in love with her, it felt too much like tempting fate.

A long time ago, I'd sworn that I would never fail someone like that again.

I scrubbed my hands over my face. "Both," I said, voice raw. "It's both."

My ass hit the seat, all my arrogance and anger gone in a breath.

Daniel nodded. "Even if you weren't ass over head in love with her, we would help her. You know that. No one deserves to live like that. But you know that your emotions and your biases are dangerous. So if we're going to get ahead of him, you're going to need our help."

They were right.

"No more letting him call the shots, right?" Harlan was wearing a grim smile.

"Right."

Daniel stood and stretched. "Then let's get the fucker."

Chapter 25

Evelyn

My fingers wouldn't stop fidgeting. It felt dangerous to be here. And indulgent. I was sitting in Dr. Rayne's office in Garnet Bend, and I'd been here for the better part of an hour. Lucas had told me that I could trust her, that she was one of the people who had helped him through his own PTSD.

That alone made me want to give her a chance. And since we weren't running, and we were taking the stance of not being afraid, I wanted to do this. It had been far too long. And for the second time ever, I told someone everything. From the beginning through to the end. I was actually shocked at the way everything poured out of me.

"I know it's a lot."

Rayne smiled gently. "It's your story. It's intense, and it feels more so because you've kept it hidden for so long. Eventually, it won't be so heavy for you."

"I hope so," I said, my fingers fidgeting again.

She noticed. There wasn't much she *didn't* notice. "Maybe at our next appointment we could meet outside? Or at the ranch with Penny, if you like. Often times meeting outside of an office can help people with PTSD. It might make you feel less trapped."

I swallowed. I did feel trapped, but it wasn't really the office that was doing that. It was Nathan. He was the reason I was still cooped up and the reason that we couldn't meet outdoors. "Until the . . . situation is resolved, I don't know that meeting outside would be safe."

"That's a fair assessment," Rayne said with a sad smile.

Lucas was keeping watch outside of the office. It felt strange to have a bodyguard—someone with me wherever I went. But at the same time, it was comforting. For the first time, I wasn't doing this alone. I was still afraid, but I could breathe, and that was better than nothing.

But I could see how tight Lucas was strung. The up and down, safety and not. Adrenaline and then tenuous peace over and over. It was wearing on him. The tiny whisper that I should leave was still in my mind.

"So that was the past," Rayne said. "Let's wrap up by talking about what's happening right now."

"There's a lot happening right now."

Rayne tilted her head and studied me. "What are you afraid of, sitting here in this moment?"

"Nathan." The answer was immediate.

"More specifically?"

My hands flared outward and then curled into fists. "Him killing me. Or kidnapping me and then killing me. Or worse, him taking me back and forcing me to live with him forever. I'm afraid he'll kill Lucas too."

"Why is that?"

The words bubbled up against my lips, and I paused.

Rayne knew Lucas really well. Was it okay to talk about him like this? Here?

"I won't share anything you say with Lucas, Evelyn. Just like I wouldn't share anything that he's said with you."

I took a shaky breath. "I'm afraid of Nathan killing him because it would be my fault. If I hadn't come here, if I hadn't . . . stayed, Nathan wouldn't know that Lucas existed." More words came crashing out, things that must have been lurking underneath. Things that I'd been pushing down. "I'm also worried that my feelings for Lucas are so strong only because he's the first man that I've let in. After . . . everything."

"But you do have feelings?"

There was no way to deny that. "I haven't felt anything like this since Nathan. And that's terrifying. I know Lucas isn't like him. I *know* that. But still."

"It's easy to worry that history will repeat itself," she said. "But you also deserve to be happy. This isn't bound by confidentiality, so I can tell you that I've never seen Lucas look at someone the way he looks at you."

That sent a little breath into my lungs.

"And furthermore, you are your own person. You know who you are and what you need. Trust that you're doing what's best for you. You have a lot of people around you now, myself included, that would tell you if things were headed in that direction. Right now they are not."

I took a long, slow breath and listened to my heartbeat slow to a more normal rhythm.

"You covered a lot today," she said gently. "And it's going to feel that way. You might be a little raw for the next few days. That's okay. It's expected when you bring stuff like this to the surface. This is a process."

I did feel lighter, and when we set our next appointment, something like hope lit up my chest. This felt like the first step toward letting everything go. I could never forget it. Not completely. My scars would never let me do that. But maybe I could let it fade into the past.

As soon as we caught Nathan.

We were closer. Yesterday there had been progress while I'd slept—though Lucas had been wrapped around me again by the time I had woken. Some location where he might be. Lucas had offered to tell me everything, and I'd said no. Only the basics. I didn't want to think about him out there lurking. He already haunted my dreams enough.

Lucas was waiting outside. His eyes were everywhere, taking everything in. But his phone was also to his ear when I stepped out of the door. "Okay," he said. "She's here now. We'll be back shortly."

He ended the call then pulled me against his body, pressed me against the side of the building, and kissed me hard. Harder than he probably should have given that we were in plain sight, but the way his mouth opened mine, tongue teasing, I didn't care.

"We got him," he said, pulling back to press his forehead against mine.

The world tumbled from under my feet, and I was glad that I had him and the wall to keep me upright. "What?"

"We found him. An abandoned cabin about an hour from here. We're going to get him. Tonight. It's a done deal. All you have to do is stay at the house. Liam will be there, and Noah too.

It didn't seem real. All I could do was stare at him. This was too easy, right? This couldn't be happening. "How do you know?"

"We traced his phone—not easy, given the amount of protection he has—and the police chief had a few reports about lights. We checked him out last night and saw him through the windows. That's where he's holed up."

My knees felt like water.

"You're free," he whispered in my ear. "As soon as I get back, you're free."

Lucas kissed me again, and I kissed him back. I couldn't believe it—wouldn't fully believe it until he was back and safe and they had Nathan. But this kernel of light in my chest was the start of something more hopeful than I'd felt in years. And that was dangerous.

I couldn't stop touching him as we drove back to the ranch, and Lucas seemed to feel the same. He kept me curled against his side, driving with one hand on the wheel and the other around my waist. I was jumpier than normal with all of my emotions at the surface from speaking with Rayne and now the possibility of all this ending. Finally.

He knew. Lucas's fingers kept moving in slow and soothing circles. Neither of us said much on the drive. He was focused on the task ahead, and just as I'd felt in Rayne's office, I didn't want to tempt fate by daring to speculate out loud more than we had to.

Freedom.

That word was an impossible thing reserved for other people. Not for me. It couldn't be real. I couldn't afford to believe it until it was.

It was all happening so fast.

Liam was already outside of the house when we pulled up, and he waved with a grin. "Ready for a fun night of waiting?"

"You bet," I said, though nerves were starting to grow in my gut.

"Give me a few minutes," Lucas said as we headed up the stairs. Aspen bounded over to me as soon as we walked in, tail wagging, pressing against my side. I scratched behind his ears.

"Noah will be around the grounds, and Liam will be in the house with you. But only if you feel comfortable with that. He can stay outside if he needs to."

I shook my head. "No, that's fine." I wasn't afraid of Liam. I wasn't afraid of the Resting Warrior men. A far cry from where I'd been when I'd first gotten here. But I'd seen their goodness and their dedication to helping me.

Lucas and I walked up to our bedroom hand in hand. Now I did think of it as our bedroom. What I'd talked about with Rayne ran through my head. I deserved to be happy, and I needed to trust myself. These feelings were real. And that made me afraid for him.

I turned to him at the top of the stairs. "Do you have to go?"

"I need to make sure that he's taken care of. I can't let my friends go and take care of Nathan alone."

"What about Liam? He doesn't feel the same? And Noah?"

He looked a little sad. "For the same reasons that I need to go, they have reasons that they want to stay."

My fingers fidgeted again, this time flaring in and out, grasping onto his arms. "I know that you know what you're doing. But I'm . . . terrified. For you."

"Don't be."

"I *am*." I pressed closer to him. "I can't take anything for granted with Nathan. Please be careful. *Please*." I could hear emotion welling up in my voice, but I kept it contained. He was going to do this, and I wouldn't send him away worried about me.

Lucas kissed me slowly. If he weren't about to throw himself into danger, he would have me on the bed in minutes. And I looked forward to doing that without this black cloud over our heads. "I will be careful," he said. "I promise."

He pulled away from me and quickly threw on dark pants and a dark shirt. I sat on the bed and watched him as he changed with ruthless efficiency. During the darkness of night, he would be all but invisible. "I'll call you as soon as it's done," he said, coming to me and pressing one final kiss to my temple. "Keep your phone with you."

"I will."

I followed him to the front door and smiled as he stepped out and Liam stepped in. Aspen pressed against the back of my legs like he knew I needed it. I wrapped my arms around myself to keep from fidgeting. I tried to stop thinking about the fact that Lucas was walking away from me and toward *danger*. For me.

Words pressed against my mouth, but they terrified me. Made my heart stutter. And I locked my lips together to keep them in. I would tell him later when he was back and we were safe and those words could be spoken in intimate darkness.

I watched him until he disappeared.

"He'll be okay," Liam said. "They all will."

"Yeah." I forced a smile. "Do you want some food? I was going to make dinner."

Liam shook his head. "Thanks for the offer, but I ate. Just do whatever you need. I'll be here in the living room." He had a laptop with him, and he set it up on the table. "Tapped into the cameras."

"Lucas seemed to think that it's a done deal?"

He shrugged. "It pretty much is. But we don't take chances with stuff like this."

I nodded. Nothing felt settled, and it wouldn't until Lucas came back. So I turned and nodded to Aspen. He came with me to the kitchen. I kept my phone tucked into my bra despite knowing it would be hours until he called or came back. The place they were going was about an hour away.

So at least two hours. I could fill two hours.

I fed Aspen and cooked myself some pasta. I took my time. Made the sauce from scratch because I didn't want to just sit with my thoughts. But still, by the time I was finished and had eaten, it had only been an hour. My phone still rested against my skin, dead and silent.

"Anything?" I asked Liam.

"No, sorry."

I closed my hands into fists and my toes curled. That was fine. It hadn't been that long. I steadied my breath and retreated to the kitchen again to make myself a cup of tea.

Now that I was here, and freedom was within my grasp, I needed to think about things to actually . . . *do*. I didn't have any hobbies. For four years, my hobby had been running and creating new identities. I hadn't had time to do anything but survive. And I doubted that creating identities for other people would be considered a good hobby.

If Lucas were here, I knew what we'd be doing. But even outside of that and the rush of heat that accompanied those thoughts, I would need other things to do. I could read a book, or anything really.

I was paralyzed by all the possibilities.

Aspen followed me upstairs, and I busied myself by taking a shower. Washing my face. Shaving my legs. Doing everything I could not to think about what was happening. And finally, I curled into bed with Aspen and willed myself to keep my eyes closed and not keep waiting for the phone to ring.

The shrill tone ripped me from sleep, and I sat up, startled, Aspen suddenly alert. I hadn't realized I'd dozed off.

Fumbling with my camisole, I got the phone out and answered without looking. "Lucas?"

"Sorry to disappoint," Lena's amused voice says. "Just me."

"Oh my gosh." I sagged back down onto bed. My entire body was thrumming with adrenaline. "What time is it?"

"Like one," she said. "I'm really sorry for waking you up, though I'm curious why you're waiting for Lucas to call like you're panicked."

Sighing, I curled toward Aspen and cuddled him closer. "I'll tell you later. I'm guessing it's not a social call at one in the morning."

"No. Bessie quit on the road home. Inconvenient as fuck, I know. But I figured you wouldn't completely hate me if I asked you to come jump it?"

My heart stuttered. Her car had died? Tonight? It could be a coincidence. But if it wasn't, we needed to get her out of there right the fuck now. I kept my voice even. "You're just now going home? Girl, you need to get some sleep."

She made a sound, no doubt rolling her eyes. "I got caught up in trying some new recipes. You know how it is."

"I don't, actually," I said, laughing. "But I need to check and see if we can come get you. I'll let you know in a couple minutes, okay?"

"Okay."

I changed out of my sleep shorts and camisole into sweatpants and a shirt with longer sleeves. The others on the ranch hadn't seen my scars, and this wasn't the time to have that conversation.

One in the morning, and nothing from Lucas. That was okay, right? Maybe they were waiting to do something until they knew for sure that Nathan was asleep.

Aspen came with me down the stairs, nearly making me trip over my own feet. "Liam?"

He looked over at me from his post. "Hey. I didn't know you were still up."

"I wasn't, but Lena called me. Her car broke down again, and she needs a jump."

"Jesus," he said. "Talk about a bad time for that to happen."

"Yeah," I said. "But I don't want to leave her out there alone. And with the timing, if it's a coincidence——"

"Lucas will fucking kill me if I take you where there's even the possibility of danger. He will also murder me in my sleep if I leave you alone."

"We can all go," I said quickly. "Noah too. I wouldn't ask you to leave me alone, I don't want to be. It will be fast. But we can't leave her out there."

His jaw flexed. "Let me call Noah."

While he did, I got my shoes and a jacket. I wanted to be ready to go.

"He'll be here in three minutes," Liam said. "We need to go fast. We're risking this because of the coincidence, and the fact that Jude would make sure that they never found my body if I left her out there to wait for a tow truck."

"I know," I said, following him. But I turned to Aspen. "Stay."

Aspen stayed obediently. I felt better, having him stay here. Quickly, I texted Lena to let her know that we were on our way.

There was tension under my skin as we waited on the porch, and Noah pulled up with a car. I tucked my phone back into my bra so that I could still feel it the second it rang. "The fact that I haven't heard from Lucas yet. That's not bad, right?"

"No. They should be getting started right around now," Liam said as I slipped into the passenger seat of the car with him in the back.

It was only a five-minute drive to where Lena was, and she was leaning against her car like a woman in a movie poster, the damsel in distress. But I could read embarrassment in the way that she was standing.

We pulled around so our car was facing hers and could jump it. The hood of her car was already up and waiting.

"I'm really sorry," she said as we got out of the car.

I laughed. "Not your fault. Though I think it might be time to give up on the car."

"Never," Lena said with a grin. "I love this car. Bessie is a good girl. I just need to pour a little more money into it to make sure she doesn't pull this shit on me."

"And go home and get to sleep at a decent time so that she can pull this shit during daylight hours," I said with a smirk.

Liam already had the cables hooked between the cars, and Noah was standing by the driver's side door, looking around in slow circles. There was nothing to see. Just a wooden fence and open fields next to the road. Ranchland, like so much out here. There weren't any lights in sight.

"Okay," Liam said to Noah. "Start it."

They swapped roles. Now Liam was the one on the lookout while Noah started the car to charge Lena's battery. She pulled me a few steps to the side. "What the hell is going on, and where is Lucas?"

I pressed my lips together, toes flexing in my shoes. "They think they found Nathan. They're all out there right now trying to catch him."

Her eyes went wide. "Holy shit."

"Yeah."

"Okay, Lena," Noah called. "Go ahead and give it a go."

She sat in her car and turned over the engine. It made a whining sound, but it didn't start. We waited a couple more minutes, and there still weren't any better sounds from the engine. Liam frowned at it and ducked his head under her hood. The car idled as Noah stepped out to keep watch.

"Nothing *looks* wrong," he said. "Give it one more try."

Lena did, and the same pitiful whine came from the engine. And then the engine stopped making any sounds at all. "Damn it." She sighed and leaned back against the seat before she pulled out the keys and locked it behind her. "I guess I'll have to call a mechanic in the morning."

"I'm sorry."

She sighed. "It's not your fault. My love for this car may not be enough to keep her alive, no matter how much I want it to."

I slipped my arm around her shoulder. "It had a good life."

"We'll see what the mechanic says. Anyway, can I get a ride home?"

"Of course," I said. "Like we would leave you out here in the middle of the night."

There was a measure of relief that we were leaving and going back to a place with walls. We were fine, everything was fine. But being out here like this was unnerving.

Liam unhooked the cables from Lena's engine and dropped the hood. It sounded with a clang. At the same time there was an electric sound. Like her car suddenly let out a zap of whatever energy had been put into it.

"What the hell was that?"

The words were barely out of my mouth before Liam

was crumpling to the ground with that same sound in the air, twitching as he dropped in front of the headlights.

My stomach plummeted, and I couldn't hear anything. The world was roaring in my ears as a dark figure bent to meet Liam's fall with a needle to his neck.

It was already too late to run. Maybe it had always been too late to run. This hadn't been a coincidence.

Nathan stood and smiled at me—the smile that haunted my dreams. "Hello, Evelyn."

Then he raised his hand and pointed a gun straight at me.

Chapter 26

Lucas

I was crouched in a bush, observing the cabin from as close as I dared. Lights blazed from all the windows, and music poured out of the house. The bastard. He was here enjoying himself while he terrorized Evelyn. Probably getting off on the fact that she was afraid.

She was safe. Hopefully asleep. And I couldn't wait for the moment that I could call her and tell her that it was done. Though the battle wouldn't be over. With the kind of protection that he had, keeping him in jail would be a struggle. But we had more than enough evidence for him to stay there.

We would make sure that he did.

He passed by the window again, and I kept my rage at bay. The plan was to wait for him to go to sleep for ease of entry, but it was getting late enough that we'd have to move anyway.

Jude's voice sounded in my ear. "Any sign of him winding down?"

"No," I whispered.

The five of us were spread around the cabin, in full mission mode. Our reconnaissance had told us about the simple security. A few cameras which we avoided, and some tripwires, which we also avoided. It was almost too easy. Was Nathan that confident in his camouflage that he didn't think he needed the security?

Something about it bothered me, tingling under my skin like we were missing something. But I could see him. I had a scope, and he'd passed by the windows enough to confirm his identity. The breach plan was solid. Three through the front door, two through the back, subdue and clear.

The cabin itself was small. It wouldn't take more than a few minutes to get control of it. "He has music playing. You guys hear that?" I asked.

"Yes," Harlan said.

"If he's not winding down, we might as well go in when we have sound cover."

A few feet away, Daniel shifted in his hiding spot. "Probably a good idea."

I breathed in the adrenaline that flooded me, the icy focus that only came when I was on a mission. Everything came into sharp relief. The air felt cooler, the sounds of the woods crisper. Every one of my muscles was ready to spring.

This was familiar territory. And even though I was glad missions weren't my life anymore, part of me craved this. The easy teamwork and the singular collective goal. It was so much simpler than everything else.

We were armed, but I'd already made up my mind not

to use my gun unless I needed to. The primal part of me wanted my hands on this man.

"On my count," Daniel said, and I readied myself.

The numbers were soft in my ear. And then, as one, we moved. The team in the front of the house breached first. I heard the shattering of wood as they broke through the door, and Daniel and I were seconds later. The back door cracked under the force of Daniel's kick, and I blinked away the brightness of going from nighttime into complete brilliance.

Music assaulted my ears, along with the shout of my friends as Harlan tackled him to the ground, Jude and Daniel breaking off into the other rooms to clear them.

And that was it.

There was no one else here, and I shut off the stereo as they came back into the room and confirmed that we were alone. My skin prickled. Something was wrong. This was too easy.

Harlan and Grant had him on the ground, the cuffs snapping over his wrists. My stomach plummeted. "Get him up."

They hauled him onto his knees, and the world fell down around me. This man was not Nathan West. He looked enough like him that he could be his twin, and at a distance it had been nearly impossible to tell. Even through the fucking scope. This man could have been his twin, but it wasn't him.

"Thank you," the man says. "I don't know who you are, but *thank you*."

"Who are you?" Daniel asked. I couldn't speak. I was locked in place, mind racing. This had been a trap.

"My name is Colin Harrington. I've been here for weeks. Or around here. Please, he has my family."

The silence that surrounded us was so thick I couldn't

move through it. My voice was deadly quiet. "Who has your family?"

"Nathan West," the guy said desperately. "He has a tracker on me. He took my wife and daughter. I have no idea where they are. If I don't do as he says, they die."

Fucking hell. This was the blond man that Charlie had seen around town. Probably the man that Evelyn had seen across from Deja Brew that had triggered her.

"You've been leaving flowers?"

He shook his head. "No. Just walking around. Wait, once I left some flowers at the coffee shop, but mostly I've been here or walking where he tells me to."

I took a step closer, but Harlan's voice cut through the red fog in my head. "Easy."

"Where is he?" My own voice was unrecognizable.

The man shook his head. "I don't know. I swear I don't. He never tells me where he goes, and he knows if I leave. I've *tried*."

I broke away from the group, and as I dialed my phone, the others asked him for more details. Where the tracker was on or in his body and any details about his family.

Evelyn's was the first phone that I tried, and it rang out. No answer. Panic spiraled inside me. She could be asleep. Next was Liam's phone. No answer there either. That was a problem. Something had happened.

I already knew that it was true before I dialed Noah's number, but I did it anyway out of sheer desperation. No answer. Fuck. *Fuck*.

Everything was spinning. Something had happened, and I wasn't there. I'd fucked up. Nathan had seen through us and what we wanted and set this up. I needed to get back there. "We need to go."

The others didn't need to ask if I'd gotten an answer. They could read it on my face.

"Go," Daniel said. "Grant and I will take care of things here."

I didn't wait, sprinting out the front door toward our concealed vehicles. They were almost a mile away. We'd parked there and hiked so there was no chance we would be seen. Once I'd reached the vehicles, the drive back to the ranch was the better part of an hour. It was a good thing that it was the middle of the night because there wasn't a speed limit in the world that was going to hold me back.

Be wrong, I begged the universe. *Please be wrong.*

Maybe a cell tower had been knocked out or there had been a fire. Maybe there had been an earthquake and they were too busy to answer their phones. My mind made up increasingly ridiculous scenarios as I ran. I knew they weren't true, but I held on to them anyway.

They were better than acknowledging the alternative.

That Nathan had played us and taken Evelyn. That once again, I hadn't been there for someone who needed me. And that there was every chance in the world I would once again be too late.

Chapter 27

Evelyn

My head pounded, and everything sounded underwater. Flickering sounds and maybe a voice. Why did my head hurt?

I tried to move, but I couldn't.

Memory dropped on me like a bomb. Nathan stepping out of the darkness with a gun. Liam crumpling to the ground, and Lena screaming. He'd moved so fucking fast. There was no chance. He'd hit me with the butt of his gun, and I'd felt a needle. I had only been conscious long enough to hear Lena try to run.

Lena.

I forced my eyes open.

The room was dim but lit with something. I didn't recognize it. The ceiling was wooden and rough. A cabin, maybe? The cabin where they'd gone to capture him? If we were there, what had happened to Lucas and the others?

Panic spiraled up and choked me, and I forced it back. I had things to live for now, and I wasn't going to let this break me. I was stronger than this.

I tried to move again, but my hands and ankles were bound.

Oh God. No.

My vision darkened. I was there again. He had me. Just like before. I wouldn't be able to get away, and he would kill me. Tears flooded my eyes, and I blinked them back.

Breathe.

The air shuddered in my lungs like it was afraid to be there.

I turned my head toward the rest of the room, the movement as small as possible so that if Nathan was here, he wouldn't know that I was awake. Lena was tied to a chair, gagged, but conscious. She saw me looking, and her eyes went so wide I could see the whites of them all the way across the room. But she didn't move. She only glanced with her eyes to the right, and I followed her gaze.

Nathan sat in a chair next to the fireplace. In it was a roaring blaze, and it took everything in me not to scream, or faint. Pure dread was a feeling I would never be able to fully describe. It was like falling into solid ice, paralyzing and infinite. It was pain and panic all wrapped up into one.

Something was leaning in the fire. Heating. I hadn't seen him heat the ring before, and this was so much worse. I wasn't naked, but enough of my clothes were gone that he could—and would—damage me. I knew that.

From his chair, he watched me with steady eyes. That was maybe the scariest thing about Nathan. With the exception of that first burst of anger and screaming, he didn't act crazy. He was always rational, explaining everything. It didn't matter that his conclusions were horrific.

I couldn't breathe. I was slipping away from everything

while he looked at me. Going back to that bed in Florida, unable to move or think because of the pain. The smell and sound of my own flesh burning. I'd blocked all those things out—I hadn't talked about them to Lucas or Rayne —but those details were fresh, and now they were all I could focus on.

Lucas would find me. Without a shadow of a doubt, I knew that he would tear down the world to get to me. I just had to give him the time to do it. I couldn't let myself go black. I had to keep thinking. But my mind was a snarl of adrenaline and fear. I could taste it.

"Most people," Nathan said, "when you warn them about something repeatedly, take the hint and change course. That doesn't seem to be the case with you, does it, Evelyn?"

I didn't say anything. It wouldn't matter if I did either way. He wouldn't listen to me. His mind was already made up.

"What did I tell you the last time we had this conversation?"

Pressing my lips together, I only looked at him. No.

He stood, and in seconds, he was over me, staring down. His face was so close that I could feel his breath. Cold anger radiated from his eyes. But I heard none of that in his voice. The words were simple and matter-of-fact. "Before we continue, I'm going to hear you say it."

What would keep him talking longer? Delay him the most? If he wanted to lecture me, I could take it. Please, let Lucas have a clue where we were. I swallowed. "You told me that I was yours."

"That you were mine until you died. I made that very clear." He turned away and walked back to the fire. His enormous shadow on the wall loomed over me the way he had.

Lena was breathing hard. Panicking. I shook my head. He didn't want her. Only me. She needed to stay invisible.

"I thought that I'd given you a good enough lesson then." Nathan ran his eyes over me. "And I see that it's held up well. But this time, Evelyn, you *will* learn."

All the breath went out of my lungs as he pulled the red-hot ring out of the fire. It glowed like the fucking sun in the half light of the room, and every bit of strength I'd thought I had evaporated. Panic choked me and I fought against my restraints. There wasn't anything in me but sheer, black terror.

"I learned it," I said, begging. "I promise that I did. You don't have to do this."

"Clearly, I do. Maybe it will be enough to remind you that you're mine. End of story."

The metal handcuffs dug into my wrists and my ankles, as he brought the ring towards me. I twisted away from him as far as I could get and already the sounds that escaped me weren't human. They were base and instinctual. Survival sounds mixed with pleading.

But the look on Nathan's face . . . He was as cold and beautiful as ever, and he was utterly unmoved.

The second the ring touched the skin of my leg the world went white. I heard a scream, but it wasn't mine. I was just trying to survive. It was Lena.

"Shut up," Nathan growled at Lena. "Shut the hell up."

She didn't. Through a haze of pain I managed to see her. She was screaming to draw his attention away from me.

But that wasn't going to work. He would only get angrier. Brand-new terror soaked my mind. My life was already spoken for. I wasn't going to let my friend die or walk out of here with her own scars. "Let her go."

Fear nearly closed my throat as I said the words. I wasn't sure how I was managing to speak, but I did. Buy more time. Get Lena out of harm's way so that Lucas could find me. Or if he couldn't find me, then find Lena.

"I'll stay with you," I said. "I'm already yours. You can have me. Just let her go."

Lena was still screaming. Nathan glared at me, and in two steps he'd crossed the distance to Lena and hit her hard enough to stop her screaming. She slumped, unconscious.

"Please," I whispered.

Nathan rolled his eyes like we were having a normal conversation. "You know I can't let her go. She's seen too much, and I need her now. Besides." He pulled the ring out of the fire again, freshly glowing. "You think that you can wipe four years of the slate clean? Come back and live our life like nothing happened? That's not the way this works, Evelyn."

He stalked closer. The grip he had on his control was thinning. It was as close as I'd seen him to that first day with the screaming. His eyes promised my death, and somehow that didn't scare me as much as I'd thought it would. Because this had always been coming. He'd promised it. And there weren't a lot of paths that didn't end up with us in these exact positions.

Not that I didn't wish it were different. I did. I wished that I could stay here and be happy. Live with Lucas and work with Lena. Train animals to help people. But that future was evaporating like morning mist.

"I gave you plenty of chances to come back. Four years of chances. I would have taken you back, and you would have been happy, Evelyn. Your entire life, I would have given you everything. But you chose your path when you let someone else touch you. When you gave yourself

234

away like a whore, knowing that you already belonged to me."

He didn't wait for a response. The ring touched my other leg and everything was pain. This time I screamed. He smiled through my sobs then did something that scared me even more.

He *stopped*.

He set the ring down on the table and picked up something else without a word. Then smiled as he showed me the needle before he slipped it into my arm.

"Wh-what? No..." The air around me became foggy.

There was still pain, but I was floating in it now. I wasn't sure that I had a body, though Nathan was able to touch it. He got rid of the handcuffs. But I still couldn't move, trapped in this interior world looking out.

I watched everything through a pane of clouded glass. I was observing a film of the last moments in my life. Was this the way it always felt near the end?

I think I made sounds of pain when he moved me. Maybe I did. Maybe I only made them in my mind.

When I'd looked at the room before, I hadn't seen the dress hanging on the wall. It was slinky and black. The kind of dress that I might have worn had I stayed with Nathan and been a part of the West dynasty. The kind of dress that cost a year's salary.

Pain seared my legs—I had legs?—when he pulled on tights. I wasn't anything more than a doll for him to dress. Sheer black tights that brought friction against new burns. New scars.

Next were shiny black high heels. I couldn't remember the last time I'd worn high heels.

Nathan lifted me onto my feet, and I flopped against his body, unable to hold myself upright. Even more than the blazing lines of pain, I didn't want to touch him. I didn't want to feel this. He got the dress over my head and let it flutter to the floor.

It fit perfectly.

He brushed my hair and dusted my face with makeup. The finishing touch was the still-hot engagement ring. It no longer glowed, but it still burned when he shoved it onto my finger—his own hand protected with a glove—along with a wedding ring. It added to the cloud of suffering I was already floating in.

Nathan leaned over me and smiled. It was the kind of smile that he used to give me when we were in love and I'd thought he was my whole world. He cupped my cheek. "See, Evelyn? I would have taken care of you. But I keep my promises. Even if you don't deserve them."

Distant horror clanged through me. He'd said that before, but here in this floating world I couldn't quite reach that memory. What had he promised me? What was he doing?

Sitting me up, he leaned me against the end of the bed and pressed a pen into my hand. Dragged my fingers across a piece of paper.

Oh my God. It was a marriage license, and now he had my fingerprints on it and the pen. This was what he'd always wanted. And now he had it. Could this be legal? Didn't I have to have a say in that?

I blinked. It was Nathan. He'd found a way. Or bought a way.

"Perfect," he said.

He took Lena first, carrying her unconscious body out of the room.

I tried to move while he was gone. Every ounce of my will went into forcing motion into my body, but nothing responded. I was powerless in my own skin. My mind cleared a little, and the panic began to rise. I was running out of time, and now he was taking me somewhere else. How would Lucas find me? How would anyone find me?

They had to find me, right? I didn't realize that I'd been holding on to that hope. But now that it was slipping away, I was unravelling.

Nathan strode back into the room and looked around. He doused the fire and tossed the poker that he'd used into the ashes.

Then he came for me, and I was blindfolded. Now there was truly nothing but pain as he lifted me and carried me. Laid me down next to Lena—her breathing was even in my ear. At least she was breathing. That was good.

Movement made me dizzy. I was in a car. Where were we going? I grasped at the straws of my memory. They were almost there. What had he promised me?

I lost all sense of time in the darkness, so I couldn't say how long we drove. But I felt the stop, and when he ripped the blindfold off my eyes, the first blush of dawn light was painting the sky. And I knew the view. We were in the park in Garnet Bend. The beautiful one where Lucas had first kissed me, and he'd asked me if this might be my place. Even then I'd known that he meant with him.

A place with flowers.

Oh, fuck.

Nathan's voice rang out of memory, and I couldn't believe that, even drifting in a drugged sea, that I'd ever forgotten those words.

I promise, Evelyn. I will bury you somewhere beautiful. In a field of flowers. Even if you don't fucking deserve it.

He was going to bury me, and there wasn't time. Lucas would never find me here. He wouldn't know where to look. I couldn't stop the tears that flowed, grief along with icy terror pouring over me like a waterfall.

"I think we can both agree that this place is beautiful."

He wasn't wrong. It was.

Lena was still in the car. What was he going to do to her? Would he bury her too? I should have run when I had the chance. She didn't deserve this.

The prick of pain in my elbow was the only warning I got before Nathan injected me again. This didn't keep me still, this pulled me under. I had seconds, maybe, and I fought it. I needed to stay awake. The longer I stayed awake, the more I would have a chance.

Nathan laid me down, and all I could see was his silhouette against the lightening dawn sky. Nathan knew that too. His smile dripped with the knowledge that his face would be the last thing I ever saw.

"Goodbye, Evelyn."

He closed me into darkness, and everything faded away.

Chapter 28

Lucas

The atmosphere in the truck was tense, and I was doing my best not to climb the walls. We were almost to the ranch. Daniel and Grant had the Nathan stand-in and were heading directly to the police station to secure him and get more help to find the man's family. But he was not necessarily off the hook because he was under duress.

And we were speeding. Not as much as we would be if I were driving, but Jude was going easily twenty over, his jaw a grim line as he monitored the rear view.

My mind was still spinning. Hoping that I was wrong, that cell service had gone down around Garnet Bend at exactly the wrong time. That she was asleep in our bed and that there was literally any other explanation than what I knew deep in my gut.

That I had *failed*. That once again, I wasn't there for the one person who needed me.

I kept calling her phone. Their phones, even though they never answered. The repetitive motion kept me sane. Barely.

The gates came into view, and we were going so fast that the truck barely cleared the edges. Dust flew up behind us. Everything looked perfect and normal. If it weren't for the thundering of my heart, it could have been any night in a hundred in this beautiful place.

Jude slammed on the brakes and the truck slid to the side, spinning to a stop sideways in front of my house. I was out of the truck before it had come to a full stop. "Evelyn!"

I shouted it. Right now I didn't give a shit. The door was locked, and I got it open faster than I thought possible, and . . . nothing. Aspen was lying in the living room, wagging his tail when he saw me. The laptop connected to the security system was still on the table.

"Evelyn?"

I sprinted up the stairs, and my stomach plummeted. The bed was unmade, and it looked like she'd gotten up in a hurry, but she wasn't here. Pajamas were tossed on the bed, and she wasn't in the bathroom either. My mind was blank with terror.

I got down the stairs and out the door, barely bothering to lock the door. Jude was still in the truck. "Harlan ran to the Bitterroot House. Let's check the main one."

"She's not there," I said.

Jude gunned the engine. "We have to be sure."

It took all of thirty seconds to confirm that the building was empty, and we came out to Harlan running up from the direction of the guest houses. He shook his head. "No."

"The cemetery," I said. There was no part of me that

wanted to imagine her there. But it was the next place that I could think of. The most obvious.

"Would he take her there before his countdown?"

"I don't know. I don't fucking know *anything*." My voice was raw. I shouldn't snap at them, but panic was wrapped around my chest and one breath was all it would take to snap me in half.

We were halfway to the cemetery when we saw the cars. "Fuck. *Fuck*."

"That's Lena's car," Jude said. Now he sounded almost as raw as I did. Please, no. Dread like ice crawled up my spine. Had he taken them both?

It was still dark, so it wasn't until we slammed to a stop behind her car that we saw the body on the ground.

Liam was crumpled. He'd been taken from behind, and the way he'd fallen looked like he hadn't fought. Or hadn't had a chance to fight. I pressed my fingers to his pulse, and a tiny thread of relief ran through me. "He's alive."

"Noah too," Harlan said. "Get them into the car. I'll take them to the hospital while you guys go to the cemetery."

We were getting too split up. Five to three to two. If this was a trap, we were walking right into it. And still I was going. So was Jude. Because it didn't matter if they pretended there was nothing between them, there was no way in hell that Jude would go in the opposite direction of Lena.

Harlan and I lifted Noah into the front seat of the car. I pulled out my phone and called Daniel.

"What's up?"

"We found Liam and Noah. Unconscious. Near Lena's car. Evelyn and Lena are nowhere. Harlan is taking the guys to the hospital, but we're going to need backup."

"I'm on my way," he said. "Grant can handle things here."

I nodded even though he couldn't see me. "We're going to the cemetery."

"Okay."

Jude and I slid into the truck, but we said nothing. I felt sick. Like my soul was shredding itself with adrenaline and panic and dread. At least the cemetery was close.

Harlan's words echoed in my mind. *We want to know how much of this is because you're terrified you'll fail to save another person and how much is because you're in love with Evelyn.*

It had never been both more than in this moment. I couldn't lose Evelyn. The truth slammed into me like boulders coming down a mountain. I loved her.

I wasn't falling, I wasn't only *in* love with her. I loved her. And if she was gone before I had the chance to actually tell her, I wouldn't survive it.

The trees blocking the view of the actual cemetery taunted me. We should have cut them down that first day and installed cameras. The only sound I heard was the rushing in my ears. Nothing else.

Jude was out of the truck as fast as I was. There was a part of me that knew I should slow down. Nathan wanted me dead too, and I should make sure I wasn't walking into danger. The sky was starting to lighten over the mountains, so everything was in shadow.

I didn't slow down.

Jude had his gun out, and I didn't stop. I ran straight for the fence and yanked the gate open. "*Evelyn.*" Her name tore from my lips the second I saw the lump of a body on the ground—right next to the open graves.

I'd never been a religious person, but I prayed to every God there was as I hit my knees next to her.

Except it wasn't her.

All the breath went out of my lungs. Lena's unconscious face looked up at me, and like Liam, she was alive. But her heartbeat was sluggish. "Jude," I called.

He held out the flashlight on his phone, and I saw how pale he was. Stricken.

"She's alive."

"Look." He pointed to her arm.

There were marks. Little bits of dried blood. Clear signs of injections on both arms at the crease of her elbow. "We need to get her to the hospital."

I didn't know what was in her system, but it wasn't good.

Jude lifted Lena out of my arms, carrying her toward the car. He held her tight, and I was glad he was here for her.

But this cemetery was empty. Where the fuck was Evelyn?

The sun peeked over the horizon and my phone rang. Unknown number. "Hello?"

"Hello, Lucas."

I went completely still. As long as I lived, I would never forget his voice. "Nathan."

Jude whipped his head toward me.

"You're not tracing my call this time, I imagine. I made sure, even if you were in a position where you could."

"We found your doppelgänger."

I heard the smile in his voice and curled my free hand into a fist. "Of course you did. You think that you found my first number or got a lock on me without me knowing? I'm fucking *untouchable* and you know it. And now you know what happens when you try to steal from me. Did you learn the lesson?"

"Where is she?" I barely recognized my voice.

A soft laugh. "It's already too late, Lucas. She's been laid to rest. Like I promised she would be."

Through the phone I heard a sound. What was that?

Bells. There were only a couple of churches in Garnet Bend, and only one had bells. And it was a church with its own graveyard.

"But maybe you could get to me in time to save her. Part of me wants to see you try."

I ended the call. She was alive, and I knew where Nathan was. That was enough.

"The Baptist church in town," I said. "That's where he is."

Jude turned the truck around without question. I dialed Daniel to tell him where to go next. For the first time in hours, I had something to hold on to.

I was going to save her.

Chapter 29

Lucas

While Jude raced Lena to the hospital, Daniel and Harlan met me at the entrance to the church's graveyard and we strode through the gate.

He wasn't trying to hide. He was relaxing against the wall of the church, perfectly at ease. He could be smoking a cigarette and not facing down three pissed ex-SEALs.

Daniel had called Charlie on the way, and the police would be here in minutes. We would have him. Finally.

The face matched the voice. Of course I'd seen pictures, but it was always different meeting someone in person and feeling their energy. I could see his charming side that could make people love him. I didn't doubt it at all.

"Where is she, Nathan?"

"I said I wanted to see you try. Where would the fun be if I told you?"

Steel entered my spine. Now that I was here and I had

him, this was familiar. He wasn't some invisible enemy with infinite reach. No longer a ghost. He was only a man, and I could put my hands on him. "I'll make sure you go away forever. For murder. We already have one body."

I lied about Lena. It was an instinct, and neither Daniel nor Harlan contradicted me.

The prick just smiled. "You know? Money can get you almost anything you want."

He pulled an envelope out of his back pocket and held it out to me. My friends stiffened. But I took the envelope. Nathan was playing a game. He wasn't going to kill me with powder in an envelope.

Inside were documents—not originals. I glanced through them. A death certificate with Ev's name on it. Rehab admission papers for Lena. And the last document, a marriage license with Evelyn's scrawled signature.

"Money can get you documents that prove someone was terminally ill. It can provide a will that shows your *wife* wanted to be buried in Montana. It can provide a history of drug abuse and an easy overdose for the naïve girl with the shitty car." He smirked at me. "No one is going to mourn a fucking drug addict, and no one is going to convict me for burying my wife in the manner she wanted."

I moved before I was conscious of doing so, and I had him up against the wall, my arm across his throat. Harlan and Daniel shouted at me, but I wasn't listening to them.

"Tell me where she is," I said, my voice as low and sharp as a blade. "Right now."

Nathan's grin was that of a snake. A snake that knew it had already won. "You'll never find her in time," he whispered.

Daniel stepped up beside me and took over the hold on Nathan. "I have him. Check the graveyard."

I didn't want to let go of him. Right now Nathan was grounding me. If I was holding on to him, there was a chance. But I let go. And I turned to the old patch of land. Not even Nathan's money could conceal a fresh grave.

Harlan was on the phone, redirecting people to check the other cemeteries in town as I jogged down the rows. I looked for any trace—fresh dirt or sod. Footprints or left-over tools. She wasn't in this graveyard. Of course she wasn't. Nathan wasn't stupid. He wouldn't make this easy.

Sirens wailed through the air, and seconds later cop cars pulled up outside the fence. I was calmer than I had been, the panic held back by the wall of steel and action that was surrounding me.

I crossed back across the graves to where Daniel held Nathan, and where he was now resisting arrest. "You can't arrest me. There's no proof that I've done anything, and you can't arrest me for standing in a graveyard. You should arrest these two for assault. They're keeping me here against my will." He pushed against Daniel's hold and failed utterly.

The police chief observed Daniel and me coolly and then looked back at Nathan. "We'll see about that once our witness wakes up. Nathan West, you're under arrest for the attempted murder of Lena Mitchell."

For one second Nathan went still. His eyes flew to mine as he realized that I'd lied. There was plenty of evidence. Who knew what Lena had seen while she was with him?

Then he started to fight. Like a wounded animal, he lashed out, and it took Daniel, Charlie, and another officer wrestling him to the ground to get the cuffs on him.

My hands twitched. There was nothing I wanted more than to put my fist into Nathan's skull and render him unconscious. But he had a point. I couldn't do shit for Evelyn if Charlie was forced to arrest me for assault. It still took everything I had to let them shove him into the cruiser.

Evelyn was still alive, but she didn't have long if what Nathan had said was true. Harlan and Daniel were standing in front of me. "Did he give you any clues?"

I crouched down, needing to just think. *Please.* "He wants me to try to find her. That must mean that she's able to be found. So she can't be far. On the phone he told me that she's already been laid to rest like he promised—" My mind went blank with realization.

"Lucas?" Daniel asked.

Standing back up, I looked at them. "He made promises to her. He told her that he'd bury her somewhere beautiful. Somewhere with flowers."

There was only one place in Garnet Bend where there were flowers in public. The same place that I'd kissed her for the first time. And it was only three blocks from here. My friends had the same thought—I could see it in their eyes.

And we ran. I wasn't going to be too late. This wasn't going to be like Emmett. I was going to make it in time. I had to.

Chapter 30

Evelyn

I was floating on a dreamless sea.

What was this place? Everything was calm and dark. I felt peaceful in a way that I hadn't in years. It was a comforting, velvet black.

But why was there pain?

Pain shouldn't exist in a place like this.

Sharp lines of fire rolled across me, even though I could barely sense my body. I think I was below ground. There was something tugging at my brain. Why did I feel like I was underneath the world?

My thoughts were growing clearer and the infinite darkness receding into a smaller space. I was here, but I hadn't chosen to be here. Where was I?

Reaching out, I brushed my hand against a ceiling a mere foot from my face. It was soft. All the walls were soft. But the movement of my arm *burned*. Why?

I shifted my legs, and the fiery lance of feeling cleared

more of the fog away. I knew where I was. I was in a coffin. *In a coffin.* Nathan had put me in here and drugged me so I wouldn't fight, but the drugs hadn't lasted long. Otherwise, I would be dead. He wanted me to panic. He wanted me to know exactly where I was and how I was dying as I suffocated.

Hauling in a breath, I held it. Holy shit, he'd actually done it. He'd buried me. He was killing me.

The urge to move and claw at the walls rose up and choked me. The panic of fight or flight. But I couldn't. I only had so much air down here, and I needed to hang on as long as possible so that Lucas could find me.

He had to find me, right?

Moving as slowly as I could, I held a hand over my mouth to keep from screaming and to try to control my breath. I was shaking with the effort to keep myself still and not claw my way out of here. I wouldn't succeed. Nathan was thorough. He hadn't left me in an open grave.

Everything in my body was burning from Nathan's attentions, and I wanted it gone. I was wearing his rings and the clothes that he'd forced me into. And his scars. He'd finally gotten what he wanted.

I didn't want to cry. I hated crying. But tears leaked out the side of my eyes, dripping down into my hair. When Lucas had left, I'd wanted to tell him that I loved him and I'd hesitated. Why? Because I was scared. And I'd thought it was too early to feel something like that.

But it didn't matter. I did feel that way. I was in love with Lucas. How could I have not told him that? How could I have doubted that the feeling was real? And I wasn't going to be able to say it now. Because it was over. Nathan had won.

I wished I could go back to that moment and tell him.

Hand muffling my breath, I breathed slowly for as long

as possible. Time didn't exist in perfect darkness. But I felt it passing. Stretching out and rushing back again. Things were slipping away. I felt thin. Like my connection to things was weakening. Pain was fading away.

Lucas's hands on me. I could feel them, but they weren't real. They were nothing more than memories comforting me on my journey elsewhere. He whispered my name. I loved the way he said it, like it was something precious to him.

Then he called me from far away, but that was impossible. My mind was playing tricks on me. So this was what dying was like. Somehow I'd thought I'd feel more . . . anything. But everything was muted now, like the volume had been turned down on my senses.

My name again. Maybe there *was* someone waiting for me beyond. Maybe there was an afterlife.

Time was running out. I knew that. My hands had fallen away from my mouth, and each breath felt less full than the last. There were sounds that I didn't understand. Scraping. And clanging. And my name. That sound was getting closer. But I wasn't. I was retreating and fading. And it was fine. Peaceful. At least it was peaceful.

A sound like thunder cracked around me and everything moved. Light blinded me, the world going white, and in the next moment there was sound and pain and *air*. Life crashed back into me all at once, my body trying to take more air than it could at once. I was coughing, choking, and my body was on fire because there were hands on me.

"Evelyn."

It was Lucas. He'd found me after all. I was lifted into the air and I felt the sun on my skin and everything hurt. In the dark, I'd felt clear, but in the real world, I knew that the drugs were still in me. I couldn't move right. Not that I had the strength to.

251

His face was above me. "Evelyn." Hands on my body. Gentle, but they still hurt. I couldn't take my eyes off him, and when he kissed me, it wasn't real. Was this real? Was this just another hallucination from the lack of air?

I couldn't take the chance either way—I needed to tell him. "I love you."

"What?"

Somehow I reached out and touched him. "I love you."

And the world faded away again. I hoped I would come back.

~

The beeping reached me first. Slow and steady. I didn't hurt as much, but my mind was clearer. There was weight on my legs. My eyes were heavy, but I managed to open them.

I was in a hospital. That was obvious. The beeping was my heart. I could feel the wires attached to my skin. The windows showed me that it was night, and the room itself was dim. But there was light pouring in from the hallway, and the sounds of the hospital filtered through the open door.

This was real, and I was alive.

I was alive.

Sudden emotion flooded my eyes, and my breath came in a ragged sob. He'd found me. Lucas was asleep, his head on my lap. But he was here. With me.

As I moved my legs, Lucas shifted with them, suddenly awake and looking at me. I saw the moment that he realized that I was actually awake. His jaw went slack with shock and then he was leaning up to me. "Evelyn."

His lips pressed to mine, and he gripped my hand. There was such impossible emotion in that kiss that it stole any remaining breath. He was here. I was here. This was impossible.

"I'm alive?"

Worry and relief clouded his face. "You're alive."

I played back those hazy memories before I'd slipped into unconsciousness. I'd been halfway gone. I held his hand a little harder. "It was close, wasn't it?"

Not a question.

"Yes."

I shuddered. "Did they . . . did they tell you—"

"That he burned you again?" Lucas's eyes were alight with a fire that could destroy worlds. "They told me. He's in jail right now, and he won't be coming back out. Ever. Not if I have anything to say about it."

That was a hard thing to believe. But the idea that they had him and he was finally gone . . . My chest felt lighter.

"I didn't marry him," I blurted out. "I couldn't move. He signed it with my hand."

Lucas shook his head. "You didn't marry him. It's illegal, and clearly not your signature."

Good. That was good. My thoughts were jumbled and another one sprang to me. "Lena? Liam and Noah?"

"She's in a room down the hall. Alive. He gave her an overdose of half a dozen drugs meant to kill her. But she'll be okay. Liam and Noah had already been discharged and are pissed as hell. They were drugged too, but nothing lethal. They'll have some pain from the stun gun, but nothing lasting."

I nodded. "Good." My breath hitched. "I need to tell you what happened. I want to know everything that happened to you. I'm so sorry—"

Lucas cut me off with a squeeze of his hand. "We'll have time for you to tell me everything, and I'll tell you as much as you want to know. But first, I need to tell you." He shifted to face me more fully. "I love you."

The words hung in the air, and I closed my eyes. I wanted to hear them again. Like he was reading my mind, he spoke.

"I love you, and the entire time I was trying to find you, I knew that I should have told you sooner. Because not getting the chance—" He had to stop and look away. "I needed you to know that before anything else."

"I love you too," I said. "I said it, right?"

"As soon as I had you out."

I swallowed. "I had the same thoughts. Before you left to go get him, I wanted to tell you, but I was scared. And then I thought that I wouldn't have the chance."

He stood up and leaned down, kissing me while holding himself back from my body. He knew what had been done. I didn't have to hide it. And whatever was flowing into me through the IV made the feelings bearable.

He was right, we had time, and all I wanted was him. "Will you hold me?"

Lucas kicked off his shoes and lifted me with infinite gentleness, settling me against his chest so we lay together. "You don't have to run anymore," he said. "And I hope, like I asked you once, that this can be your place. I want you to come home with me, Ev. I want my house to be your house, my bed to be your bed. I want to take you back to the lake and finish making love to you against one of those trees. I want to do everything with you, if you'll stay."

I pressed my face against his chest, breathing in the rich, pine scent of him. "I don't want to go anywhere. Except with you. Garnet Bend isn't my place. You're my place."

Lucas kissed my hair, and his hand stroked down my

back. Being here with him wasn't something I'd ever thought I'd feel again, and now, I got to do it forever. Tension so deep I hadn't known it was there slipped away, and I melted into Lucas. That relief brought a brand-new wave of exhaustion, and I fell asleep in his arms.

Safe.

Finally.

Chapter 31

Lucas

I didn't dare close my eyes again. I'd fallen asleep, and she'd woken. Now, I didn't want to miss anything. Especially since she was in my arms.

There was a part of me that wondered whether it was real. Whether I'd really found her. If she was here.

Nathan hadn't bothered to hide the grave in the flower bed. He'd thought that we wouldn't find her in time, and that with the documents he'd forged, it wouldn't matter. He hadn't bothered to move the tools that he'd used to bury her.

Harlan, Daniel, and I had dug as fast as possible, and I'd ended up using my hands for the last bit because it was faster. And when I'd opened the lid—

I'd thought she was gone. She'd been so pale and still that the world had crashed down on me in a second, thinking that I'd been too late and she'd suffocated waiting for me to find her. But then she'd breathed, and I couldn't get her out of there fast enough.

She hadn't stayed awake long enough for me to tell her that I loved her. I'd just been glad to see her alive. Even when I'd seen the new angry red marks on her arms. And her legs. Creeping beneath her clothes. The ring burned onto her finger. The paramedics had put her into the ambulance, and it had taken both Daniel and Harlan to keep me from going to the police station and killing Nathan right then.

My arms tightened around her sleeping form. She was here with me. And she was going to stay. That's all that mattered. I didn't give a shit that she had new scars—there wasn't anything that would make her not beautiful to me. But Ev would need to be shown that.

In the darkness and solitude, I finally let in the emotions I'd been pushing back. All that panic and fear and rage. It shuddered through me, and I let it. I pressed my face deeper into Evelyn's hair. She smelled like sunlight and coconuts, despite everything.

When I was too tired to stay awake, I let myself drift. The others were keeping tabs on things here at the hospital and the police station. They'd ordered me in here and to not even think about anything else, and I'd listened. But the feeling of needing to watch our backs hadn't quite faded. It never did right away.

There was always a period after missions when my senses were heightened, and it took time for them to come back to normal. Given how personal this was, it might take longer.

Evelyn moved in my arms, shifting closer, her fingers curling into the fabric of my shirt. And together, we slept.

I surfaced again when the sun was shining. It was still morning, but late. I'd slept more deeply than I'd intended, and Evelyn was still passed out. She needed all the rest she could get.

I eased myself from her and laid her on the pillows. I needed to check in with the others, and my stomach was growling. I didn't actually remember the last time I'd eaten, and Evelyn must be the same. There was a vending machine down the hall. I'd grab something for us while I made some calls.

"How is she?" Daniel asked as he answered on the first ring.

"Sleeping. She woke up for a little while last night."

"Good. Listen, I was waiting for you to call."

I punched the numbers into the vending machine for a granola bar for myself, one for Evelyn, and a chocolate bar. There wasn't anything that chocolate didn't make better. Hopefully she'd like that when she woke up. "What's going on?"

"Don't panic," he said, which made me freeze. "Everything is fine. But Nathan was transferred to the custody of the state troopers."

"*What?*" He wasn't supposed to set foot outside of his cell. "Why?"

I looked in both directions down the hallway, my senses reaching out and searching to make sure nothing was wrong. This machine was going too damn slowly.

"There was nothing we could do," he said. "*Believe me*, we tried. I guess he used his phone call wisely. In the middle of the night, an army of lawyers stormed the station. They didn't want him in jail. And since Lena wasn't awake, there wasn't enough proof to hold him in a cell. Both the lawyers and the state troopers promised to take him to a hotel and keep him close until Lena and Evelyn could be questioned."

I swore. That wasn't any promise at all.

"We followed them. Grant has been on the hotel and Harlan has been circling it. No movement that we've seen, but—"

"But don't leave her side," I said. "Got it."

The last thing fell from the vending machine and I snatched it out of the bottom before walking back down the hall. The only reason I didn't run was that I didn't want to make the nurses panic for no reason. They were watching. We'd be okay.

But maybe there was a reason my instincts hadn't settled.

I spun around the corner and took in the nurse's station and her doorway. No one suspicious. Good. And when I stepped into Ev's room, she was exactly as I'd left her. Perfectly and peacefully asleep.

Shutting the door behind me, I took a breath. It took me stepping into the room to see the black rose lying on the foot of her bed.

The movement registered before I'd fully seen it, and I spun on instinct. Nathan was there with a knife, already in motion. Thank fuck that SEAL training went deep. I lunged out of the way of the knife barely in time to avoid having my guts spilled on the floor and pushed his next thrust to the side.

My foot slipped on the granola bar that I'd dropped, but I recovered enough to knock aside the next blow. I was at a disadvantage here—I was no longer armed and was on the defense.

It was clear that Nathan had training. This was more than an angry man with a knife. He had skills. And knives were not my specialty.

He was screaming at me. There might have been words, but I didn't hear them. I was focused on the movement of his blade and circling away, trying to get an advantage while also keeping him as far away from Evelyn as possible.

I was detached, observing him. It was the only way that I could be. If I let him in, I would lose control. And keeping control was the only way that this wouldn't end in Evelyn's death. I didn't give a shit about mine.

The wall was too close behind me, and the slash that Nathan used grazed my forearm as I put more open space between us. I hissed in pain, and Evelyn screamed. That was all he needed. I looked over at Ev, and Nathan lunged.

He tackled me to the ground, knife coming straight at my face. I barely caught it in in time. On any given day, I was easily stronger than Nathan. But if my life experience had taught me anything, it was that there was no comparison to the strength of madness.

"She will never be yours," he hissed. His eyes were close and mad, arms shaking with the force he was pushing down on me.

Evelyn screamed again. "Nathan, *stop*."

But he wouldn't. We both knew that. I could see it in his eyes. He was going to die, or I was going to. And it didn't matter if I won and sent him away, he would never stop. Ever.

Out of the corner of my eye, I saw Evelyn move. She was out of the bed and I didn't dare look at her or tell her to stop because I wanted his attention to stay on me.

"She doesn't belong to anyone," I said, air hissing through my teeth.

The glint in his eyes sharpened, and I slipped an inch. He was groaning with the effort of pushing that knife toward my heart, and there was only so much I could do. Any move I made that took away from my concentration would cost me my life. And then Evelyn's.

Evelyn yelled, and the sound of glass shattering made

me close my eyes. Nathan went limp, and I didn't hesitate. We rolled together as I flipped the knife, and it slid into his body far too easily. He stared at me for a moment and blinked. The madness died, and in the moment before he was gone, I saw who he might have been.

Then he was gone.

The door crashed open, followed by a screaming nurse.

Ev was swaying on her feet, and I moved to catch her. "Watch out." I lifted her off the floor. Her feet were bare and the shards of the lamp she'd broken over Nathan's head were everywhere. "Are you all right?"

She looked up at me, eyes glassy with tears. "Am I all right? He almost killed you."

"But he didn't," I said. She was still in my arms and for the time being, that was where she was going to stay. "You saved me."

"He—" She swallowed. "He's gone?"

"Yes."

Evelyn melted into tears. In the time I'd known her, I'd never seen her cry. Not truly. She'd teared up, but nothing like this. These sobs came from somewhere deep. Relief, because the nightmare was finally, truly over. Nathan was dead. He couldn't hurt her anymore.

I held her close until her crying slowed. Nurses and the police came while she cried, and I waved them away. They went. Nathan's body wasn't going anywhere.

Finally, when her breath had evened out, I tilted her face up to mine and kissed her. "It's really over now. He can't hurt you anymore."

She shuddered, and I reached over to the bedside table to get a tissue and helped her dry her eyes.

"The police are here," I said gently. "They're going to want to talk to you."

She nodded. "Just about this though, right? I'm not ready for the rest of it."

"He's dead. You don't have to press charges to keep him in jail. As far as I'm concerned, you don't have to tell anyone what happened. Ever."

With all the pain and anguish that Nathan had caused, it felt like he would have gone less quietly. But from where I sat, I could see the blood pooling on the floor, and I wished that I could feel the slightest sliver of guilt for killing him. I didn't. Neither Evelyn nor I would have to look over our shoulders again, wondering if he was out there.

When Charlie came back to the door, I nodded. I didn't let go of Evelyn as they took the body away, and she hid her face in my shirt as the gurney was wheeled out.

The statements were short and simple. Knowing what he did about Nathan, Charlie believed me when I told him that he'd come at me with the knife. And the broken ceramic all over the floor proved that Ev had thrown the lamp.

Nathan's biggest asset had been money. The kind of money that could pay off lawyers and cops to get him out of jail or buy fifteen custom gravestones and protection so tight that no one could find him. But even money couldn't fight death, and his death was clear-cut self-defense. He'd known that Ev and Lena would send him to jail, so he'd taken one final chance and lost.

The cops left soon after, and we moved to a different room, away from the blood and the carnage, leaving the final black rose behind.

"Evelyn!" Lena burst through the door in a gown and still hooked up to an IV, a harried Grace running in after her.

I'd finally put Ev down, and Lena practically tackled her friend. Though she was mindful of her wounds.

"You're okay. You're *okay*." The bakery owner was crying, and Evelyn was too. There was something different about Lena. Even at her most vibrant, she hadn't sounded like this. Words poured out of her. "I'm so sorry. I tried to do something. I tried so hard, but I couldn't move."

Nausea filled my gut as I realized that Lena had been forced to watch Evelyn be tortured. If I'd seen that . . .

"There's nothing you could have done," Ev said. "And you're okay?"

"I'm high as fuck right now," Lena said. "And I'll be honest, I probably won't remember any of this. But I'm okay."

Ev looked at Grace, who was smiling. "She'll be all right," the redhead confirmed. "She's going to stay with me for a few days."

Harlan stepped into the room, and the second he did, Grace's eyes were on him. I didn't fail to notice the way she looked him up and down like she was making sure that *he* was okay. "Grace."

"You're in one piece, I see." Her tone was sarcastic, but I heard relief too.

"We all are. Thankfully."

"It was close," I admitted.

Harlan scanned me head to toe. "Yeah, from what I hear, I need to start kicking your ass in some knife drills."

"I'm hoping I won't need them." I reached down to take Ev's hand. "Any word?"

He nodded. "We found the family. Nathan was keeping them under guard near their home in Texas."

Texas. Holy fuck.

"They're letting the guy go. He really was forced."

Now that Nathan was gone, I didn't care. The man he'd kidnapped would be traumatized, given what he'd been a part of, and that his family's lives had been at stake. No doubt Nathan hadn't been bluffing.

"I can actually come back to work," Evelyn said. "If you want me."

"Hell yes, I want you." Lena's voice was way too loud. "But not before you're ready. But when you are, we're going to tear down this town with new recipes!"

I looked at Grace, and she nodded. She came over and put a hand on Lena's back. "Speaking of that, let's let Evelyn rest."

"Okay." Lena hugged Ev one more time, and as she turned away Grace stepped down and hugged her too.

"I'm so glad you're alive. When you're ready, I still owe you dinner at Ruby Round."

"For sure," Evelyn said with a smile.

Grace guided Lena out of the room, and Harlan's eyes never left her. He stared after the two of them long after they'd disappeared.

"Everything else okay?"

His gaze snapped to mine. "Yeah. And I'm the envoy."

I raised an eyebrow, but he looked at Ev. "We didn't want to overwhelm you with all seven of us in here. But all of us wanted to tell you that we're glad you're all right, and we're happy that you'll be staying as a part of the family."

Ev's hand tightened on mine. "Thank you."

Harlan nodded to me and left. They were right not to overwhelm her. She was already reaching her limit. So when the doctor knocked on the door apologetically, I gave her hand a comforting squeeze.

"Quite a lot of excitement," the doctor said, flipping through the chart and checking the nurse's notes. She didn't look alarmed at all, so that was comforting. It was the same doctor I'd seen last night, and she'd been leery of letting me stay. But given the unique circumstances, she'd relented.

"Yeah." Ev's voice was weak.

"I know it's going to be a complicated answer, but how are you feeling?"

Evelyn laughed, her voice hoarse. "Everything hurts."

"We can help with that."

"Is there anything that you're going to do here that I can't do at home?" Her voice shook a little, and I knew that she was scared to ask. "I really just want to go home."

The doctor looked at her for a long moment. "I'd like to keep you for a couple more days, but you're in good shape, and I know where you're going. If you'll come back once a day to make sure that the burns are healing well, and follow the instructions that I give you to the letter, I'll let you go home."

"I'll make sure," I said.

The doctor smiled. "I'm sure you will. I'll give the nurse my discharge instructions and order some prescriptions that you can pick up on the way home, then we'll get you out of here. But I wanted to mention something." She put the chart at the end of the bed and leaned against the end of it. "One of the best plastic surgeons in the country lives over in Bozeman. I don't know why he's holed up in Montana when he could be making a shit ton of money in a bigger city, but he's here. And one of his specializations is burns."

Evelyn let out a tiny gasp.

"I'm not saying it's necessary," the doctor said. "Your scars will heal well. But if you ever want to explore that as an option, I'll be happy to refer you."

"Thank you," she whispered.

The doctor smiled. "Hang tight, and we'll get you out of here, okay?"

She disappeared, and I sat on the bed with Ev. "You okay?"

She leaned back against me, and even in pain, she was more relaxed than I'd ever felt her. "I am."

"Good." I slipped my arm around her and hugged her close. "I love you."

"I love you." Her voice was a smaller echo of mine, but no less fervent.

I breathed in the freedom of holding her without anything over our heads. We were going home. Together.

Epilogue

Evelyn
Six Months Later

I'd given up on ever seeing Florida again. First, I hadn't thought I'd ever get to return because of Nathan, and then after he was gone, because I wasn't ready.

After everything, I didn't know how seeing all my old places would affect me. But when it was time, I knew.

Dr. Rayne and I had been meeting regularly since everything had happened. Sometimes in her office, sometimes outside, and sometimes with Lucas too. Now that we had shared trauma, it was good to process it together.

The past six months had been . . . amazing. I'd gone back to work at Deja Brew, helped Lucas with the animals, and *lived*. He did take me back to the lake—and very thoroughly kept his promise of using a tree. He'd encouraged me to apply to vet studies programs, and even though I wasn't ready for that, I was thinking about it.

My birthday had happened. I'd almost forgotten about it. After so long not celebrating, and not knowing if I would be alive to celebrate another one, it had snuck up on me. That celebration had been private, just the two of us, and I was grateful for that.

I'd even had consultations with the plastic surgeon about my scars. I wasn't ashamed of them. Not anymore. Not when Lucas took the time to make sure I knew how brave I was to have them and how beautiful I was anyway. There wasn't a second where he'd flinched or looked at me as anything but perfect. And he would never know how much that meant to me. It would be a long and slow process, and not every scar could go. But some of them . . . it would be good.

Most of all, I settled into a life. One that had normalcy and friendships and no more fear. So after our first Christmas together with all of our friends, and after we were buried in snow, when Lucas asked if I finally wanted to go to Florida, I said yes.

Now I was standing on the beach in the warm air. Winter wasn't hot in Florida, but it was a hell of a lot warmer than Montana was. The tang of humidity brought memories both good and bad.

Honestly, I'd thought I'd miss it more. Yet now that I'd experienced the clear Montana air, there was no comparison. But I felt lighter being here.

Lucas had arranged everything, and this afternoon I'd seen my sister, Melanie, for the first time in years. I'd cried. Hard. Now that I had the freedom to, I cried more often than I felt like I should. But it had been amazing to see her, and we were going to see her again tomorrow.

I wasn't ready to see the rest of my family after what they'd done and believed. Maybe I'd never be ready. But Melanie was the one who'd saved me, and we were already making plans for her to come visit the ranch in the spring.

Arms snaked around me from behind and a kiss warmed my neck. "Hey."

"Hi," I said. The sun was setting now, and I was enjoying the wind blowing on my skin. That was one of my favorite parts of the beach, and probably the one that I'd miss the most.

"You ready?"

"For what?"

"For a surprise." He smiled, curling himself further around me. Lucas was still so big, and I'd gotten so used to it that I sometimes forgot. But when he curled around me like this, I remembered and felt small. Protected. Loved.

"This is already amazing. You don't need to surprise me."

He laughed, the soft sound rolling across my skin and making me hope that the surprise involved going back to our hotel room. "Too late."

Lucas pulled me down the beach in the direction of our hotel, but not all the way. We drifted toward one of the many restaurants that dotted the area behind the beach, and one in particular seemed to be his goal.

I found out why.

A whole section of the restaurant that was open to a view of the beach was covered in candles. It was set for two people. Us. "You did this?"

"I did."

The candles were far enough away from the table that I wouldn't be nervous. I'd gotten better with fire, and I loved our fireplace back home. But open flames still made me anxious. He'd thought of that. He thought of everything.

But we didn't go up to the table. Lucas sat down on the

sand and tugged me down in front of him so I was bracketed by his legs. "We have some time to finish the sunset."

"Okay." I snuggled back into him.

No matter how many times he held me, I would never get tired of it. Every time it felt like safety and comfort. It felt cliche to say that it was my happy place, but it was.

"Are you happy that we came?" he asked.

"Yes. It was time. And Melanie will love Montana. Watch her ditch Florida once she sees it. She's always hated it here."

Lucas chuckled. "Well, we do have guest houses if she wants to get on her feet."

I laid my hands over his where they rested on my stomach. If he hadn't done that, given me that chance, I probably wouldn't be here. *We* wouldn't be here.

"I want to ask you something," he said.

"Mm?" The sunset was a blaze of orange and pink in front of us, and I was so relaxed I could just fall asleep.

"Will you marry me?" he whispered.

My whole body went still. "What?"

"I know that it might be difficult for you to say yes, given what happened the last time someone asked you that question."

I scrambled out of his hold and turned around. He wasn't joking. There wasn't a shred of humor on his face.

"And if that's the case, then I'll wait. Even if it's something you can never do, I want you to know that I'm in this forever. It's you and me, for as long as you want me."

"You want to marry me?"

Lucas slipped a hand around the back of my neck and wove his fingers into my hair. "Evelyn, I've wanted to marry you for as long as I've loved you. And I loved you a lot sooner than you realize. But no matter what you answer, I'm still yours."

I crushed myself against him with a kiss that could have melted the whole beach to glass. Lucas's other arm came around me, and his hand sank deeper into my hair. I wanted to breathe him in and never let go. "Of course I'll marry you."

He smiled against my lips. "Really?"

"Really."

Reaching into his pocket, he pulled out a square of black fabric. My heart stilled. Not a jewelry box. He'd thought of that too. "Given everything, I didn't want to get you a ring. And I know you'd say that it was fine, but there are no rules. And we don't have to force ourselves to go by tradition when it's going to make it that much harder."

He unfolded the velvet. Nestled inside was a necklace. A simple, beautiful chain with a teardrop diamond that sparkled in the fading light of the sun. It was beautiful.

He was right. I would have worn a ring for him. But my finger was scarred, and it would have kept the memories lurking.

"It's perfect."

As he lifted the chain, it seemed to go on forever. "It's long so you can wear it beneath your clothes if you want. Or shorten it too."

I ducked my head as he looped it around my neck. The length placed the diamond near my heart, and I put a hand to my chest. I didn't have to say it out loud. He already knew. "I love you," I told him anyway. There wasn't anything truer that I could say.

"I love you more."

"Doubtful," I said with a laugh.

Lucas spun me down onto the sand so he was hovering over me and kissed me again. Hard. "I guess we'll just have to see who wins."

"Kind of hard to do that if we're together forever."

Lucas smiled. "That's exactly the point."

The sun blazed bright in its final moments before it disappeared, and Lucas wrapped me up in him. The first and only place that I never wanted to leave.

•••

Acknowledgments

A very special thanks to the Calamittie Jane Publishing editing and proofreading team:
  Marci Mathers
  Denise Hendrickson
  Susan Greenbank
  Chasidy Brooks
  Tesh Elborne
  Marilize Roos

Thank you for your dedication to this new series.

Ghost

Shadow

Echo

Phoenix

Baby

Storm

Redwood

Scout

Blaze

Forever

INSTINCT SERIES (series complete)

Primal Instinct

Critical Instinct

Survival Instinct

THE RISK SERIES (series complete)

Calculated Risk

Security Risk

Constant Risk

Risk Everything

OMEGA SECTOR SERIES (series complete)

Stealth

Covert

Conceal

Secret

OMEGA SECTOR: CRITICAL RESPONSE (series complete)

Also by Josie Jade

See more info here: www.josiejade.com

RESTING WARRIOR RANCH

Printed in the USA
CPSIA information can be obtained
at www.ICGtesting.com
CBHW020344260824
13582CB00053B/1174